EVERYTHING YOU ALWAYS WANTED TO KNOW ABOUT DI AND FERGIE —AND MORE!

THE GIRLS' BEST FRIENDS: What fabulous London jeweler fashioned Diana's dazzling sapphire engagement ring *and* Sarah's favorite gift from Prince Andrew?

MAJESTIC HOMES: If you were paying a call on Princess Di during a visit to London, where would you go? If she wasn't home, where could you look up Fergie and Andrew?

THE TIARA TRIANGLE: What area of London can you expect to find the glittering duo doing a lot of their most *exclusive* shopping?

FABULOUS FEASTS: Where does Di go to have lunch for two—and rub elbows with Joan Collins, Liz Taylor, Robert Redford and Dustin Hoffman?

EXQUISITE UNMENTIONABLES: Which stores provide the same type of sensual silk undergarments ̲ ̲ ̲ ̲ ̲ ̲ ̲ ̲ ̲ ̲ ̲ ̲ Di's own designers ̲ ̲

The answers ̲ ̲ ̲ ̲ ̲ ̲ ̲ ̲ ̲ ̲ ̲ ̲ a follower of the ̲ ̲ ̲ ̲ ̲ ̲ ̲ ̲ w!

THE
PRINCESS
& THE
DUCHESS

JOSEPHINE FAIRLEY

A 2M Communications Ltd. Production

SMP
ST. MARTIN'S PAPERBACKS

THE PRINCESS AND THE DUCHESS

Copyright © 1989 by Josephine Fairley.

A 2M Communications Ltd. Production.
Photo Research by Amanda Rubin.
Cover photo by G. de Keerle.

Library of Congress Catalog Card Number: 89-30136

ISBN: 0-312-92152-7

Printed in the United States of America

St. Martin's Press hardcover edition published 1989
St. Martin's Paperbacks edition/September 1990

10 9 8 7 6 5 4 3 2 1

Contents

Introduction

All over the world, there are little girls—and big girls—who dream of Cinderella, of being swept off their feet by a handsome prince and spirited away to live happily ever after in a castle, with uniformed footmen to wait on them, extravagant gowns, priceless jewels, and the eternal love of a man through whose veins regal blood flows. In most cases, of course, it is nothing more than harmless escapism, a fantasy to transport them, even fleetingly, from a world of homework, household chores, or puppy fat. But for two very special little girls—two extraordinary young women—the dream came true. And for them, real life has turned out to be stranger than the fiction of that favorite fairy tale.

The Princess of Wales and the Duchess of York—Di and Fergie, as they've become affectionately known the world over—are not royal by birth. But they have been plucked from obscurity, chosen by a duo of charming princes as consorts. And one of them, destiny willing, will even become queen.

But life as a modern royal is a far cry from that glittering children's fable. A princess's life, as Diana and Sarah have discovered, can be something of a nightmare, too. These days, there is a high price to be paid for marrying a prince.

It all began, of course, when—once upon a time, after years of speculation about a future bride—Prince Charles was first linked in public with the eminently suitable Lady Diana Spencer, a refined English aristocrat who had been invited by the Queen to spend the weekend at Balmoral, the family's Scottish Highland retreat. It was an event which sent the world's news hounds and paparazzi into an unprecedented frenzy. They swooped with glee upon the slightly chubby, overwhelmingly shy young nursery-school teacher whose gauzy cotton skirt, chosen for her first official photo session, just happened to display a show-stopping pair of legs when she stood against the sun. The appearance of this demure but blossoming English rose upon the royal scene could not have been more timely. The British monarchy, loved the world over, had nevertheless begun to lack glitz and glamour. It was crying out for an injection of magic, and Diana Spencer was heaven-sent.

As the romance heated up, and as the world's hunger for a new princess grew, "Shy Di"—as the seemingly timid Diana was known—was taken under the wing of the elderly but still sprightly Queen Mother, a woman who had unique firsthand knowledge of what marrying a prince actually entailed. As Lady Elizabeth Bowes-Lyon, she had been chosen by "Prince Bertie" (then Duke of York and second in line to the throne). Later, she unexpectedly became queen when Bertie's brother dropped the bombshell that he would abdicate for the love of the twice-divorced Wallis Simpson. The Queen Mother knew better than anybody what Diana must learn and made it her special duty to help in every way. But even the Queen Mother could not prepare Diana for the assault on her privacy, the sudden jolt of superstardom that was to come her way.

A combination of diet and a diary so packed with engagements that Diana was rushed off her feet made the pounds literally melt away, and with the guidance of fashion experts and top stylists, Diana—with her aristocratic bone structure and fashion-model's stature—was transformed into a ravishing, radiant beauty. The public could hardly fail to be seduced, as Charles so obviously was, by her. The world couldn't get enough of the royal love affair, and it still can't, even though speculation is rife about whether or not the romance will have the "happy ever after" ending we all wished for and believed at the time was preordained.

Diana was at first dazzled by the quick-fire burst of a thousand popping flashguns, by the pack of notebook-carrying reporters whose pursuit of the twenty-year-old ingenue was reminiscent of a "Kojak" car chase, and by the glamorous upheaval of her cardigan-and-pearls, "Sloane Ranger" lifestyle—so called because the aristocratic young men and women this tag refers to almost inevitably live (and occasionally work) in the upmarket Sloane Square area of London. She rocketed to celestial status faster than any Hollywood starlet in history and thrived on the sudden attention. But as the gold dust settled, she began to yearn for a little companionship. Nobody, it seemed—even close girlfriends and roommates from her single days, who had stood staunchly by, deftly deflecting press probing and remaining tight-lipped about the royal family's newest recruit—quite understood the pressures of juggling marriage, motherhood, and a relentless itinerary of appointments and public engagements at which Diana is expected to appear and to behave every inch the princess she has become.

Cut off from the outside world, she began, not surprisingly, to yearn for a playmate. Her husband, twelve years her senior, loves polo, painting, and trout-fishing holidays on the rivers that flow through Balmoral. Diana, although deeply committed to her royal duties, gets itchy feet when she's cooped up with Charles's family for too long; she adores dancing and rock music and can contentedly shop till she drops—activities which are known to bore the pin-striped pants off Prince Charles.

So when Prince Andrew—nicknamed "Randy Andy" after his dalliances with unsuitable young women, among them a "soft-porn" star named Koo Stark—began to date Sarah Ferguson, the flame-haired, freckled daughter of Major Ronald Ferguson, Prince Charles's polo manager, and a friend (though not exactly the bosom buddy we've been led to believe) of the Princess's, Diana did everything she could to encourage romance to flourish between Charles's younger brother and the effervescent Sarah. Here was a woman whose company Diana enjoyed yet who seemed to pose no threat to her own star status (which there is absolutely no doubt she laps up). In many ways, their lives had run along parallel lines. Their mothers had both abandoned their young families and left their husbands behind in the United Kingdom, and the two girls were raised, unusually, by single-parent fathers. They knew many of the same people and were both related—albeit several generations back—to royalty. And they both loved to have a good time.

As the relationship between Prince Andrew and Sarah became increasingly serious, it must have seemed to Diana that here, at last, was a woman she could get along with, giggle with, and consider an ally in the royal camp. The pair of them would be able to let their hair down together and poke affectionate fun at the stuffier royals. Here was a comrade who could rapidly become a sympathetic shoulder to lean on, as Sarah learned for herself about the pomp, pageantry, and painful lack of privacy of modern royal life. The pair would be able to share the upside and commiserate with one another about the downside of marrying a prince. Sarah's arrival on the scene meant Diana was no longer the royal new girl. Like a wise older sister, the Princess could pass on tips about protocol and even lend the newcomer cast-off clothes, since Sarah's income, as an editorial assistant for a Swiss-based publishing firm, couldn't be expected to stretch to a new designer outfit every time she appeared in public.

Crucially, however, in her heart of hearts, Diana must have felt that in Sarah she had no real competition. She couldn't have anticipated, when Sarah made her rather frumpy debut on the royal scene, that the plump, somewhat rowdy girl who'd won Prince Andrew's affections with her sporting, gregarious nature would ever threaten her position as royal family favorite. Diana may have begun royal life full of trepidation, hiding behind thick bangs and speaking so softly others sometimes had to strain to hear her, but she was now ranked as one of the world's best-dressed women, acknowledged as a legendary beauty, and greeted with applause and admiration everywhere. She had been showered with jewels by international heads of state and met many of the world's most powerful personalities. She was married to the man who will be king and is mother to Prince William, who'll one day succeed him. Her place in the history books was assured, and so, Diana believed, was her place in our hearts.

What nobody, least of all Diana, had anticipated was how the extrovert Fergie (as everyone now called her) would rise to the royal challenge, showing the world a multifaceted character and a daredevil streak. Anything Prince Andrew could do, Sarah Ferguson seemed determined to try her hand at, too. Diana's show-stopping glamour was one thing, but to many people it began to seem rather two-dimensional beside the relaxed style of her new rival. And Fergie, too, was undergoing something of a "makeover." While her image was being polished, she was working out regularly at a gym, slimming her rather matronly proportions down just slightly to the point of ripe voluptuousness. Her womanly curves made her the heroine of millions of women only too ready to shred their diet charts.

Who could deny that Prince Charles's wife was utterly beautiful? But the characteristics which had attracted Prince Andrew to his bride-to-be were more than skin deep, and her casual, confident air and infectious humor appealed to royal watchers around the world. Her popularity was contagious, too, rubbing off on her beau, whom many had dismissed in the past as bumptious, arrogant, and egocentric. All the world loves a lover, and the "can't-keep-their-hands-off-each-other" passion between Fergie and Randy Andy was plain to see. At the same time, she revealed that the Queen's second son had a caring side, which only those behind closed palace doors had previously glimpsed.

Sarah rapidly became very close to her future mother-in-law, seeming not at all awed by the Queen—though always careful to remain polite and respectful. Within a very short time, she'd enjoyed the privilege of dining alone with Her Majesty in her sumptuous private apartments while Prince Andrew was away completing a naval training course. (For as long as anyone can remember, the only other person to enjoy regular, secluded tête-à-têtes with Queen Elizabeth has been her beloved elder son, Prince Charles.) The Queen and Fergie share a love of the outdoors and in particular of horses. It's doubtful that the conversation—or the laughter—ever dries up at the dinner table with the two of them around.

Everyone, it appeared, had fallen head-over-heels in love with Sarah, and Diana must sometimes have felt that she'd been left behind in the stampede. Once upon a time, the Princess of Wales would joke to the assembled press corps, "I know you'll all grow tired of me one day when Prince Andrew runs off and marries some exotic beauty." The exotic beauty, in fact, turned out to be rather more the girl-next-door variety, but there must be moments, nevertheless, when Diana senses that her joking prophecy may be coming true.

Sarah Ferguson has enjoyed a taste of freedom, a fact that must rankle the Princess of Wales. Sarah had played the field, as many contemporary women feel entitled to do, before making her decision to settle down. She'd had her heart broken at least once and had no illusions about what she'd be giving up to marry her prince. Diana, by contrast, was totally inexperienced romantically when she met Charles. ("The only virgin left in England," people joked at the time, and while that wasn't exactly true, nineteen-year-olds without a sexual skeleton or two in the closet were not exactly the rule.)

In the blue-blooded world to which Diana was born, most young women are still encouraged to make a good match—to snare a wealthy and wellborn husband. It is a role for which, even now, aristocratic young women are groomed from birth. Girls are allowed to dabble as Montessori schoolteachers, take Cordon Bleu cookery courses, or learn about fifteen different types of glazed chintz curtains in an interior design course— all useful domestic skills that, it's hoped, will give their marriage prospects a boost—but a fully fledged independent career is frowned upon. Many "Sloanes" like Diana (a nickname taken from Sloane Street and Sloane Square, the main shopping area of her set) enjoy a private income or trust funds and needn't work at all.

In marrying the future king, Diana couldn't have landed a bigger catch. Discussing whether or not Lady Diana Spencer was naive in accepting Prince Charles's proposal, I've several times heard the opinion expressed that she must have been out of her mind to restrict her freedom voluntarily, even for a man she was obviously crazy about. In reality, however, Diana was living up to—if not exceeding—the expectations of her family and her class. Nobody could have warned her of the media circus that would trail her around the world, intruding on her privacy, because she herself unwittingly sparked it off. Before Diana joined the royal cast, there would be only a handful of press at all but the most dazzling events. For Diana's first "photo opportunity," at the Young England Kindergarten where she helped out, 432 photographers showed up. She may well have believed that all the fuss would die down after her marriage.

The pressure had long been on Prince Charles to settle down, find a wife, and produce an heir, and virgins (with no boyfriends lurking in the background to spill the intimate beans to the yellow press) were becoming increasingly few and far between. Less than one year after the legendary "wedding of the century" in St. Paul's Cathedral, beamed around the world by satellite to billions of rapturous viewers, the Princess of Wales had produced the son Prince Charles so desired, a baby boy who would one day inherit his father's crown.

No longer was Prince Andrew second in line to the throne. By efficiently producing a son and heir, Diana had taken the pressure off her brother-in-law, who—barring some terrible catastrophe—would never now become king. Soft-porn stars were still out of the question, but his choice of bride wasn't so crucial anymore. Diana had also, therefore, freed the woman Prince Andrew ultimately settled for. And with fewer official engagements, the Duchess of York was able to keep her job (the first royal to be permitted to do outside work from the gilded confines of Buckingham Palace) and maintain diverse interests. Sarah's family, although extremely wellborn, aren't top-drawer aristocrats (like the Spencers) with seemingly unlimited financial resources, and it's likely that Sarah worked not merely from choice but also of necessity. Her decision to keep her job—hardly demanding and also flexible enough to be slotted into her royal schedule—showed a highly independent streak and a wish to keep her feet planted as squarely on terra firma as she can.

By contrast, as future queen, Diana—who, for reasons of security, gave up her job as soon as her engagement was announced—must put her duty to her country first, undertaking, in preparation for her future role, an often tedious round of official engagements that are far from glamorous: opening factories and laying endless foundation stones, planting trees, and shaking thousands of strangers' hands without yawning from boredom. Contrary to popular belief, a modern princess's life is not one long round of dress fittings and hairdressers' appointments, although she must never be glimpsed with laddered pantyhose or a frosted strand of hair out of place. She has had to become a princess by profession, and sometimes—with official trips overseas—even motherhood has to take a back seat, with willful Wills and Harry often left behind.

Most of all, however, Diana must be frustrated by the way Sarah is allowed—and encouraged by her husband—to be utterly herself, to relax in public and in private. It is possible for the Duchess to get away with antics that would be unthinkable for a future queen of England. Sarah, who has taken to speech making like a duchess to water (unlike Diana, who still blushes whenever she has to open her mouth on a rostrum), has developed a quick-fire badinage almost worthy of a standup comedienne. It is hard to imagine the Princess of Wales standing onstage in Los Angeles and, quick as a flash, responding "I'll see you later" to an "I love you" shouted by a male admirer in the audience. It is harder still to imagine her being allowed to get away with it. But that is just one of the freedoms afforded the Duchess of York and denied to Diana.

A pair of real-life Cinderellas, the Princess and the Duchess are similar in age, in background, and in their selection of royals as husbands. They are uniquely qualified to guide, help, and support one another in their roles. Until Sarah Ferguson came along, nobody in the world but Diana understood what it's like to trade freedom and anonymity for the opportunity to sit inside the famous glass carriage and be transported through London, drawn by immaculate horses; to walk up the aisle in yards of spun silk and a halo of tulle; to bring tears to the eyes of millions as she exchanged vows with a prince. From the start, it looked as if, when Prince Andrew proposed to Sarah, it would be the answer to a lonely princess's prayers. But has it turned out that way?

1

Once Upon a Time

One factor, above all else, has endowed the Princess of Wales and the Duchess of York with a steely determination to make sure that, in an era when divorce is commonplace, their own marriages will work out. Diana and Sarah each remember only too well the pain of being the victim of a broken home, and they don't want to repeat their parents' mistakes.

The breakup of their parents' marriages was remarkably similar and left each young woman with a legacy of self-sufficiency which, actually, proved perfect preparation for their newfound, isolated roles in life, while also giving Sarah and Diana shared, common ground. It is still extremely unusual for wives and mothers to abandon their family homes—and their children—but, heartbreakingly, both Sarah and Diana's mothers did just that. "Bolter" is a cruel, upper-crust word used to describe a woman who abandons her family. But "bolting" is still comparatively rare; it is usually, even in 1989, the man who moves out.

Not so in the cases of Diana and Sarah. Lady Diana Spencer was born the youngest of Earl and Countess Spencer's three daughters (to be followed by a son, Charles). Hers is a family which, technically, has more royal blood in its lineage than does Prince Charles's, the House of Windsor. Frances Roche was the daughter of the fourth Lord Fermoy, a former Conservative member of Parliament for the Norfolk constituency of King's Lynn. Her mother, Ruth Fermoy, was a close friend of the Queen Mother and has served as her lady-in-waiting since 1956.

Tall, blond, and slender, Frances Roche was just eighteen when she was swept off her feet by Viscount Althorp (pronounced All-trup), who was actually then engaged to another. She met Johnnie (as everyone knew him) Althorp, then aged thirty-two, at her debutante coming-out ball in April 1953. He was heir to Lord Spencer and considered the most eligible of bachelors. Ironically, the nuptials of Frances and Johnnie, Diana's parents, constituted the society wedding of the year. And the perfect picture seemed complete when their first daughter, Lady Sarah, was born just nine months later.

In fact, the sad seeds of discontent in her parents' marriage were sown long before Diana made her appearance in the world on Saturday, July 1, 1961. To begin with, the couple had endured a less than ideal domestic setup, living for a time under the same roof as Johnnie's irritable father. Then, when Frances's own father died, her mother invited the expanding family to move into the ten-bedroom Park House. Located on the Royal Sandringham estate (the venue for the Queen's extended post-Christmas break), Park House is, in fact, just a stone's throw from the place where Diana's future husband spent annual holidays. The Spencer children were raised, as was the custom, by a strict nanny in a nursery wing. They were taught impeccable manners, to "mind their p's and q's," and always to say "please" and "thank you." The general notion was that "children should be seen and not heard."

After Sarah, another daughter, Jane, was born. Then, before Diana arrived, Frances gave birth to a son, who survived only ten hours. In aristocratic circles, the birth of a son is a crucial event, for titles pass down only through male children. Frances must have felt a sense of failure compounded by the inevitable grief over the death of a child.

By now, the age gap between Frances and Johnnie was yawning. Surrounded by a family he loved, Johnnie was rapidly sliding into middle age—which must have seemed deathly dull to Frances, still so youthful and so full of life and beauty. (She is still an incredibly lovely woman, with a quiet elegance, translucent skin, and the clearest blue eyes. Only recently I sat next to her on a bus, traveling down—where else?—Sloane Street, where she blended perfectly with the other beautifully turned out shoppers. It must be strange to sit on a bus, unrecognized by almost anybody, and ponder that your daughter will one day be queen of England.)

Although it was obvious to many around her that she was unhappy in her marriage, Frances persevered, still hoping to give her husband a son. She was thwarted (though nevertheless delighted) when along came Diana, a pretty baby instantly adored and treated like a living doll by her elder sisters, who loved to brush her hair and dress her up. It was an idyllic childhood. Diana grew up not far from the beach, and in summer the children looked forward to frequent picnic expeditions. Sandringham, a striking sandstone mansion, is set among woods and fields. Johnnie, in fact, had bought some land near Park House to farm beef cattle, and the arrival of new calves in the herd was a particular thrill to Diana and her sisters. The sight of royalty, out riding in the park, wasn't unusual, and the Queen—who so loves children—would stop and chat with the little Spencers. Invitations to tea would be exchanged, and the Spencers and the younger Windsors would attack their cakes and buns together. The royal family's Sandringham sojourns, however, are restricted to a few weeks a year. Diana and her sisters were more acquaintances than close friends of the Queen's children.

Diana was three years old before her brother Charles was born, in May 1964. At last, Johnnie had an heir—but Frances's discontent was gnawing away at her. So far, Diana had enjoyed a happy, very privileged childhood, surrounded by her parents' love in a comfortable, homey house filled with valuable antiques and family portraits. All that was to change. First of all, her two elder sisters were sent away to boarding school— to West Heath, where Diana would later follow. It was a prelude to a trial separation between Frances and Johnnie, which Frances painfully and painstakingly explained to her children. At the time, Frances's intention was to retrieve her children once she'd established herself in a new home. There's no doubt that she would have been devastated to learn that, as fate would have it, she was leaving her children for good.

Frances had fallen in love with another man, a dashing, rich gentleman who seemed to offer all the excitement that Johnnie could not. At the time their eyes had met across a crowded dinner table, when Frances was thirty-one, forty-two-year-old wallpaper heir Peter Shand Kydd was still married, with a family of three young children, and the affair must have seemed all the more thrilling for its forbidden nature. When the Shand Kydd and Althorp families took a skiing holiday together, romance truly blossomed—to everyone's shock. Frances moved to London—and to start with, Diana and her younger brother Charles went with her. The whole family was reunited for one very strained Christmas, but by then the writing was on the wall. Johnnie's and Frances's marriage, to their great sorrow, was irretrievably on the rocks.

For the moment, the children were to remain in Norfolk with their nanny, governess, and father, to spare them emotional and physical upheaval until the divorce was settled. Nobody but Johnnie and Frances know precisely what went on behind closed doors in the Spencer household—Frances still finds it far too painful to talk about—but in late 1968, Frances filed a divorce petition on the grounds of her husband's cruelty, believing, as was customary, that she would then automatically receive custody of her four children.

But Johnnie was—still is—a powerful man, and he was determined to counter his wife's divorce action. He rounded up his supporters to testify against his wife—even Frances's mother, Lady Fermoy, spoke out against her daughter—and was ultimately granted a divorce on the grounds of Frances's adultery with Peter Shand Kydd. She was branded something of a "scarlet woman"; the "Swinging Sixties" liberal attitude had not yet filtered into the upper echelons of society, whose doors were slammed in her face. An insider declares, "Frances was completely cut off from everyone."

She was instantly persona non grata. Even though her mother was lady-in-waiting to the Queen Mother, it made no difference. She was just "pushed out." Nevertheless, the lovelorn couple later married—very quietly, with no fuss, due to what were, even in the late sixties, the somewhat scandalous circumstances of their romance. They were extremely happy and divided their time between the United Kingdom and Australia, where Diana has visited. Sadly, the new Mrs. Shand Kydd was a victim of bad timing: just two decades later, barely an eyebrow would have been raised. So she fled into a kind of exile with her new husband, a Marlborough-educated naval veteran once described by one of his friends as "a bit of a gypsy, never happy in one place for long, dabbling in different adventures."

Life was a little sadder at Park House without Frances, but the children coped admirably. Jane and Sarah were old enough to help care for their little brother and sister during the school holidays. Although it wasn't unusual for aristocratic children to be educated exclusively at home, the decision was taken for Diana and Charles to attend a small local day school,

Silfield School, a short drive from Park House. It provided a welcome distraction for both.

Academically, Diana has never excelled. She's been the victim of cruel jokes about her relative lack of formal schooling, but it's clear to everyone who meets her that Diana is anything but a dumb blonde. She simply realized that the future carved out for her didn't require a string of certificates and degrees. Everyone at the school was impressed by Diana's friendliness and warmth, her manners, her tidiness—she still can't bear a mess—and, in particular, by her love of little children. Small children have been a passion with Diana probably ever since the arrival of her own younger brother, and she's famous the world over for being crazy for babies.

There's no doubt that, deep in her heart, Diana suffered greatly over her parents' divorce. But so did Fergie, whose mother also ran off with another man, creating scandalous ripples in society circles. Susan Wright, Fergie's mother, was the daughter of a well-to-do Derbyshire family—her father, who had the unusual Christian name of Fitzherbert, had served in the Hussars, and her mother was a viscount's daughter. Susan, like Frances Roche, had followed the custom and enjoyed a year of social whirl as a debutante. She fell for Ronald Ferguson, a polo-loving cavalry officer, at the age of twenty-one, married him, and had two daughters, Jane and Sarah. They were the picture of social propriety, on the fringes of the aristocracy—though actually upper-middle-class in background—with a lovely Hampshire home in the village of Dummer. There, Sarah grew up in Dummer Down House, a home handed down to Major Ferguson by his own father and set among 871 wooded acres sixty miles or so from the center of London.

Sarah had a blissful, bucolic upbringing, with picnics by the seaside and holidays in Cornwall. She loved tennis, swimming, and most of all riding. Her first pony soon became too small for her, and she had her best times on horseback astride another family steed, Peanuts. Together they scooped rosettes and prizes at many local Pony Club competitions. At bedtime, there would be stories read by Daddy as little Sarah snuggled up in bed with Mr. Rabbit, her favorite soft toy, loved so much that eventually he grew rather threadbare.

The Fergusons were part of a group who mixed regularly with the royals, linked by a common love for polo, the ultimate rich man's sport. (A photo actually exists of Sarah with her future husband standing just beside the Queen at the Windsor horse show in the mid-sixties. Apparently, the pair would tweak each other's hair and tease one another, just as they do now.) There were invitations to Windsor and to Buckingham Palace; later, Major Ferguson (following a distinguished twenty-year career in the British Army) was to be appointed Prince Charles's polo manager. Charles himself was a big fan of Susan Ferguson, an extremely youthful woman with, even now, a figure most models would kill for.

In 1973, after twenty years of conventional marriage to Ronald and growing frustrated at being left at home by a hardworking husband, Susan was struck by Cupid. Out of the blue, she fell rapidly and madly in love with an Argentinian named Hector Barrantes, a professional polo player on Lord Vestey's Stowell Park team, known as one of the "hired assassins" for his ruthless horsemanship. He's been described by Patricia Hipwood (who's married to Englishman Julian Hipwood, Barrantes's polo-circuit friend) as "a great bear of a man with the manners of the most civilized of Europeans." If she was to make a life with this new Latin love, she would have to leave behind her two daughters—a decision which, after much soul-searching, Susan made.

Long before her mother fled, Sarah had been dispatched, at the age of seven, as a day pupil to Daneshill House (where her mother actually gave riding lessons to the girls). Interestingly, it was Sarah's elder sister Jane who was first tagged "Fergie"—the nickname by which Sarah's now known around the world and which she and her husband hate. Jane recalls, "I was originally called Fergie. But then later it somehow got that a few girls still called me Fergie while others called me Jane. Sarah—she got stuck with Fergie."

A few years later, Daneshill closed down and the Ferguson sisters were accepted by nearby Hurst Lodge—a happy environment where the emphasis on academic achievement wasn't too strong—housed in a sprawling suburban building. Sarah's sunny nature made her instantly popular among the other girls, many of whom were prominent businessmen's or celebrities' daughters. These included Florence Belmondo, French actor Jean-Paul Belmondo's daughter, who is still a firm friend. (The pair holidayed together beneath a blazing Caribbean sun just before the royal wedding and more lately, in Megève, the French ski resort.)

In typical boarding-school style, the girls had plenty of innocent fun together, and Sarah loved playing pranks and organizing midnight feasts. Her sister recalls, "We were both pranksters and practical jokers when we were young, and I wouldn't be surprised if she still enjoys such things." The duo, united in their sadness at their mother's departure to South America, spent a lot of time in one another's company. Tricks played on fellow pupils by Fergie and her gang are alleged to include slipping frogs' eggs into one girl's pockets as her clothes hung in the changing room, cream-bun fights, and frequent "apple-pie beds," where the sheet is folded back so that an unsuspecting sleepyhead will discover with chagrin that she can't slip between the covers without first remaking the bed.

Sarah's dormitory was known to one and all as "Peach Dorm," shared by six blossoming adolescent girls. One roommate is quoted as saying, "Ninety percent of the talk was about boys and one percent about food. It was all pure fantasy—we talked about boys we had seen in the holidays. Boys we had seen in films or magazines. We were terribly innocent." One of the girls Sarah shared with, Sarah Alexander, left Peach Dorm and Hurst Lodge to attend the rugged Scottish public school called Gordonstoun, where she was due to become a classmate of Prince Andrew's, the subject of much excited speculation and girlish giggling among the boy-mad coterie of classmates. In schoolgirl tradition, her friends wrote farewell messages in Sarah's autograph book. Years later, faded handwriting reveals a supremely ironic au revoir to Ms. Alexander, which reads: "Good Scotish [sic] luck! Mind Prince Andrew, lots of love Sarah Fergie (Ferguson)."

One weekend—Sarah always went home to Dummer Down House to see her darling dad—she was able to surprise her father with the good news that she'd been chosen as one of Hurst Lodge's two head girls. She also became captain of the netball team and was hugely popular with teachers. At the time of the royal engagement, her former headmistress recalled that "from a very small girl, Sarah always had charm, humor and a sense of fun. She was enormously cheerful, bubbly and fun-loving. She was not a superficial girl. But she also had a stubborn streak. I should think she will suit the young prince very well. She is a strong enough character to keep him in order."

Sarah banished any thoughts of college; she wanted to escape into the big wide world. At the time Sarah left Hurst Lodge, it was generally thought that a good secretarial education would open many career doors—although Sarah was never particularly ambitious. So she signed on, like many of her set, at Queen's Secretarial College in South Kensington, where her fellow pupils were debutantes and diplomats' daughters. Again, ebullient Sarah was a popular student with teachers and classmates. An assessment of the young Miss F. declared her to be "a bright, bouncy redhead. She's a bit slapdash, but has initiative and personality which she will use to her advantage when she gets older. Accepts responsibility happily." Even at seventeen, it seems, Sarah's character was fully formed.

She didn't turn out to be one of Queen's College's high fliers, however, clocking up speeds of just 90 words per minute shorthand and a mere 37 w.p.m. typing. Next stop was a course in cookery (deemed by the aristocracy and upper classes to be an essential part of any future bride's training); Major Ferguson's verdict on her culinary skills is that "she's a good cook, if a bit basic."

Meanwhile, his young redheaded daughter had a yearning for adventure—she seems, from her apparent love of travel, to have inherited more than a little of her mother's wanderlust. The endless round of London cocktail parties, dinners, and evenings spent in wine bars were not enough to satisfy Sarah. And the fact that her mother had settled in the Southern Hemisphere gave the flighty young secretary the perfect opportunity to see more of the globe than the four square miles of central London from Pimlico to Fulham and Belgravia to Kensington—which seemed to be all the world her contemporaries were interested in, barring the odd country weekend and an annual skiing trip, that is.

Despite their mothers "bolting," both Diana and Sarah have managed to remain on the very best of terms with these women; indeed, each has had a soft spot for the new man in her mom's life. And with her father's blessing, Sarah departed on the adventure of a lifetime with Charlotte Eden, daughter of Sir John Eden, a former Conservative government minister who is now Lord Eden. First stop was a visit to Mummy in Argentina, to stay at the Barranteses' thousand-acre chalet-style pony ranch named El Pucara (or The Fortress) near Buenos Aires, a home that was actually ordered from a catalogue!

The Barrantes also have a home at Palm Beach in Florida, where some of the world's finest polo is played. They spend much of the year traveling on the international polo circuit, and they share a deep love of horses. Theirs is a true love match. Sarah's mother confesses: "I am not a feminist in the strict sense of the word. I go where Hector goes. I find my happiness in him. Hector is my home." Or, as their close friend Mrs. Hipwood describes fifty-one-year-old Susan's twin passions for her husband and his sport, "Susie darts backwards and forwards during matches, checking tack on horses, holding replacement mallets, issuing orders to grooms. After the game is over, Hector sits comfortably in a folding chair while Susie unbuckles his spurs and takes off his knee pads. She produces a gourd of maté tea and a towel to wipe away the sweat of his exertions." Others on the polo circuit are touched and somewhat surprised at the couple's enduring passion for one another.

Sarah's elder sister Jane has spoken out about the breakup, revealing that "it affected us both. We are still close to our mother, though we never saw as much of her as we did of Dad following the divorce. When our mother attended Sarah's wedding, it was the first time we'd all been together for fifteen years." Sarah often manages to catch up with Susan Barrantes on the whistle-stop, jet-set polo circuit, but that first voyage around South America was special. The two young English girls used El Pucara as their base (having been instructed, like all guests from Britain, to pack their suitcases with ample supplies of flea collars, silver polish, and Mrs. Barrantes's orange marmalade, which are all hard to find in Argentina. And then, as Charlotte recalls, "We traveled by bus. It was pretty rough. We had a guidebook and used to find all the cheap places to sleep." Dressed in jeans and carrying knapsacks (Sarah, who burns easily, had plenty of sunscreen stashed in hers), the pair were the center of attention on their bargain-basement adventure.

Just like all hippie hitchhikers, of course, they found themselves desperately short of cruzeiros (and the English, unlike many American parents, don't furnish their wandering offspring with American Express cards to buy their way out [of] trouble). "We had our bus and air tickets," Charlotte remembers, "but by the time we got off the bus at Igazu Falls [on t[he] borders of Argentina, Paraguay, and Brazil], we'd run out [of] money."

They had a precarious time, sleeping on benches in the b[us] station, their tummies growling with hunger, so they thoug[ht] up a ruse to get food. The local bar owners and innkeepe[rs] traditionally put down cheese for customers to snack on wh[ile] they're enjoying a drink. "So trying to look as prosperous [as] possible, we sauntered into a nearby hotel and asked for tw[o] glasses of water. They brought the water and put down t[he] cheese. We scoffed the lot and ran." It may well have been t[he] last time that the Duchess of York would go hungry in h[er] whole life. On her overseas visits these days, she is more oft[en] feted; sleeps on crisp, clean sheets laid on comfortable, inne[r]-sprung mattresses and is fed five-course meals accompani[ed] by only the finest wines. But it's doubtful that even the[se] magical moments of luxury abroad, as Prince Andrew's w[ife] and consort, have quite the same impact on her life as sleepi[ng] on a slatted bus-station bench surrounded by Indian nativ[es].

After her marriage, Frances Shand Kydd was happy to u[n]dergo a major life-style change, too, trading the grand l[ife] she'd enjoyed as the future Countess Spencer for a mu[ch] humbler existence as a sheep farmer's wife. The Shand Kyd[ds] had two farms, one on the far-flung, bleakly beautiful isla[nd] of Seil off the coast of Scotland, and the other in New Sou[th] Wales, on the other side of the world in Australia, somewhe[re] they retreated to for sunshine when the icy Scottish winds b[lew]. They kept themselves very much to themselves, away fr[om] prying eyes in these remote locales. But sadly, this marria[ge], too, has crumbled, and Mr. and Mrs. Shand Kydd are n[ow] separated, a fact which is known to have brought Diana gre[at] sadness. Now, however, at last, the doors that were slamm[ed] in Frances's face seem, slowly, to be opening up to her on[ce] more. As Margaret Holder of England's *Royalty* magazine explains, "There's no one quite like Mrs. Shand Kydd in the royal family. She has a unique advantage, being the daughter of Lady Fermoy, the Queen Mother's best friend. But beyond that, she is recognized as a woman of independent means and independent views."

Despite the miles that now divide Frances and her daughter, the royals' former press secretary Michael Shea revealed that they are "closer than you think. During the time before the Princess's marriage, her mother was a great source of strength to her." Soon after Prince Charles proposed, Diana sought the privacy and comfort of her mother's Australian ranch, where, Mrs. Shand Kydd declared, they were "determined to have what my daughter and I both knew to be our last holiday together." During that holiday in 1981, they made up for the lost years, with cozy talk of men, motherhood, and marriage.

Indeed, it is believed to have been to her mother that Diana turned when her own marriage seemed to be going through a rocky patch two summers ago. At that time, Frances, with her insight into the traumas of a crumbling marriage, was able to counsel her distressed daughter. According to Harold Brooks-Baker, publisher of the upper-crust directory *Burke's Peerage,* Frances Shand Kydd's advice was crucial. She helped her daughter to understand "that they *had* to stick it out and be successful in their marriage." If the world's most glamorous and attractive man came down the road and the Princess was interested in him, she must not budge. Her marriage *must* work, in a way that her mother's did not. As anyone who saw pictures of a radiant Diana and her husband affectionately exchanging glances in public earlier this year should be able to divine, Diana appears to have heeded her mother's sound and expert advice. Mrs. Shand Kydd declares, "When children marry, you are maternally redundant. But if they want to ask for your opinion, that's nice."

In exchange for that counseling, Diana was able to give her mother an insight into a wide world Frances may never see for herself—impressions of an AIDS ward's dying patients, orphaned children, or the grief of relatives or victims directly stricken by a national tragedy like the sinking of the ferry *Zeebrugge* or an IRA terrorist attack. Frances Shand Kydd must be extremely proud of the way her daughter takes it all in her stride, with constant compassion and concern.

It's a matter of sadness to both, however, that these mother-daughter heart-to-hearts happen all too rarely. But at least there is the occasional hilarious moment to ease any loneliness Mrs. Shand Kydd might now feel. Until recently, Frances owned and managed a small Scottish gift shop. Amusingly, she was standing behind the counter one day when she overheard a woman customer raving to her husband about the marvelous, beauteous Princess of Wales. The customer then turned to Mrs. Shand Kydd and asked what *her* opinion was of the future queen. Frances remembers replying, with diplomacy, "It's a bit difficult for me to say." "Quite right, my dear," said the woman, "as a shop assistant you shouldn't give an opinion!"

When Diana was just a child, however, having notched up a couple of years at the local King's Lynn school, Silfield, a decision was made to send this shy, pensive child—just eight years old—to boarding school. To most Americans, it may seem cruel and unnecessary to wrench such a young person from her family, but among the British upper classes it raises no eyebrows. Johnnie Althorp could no longer guarantee to be at home during weekends and evenings, and it was generally felt that Diana would be less lonely in an environment with playmates her own age. To Riddlesworth, then, a cozy school less than two hours' drive from Park House, she went—taking her own guinea pig, Peanuts (coincidentally the same name chosen for Fergie's pony), to join the school's Pets Corner menagerie.

As it turned out, Riddlesworth was just what shy Di needed to coax her out of her shell. She thrived on the warmth and friendliness of her school friends and enjoyed the gentle routine, with frequent breaks during which the girls would beat a hasty retreat to check out their furry friends in Pets Corner. She looked forward to the regular visits of Frances and Johnnie, who took pains to take turns, and wrote them weekly missives about school life, no doubt omitting details of innocent pranks such as writing her name in pencil on the school walls.

The time came, however, for a spot of serious education—at least, that was her parents' intention. Diana followed in the footsteps of her two older sisters, packed her school trunk with framed photographs of her family, her pets, and home, sweet home, and was admitted to West Heath School at Sevenoaks, in the picturesque Kent countryside about thirty miles from central London. Perhaps armed with an intuition that she'd never need to call upon a litany of academic credentials, she was never a genius in the classroom, preferring, for her reading matter, the latest romantic paperbacks by Barbara Cartland (who, ironically, became her stepgrandmother when Diana's father married Miss Cartland's daughter Raine). "We used to spend all our time reading them," remembers a friend. "They were awful, really awful, romantic slush novels when we were supposed to be doing prep. We had a craze on them."

She was good at sports like swimming and tennis and a popular pupil—though she never had a particular "best friend"—who, in her last year, was made a prefect and awarded the Miss Clark Lawrence Award for service to the school, "for anyone who has done things that might otherwise go unsung." The school's headmistress remembered "her telling me that winning it was one of the most surprising things that had ever happened to her." Her yearning to improve the quality of others' lives was apparent even then.

Diana recently made a nostalgic visit to her old boarding school to open a gymnasium named after the school's head-mistress, Ruth Rudge, who was retiring. For fun, she took along her two sisters, now Lady Sarah McCorquodale and Lady Jane Fellowes, and her own lady-in-waiting, Anne Beck-with-Smith, another West Heath graduate, to share the day of memories. The quartet giggled almost constantly.

Diana, confronted by 150 girls dressed in the identical uni-form she'd had to wear—a navy pullover and blue skirt—noticed fashion's inevitable impact. "Wow, your skirts are short," she laughed. Diana later referred wistfully to her four years at the school (where fees are now a hefty £1,925 a term). She sniffed the air on arrival and threw back her head with laughter, declaring, "It smells as it always did!"

Blushingly, Diana recalled, "I made many friends whom I often see, and—in spite of what Miss Rudge and my other teachers may have thought—I did actually learn something. Though you wouldn't have known by my 'O'-level results!" (Diana left West Heath without having passed a single "O," or ordinary-level, examination. It is hardly a record to be proud of when many of her classmates scooped a dozen or so.) Referring to the sports hall itself, Diana, recalling her mischie-vous, rule-breaking misdemeanors, commented: "Perhaps now, when future generations are handed out punishments for talking after lights" (the moment of curfew, when lights in the girls' shared dormitories, which the students referred to as "cowsheds," must be switched off, prompting many girls to read with flashlights under the bedclothes), "pillow fights and illegal food, they will be told to run six times around this hall. It has to be preferable to the lacrosse pitch or weeding the garden, which I became expert at!"

Diana's former headmistress and other teachers clearly re-membered the tall, titled young woman who'd spent four years in their charge, where—reunited with her sisters—she'd discovered a home away from home. Her headmistress revealed, "This is an occasion neither of us could have imagined ten years ago." With a note of humor, her former geography teacher declared, "She hasn't changed at all. She is more elegant, but still the same Diana we knew," adding, with a wry smile, "although I imagine she has learned a lot more about geography since she left here. . . ."

It's a comment that rings equally true for both globe-trotting princesses. But when you're a royal, qualifications don't count for much. The most important lesson of all for the new princesses—one Sarah and Diana learned firsthand—is not to repeat their parents' tragic errors.

2

Family Ties

For Sarah and Diana, catapulted to international stardom and wealth beyond the dreams of avarice, keeping close links with their families is the best way to keep their glass-slippered feet planted securely on terra firma. Only in the privacy of their families, surrounded by people who've loved them all their lives, can they lose themselves completely and forget about the royal roles and responsibilities they have both assumed. They can kick off their shoes, put up their feet, take down their guard, gossip wildly, and be just like any other sister or daughter.

Because their mothers lived abroad for much of the year, both Diana and Sarah forged a bond stronger than Superglue with their respective fathers (known as Daddy to Diana, Dads to Sarah). On the mornings of their weddings, pride positively shone from Major Ferguson and Earl Spencer's faces as they escorted their daughters in the famous glass coach to take their vows, pointing excitedly at the thousands of people lining the street—some dressed in funny hats or Union Jack

T-shirts—to see *their* little girl. Whoever would have thought it?

But as Sarah and Diana each took her father's arm, to glide slowly up the aisle while millions watched, the emotional dads, who exchanged loving glances with their girls, must actually, inside, have wanted to weep. (Sarah reputedly said that, on telling her father of her intended engagement, "It's the only time I have ever seen my father cry.") More than most fathers, they were losing their daughters. Having a princess for a daughter could surely never compensate for the fact that neither the Duchess nor the Princess would have the freedom to spend as much time in the bosom of her family as she'd like.

Take Christmas: traditionally, once you marry into the royal family, the Yuletide holiday must be spent at Windsor (although last year, due to renovation work, the festivities were shifted to the Norfolk estate of Sandringham). No more joyful faces as their daughters reached into the pillowcases that had been hung at the ends of their beds, to discover tangerines and bags of chocolate money and paperback books. No more pulling of Christmas crackers as a whole family, or sitting down after turkey and roast potatoes to watch the ritual of the Queen's speech on television. These days, an occasional glimpse of news footage of Sarah or Diana during this annual Christmas Day broadcast may be all the young women's families get to see of them during the holidays.

And in public, formality is the order of the day. Protocol demands that Major Ferguson and Lord Spencer's sons-in-law must, for example, be addressed as sir. And, although they're still allowed to call their daughters by their Christian names, the Ferguson and Spencer parents must bow and curtsey to the Princess and Duchess in public—with all and sundry trying desperately to keep a straight face, no doubt!

In his heart of hearts, every father yearns for his daughter to marry well. To wed a prince is surely the ultimate; but for the girls' fathers, it is a mixed blessing. During intense press speculation over another royal romance—between the princes' younger brother Edward and a twenty-two-year-old brunette financial adviser called Georgia May—the young lady's father spoke out of his anxieties. "Somebody who marries into that family lives in a permanent goldfish bowl, under a microscope," said millionaire boat builder David May. "I do not think that is a very happy way to live." It is a sentiment that any father might echo if he saw his darling daughter harassed and pursued relentlessly by paparazzi and reporters wherever she went.

It was a particularly poignant moment when Johnnie Spencer stepped onto the red carpet of St. Paul's Cathedral to lead his daughter up the steps to her future husband. Viewers may have noticed his slight limp, and anyone who hears him speak can detect a slurring of the words. In fact, Diana's father battled back to fitness from a massive stroke, coaxed by his daughter and by his second wife, Raine (who is the daughter of romantic novelist Barbara Cartland). They bullied and cajoled him to rude health, and Diana is known to have worried about whether the stresses and strains of her big day would be too much for him. In the end, of course, it went off without a hitch, but just to make sure, medical staff were standing by on alert.

During Sarah's courtship, Major Ferguson is reported to have joked, "Do you know how much this is costing me in dressmaker's bills?" The £3,500 or so he shelled out for what was undoubtedly the wedding dress of the century must, however, have seemed a bargain when he first caught sight of his youngest daughter descending the stairs at Clarence House, the Queen Mother's home. "That dress, the flowers in her hair . . . it was breathtaking. I shed a tear." It was the prelude to a magical—but mirthful—journey to Westminster Abbey. In an interview with *London Daily Express* reporter Jean Rook (which reveals his healthy English sense of humor), Major

Ferguson recalled: "I thought of saying all sorts of things to calm her down—well, to calm me down—and then I saw the happiness and confidence in her face and I knew we'd have no trouble. When somebody trod on her train and she let out a swear word, I thought, "Everything's normal, we're home and dry.'

"In the coach, it took a while to get used to talking to each other, waving and facing the other way. About halfway down Whitehall, I nudged her and said: 'Just look at all those people, why are they here? All come to see my smelly little daughter.' She nearly fell about, and hissed, 'Shut up, Dad.'

"Going up the aisle, it was personal father-and-daughter stuff—most of it unprintable. But we didn't stop chatting until we got to the archway in the Abbey and realized, 'this is serious stuff.' " It marked both a beginning and an ending. Life at Dummer had been lonely for a while after the Major's wife, Sarah's mother Susan, ran off with Argentinian polo player Hector Barrantes when Sarah was just thirteen.

"Of course, it affected her, but I don't think it changed her," is Major Ferguson's considered verdict. He went on to raise his daughters with a firm but loving hand during their holidays from boarding school, and under his tutelage—he is a former commander of the Household Cavalry's Sovereign's Escort (the mounted soldiers who accompany the queen on processions)—both have become fine horsewomen. Sarah could ride almost as soon as she could walk and first sat on a pony at the age of three. Her spirit was evident from the word go. Her father remembers, "When she took a fall, she'd sit beating the ground with frustration, because she knew perfectly well it was her fault, not the horse's."

It is a shared love of equestrianism which has linked Major Ferguson with the royal family over the years. As Sovereign's Escort, he was well known to the Queen, who is said to have remarked once, smiling, when his horse advanced in front of her open carriage en route to the State Opening of Parliament, "Ronnie, the people have come to see *me*, not you!" The Queen and Prince Charles both liked Major Ferguson enormously, and an occasional invitation would make its way through the Dummer House letterbox, requesting the pleasure of the Fergusons' company at Sandringham or Windsor Castle. Sometimes Jane and Sarah would encounter their royal contemporaries, the Queen's children, but (little guessing what destiny had in store) they never became close.

Ultimately, Prince Charles selected Major Ferguson as his polo manager. This blue-chip rich man's sport—requiring players to maintain a string of ponies priced anywhere from £5,000 upward—is almost two thousand years old. It is a virtual obsession with the Prince of Wales, a total diversion from duty. "Everything is geared to his polo," reports one of the Prince's aides; "the rest fits in around it." Every summer weekend and some weekday afternoons, the game is played at the Guard's Polo Club headquarters at Smith's Lawn, in Windsor Great Park, and at a handful of other, less important venues. During a chukka—as each section of the match is known—the supremely fit players (who practically have thighs of cast iron from the effort of staying in the saddle) thunder up and down the field, expertly wielding mallets and aiming to score off the opposing team. Some professional players earn up to £100,000 a year and take their sport deadly seriously.

Off the pitch, however, a different sort of game is going on, as the elite—beautiful women and suntanned men—mix and chat, sipping Pimm's cocktails or chilled Krug champagne, lunching on smoked salmon and gossiping wildly. It is an occasion for dressing up and occasionally resembles the world's most upscale singles bar. Only here, people have impeccable backgrounds or they wouldn't have made it to the Member's Enclosure at all, and men and women are always introduced formally. It is a heady, seductive atmosphere, where the scents of Chanel No. 5 and horses' sweat mingle on the breeze. It was at a polo ground that Major Ferguson's first wife met and fell in love with the Argentinian horseman Hector Barrantes, prompting her famous remark, "Where else does one meet one's husband?" (Upper-crust English beauties know that one of the finest investments they can make—if their quest is a rich, bronzed husband—is the £100 per annum nonplaying subscription to the Guard's Polo Club.)

The royal family have been fans of this glamorous, sophisticated sport for years, and Major Ferguson—the expert horseman with excellent administrative skills—was a popular choice when Charles appointed him manager thirteen years ago. (He can be feisty at times, and behind the pony lines is occasionally referred to as "Major God" or "The Ayatollah.") On summer afternoons, the Windsor tribe loves to cluster at Smith's Lawn, and Di is a keen polo watcher who gives rousing support to her husband's team, Les Diables Bleu (The Blue Devils). She and Sarah both lap up the social side, too. But there are nail-biting moments; Prince Charles has taken some nasty tumbles from his pony and been carted off to the emergency room for stitches on more than one occasion.

For half the year, polo rules the Major's life. From the third Saturday in April until the second Sunday in September, he has to work a seven-day week, combining his role as the Prince's polo manager with deputy chairmanship of the Guard's Club. Every day, all year round, his "built-in" alarm clock sounds reveille, rousing him out of bed at Dummer Down Farm. Reaching for a "royal wedding" mug featuring his daughter's and son-in-law's faces, he takes a quick cup of coffee and, all polo season long, is on horseback by 7 A.M. "I ride for as long as the horse needs the exercise, but everything has to be geared for me to leave for the polo club at 8:30 A.M.," he explains. After driving from Dummer to Windsor Great Park, listening to sports coverage on BBC radio to pass the journey, the Major may make a quick call to Prince Charles to confirm the day's order of play or to report on the horses' fitness. "Otherwise, we have our talk when he arrives to play later in the day," says Major Ferguson. It is he who decides which of the club's polo pitches are perfect for playing on and who organizes endless polo practice.

Major Ferguson is now married for the second time, and the new Mrs. Ferguson—also, confusingly, called Susan—is a devoted spectator who nowadays finds herself in the spotlight during the summer polo season, a spin-off from her stepdaughter's new royal role. On Sundays, she always goes to Windsor to watch the matches, "to support Ronald, to take part in his life." In fact, it's virtually the only time she gets to see her husband during the glorious summer months, which coincide so absolutely with the polo season that at home, to Sue's regret, the Major "doesn't even have the time to walk to the bottom of the garden and see the roses." To Windsor, then, for balmy Sundays. "I just want to be there with him, although I don't expect him to talk to me. He has his mind on other things and hardly notices me, but that doesn't worry me. He is working."

And there is not a moment to be lonely. Beautifully dressed in summer silks, her English rose complexion protected from the (occasional!) English summer sun by a stylish straw hat, Sue Ferguson is a popular and striking figure in polo's social circle—and there may even be the joy of running into her stepdaughter, down to watch Prince Charles in the saddle, perhaps weekending at Windsor as is the royal family custom, while waiting for her own marital home to be completed.

After Sarah and Jane's mother left (and before he met his second wife), there was a time when the Major, encouraged by his daughters, dated other women. They had alw s hated the idea that their father might be lonely. It was a time referred to humorously inside the family circle as "intermarriage," when "Sarah and Jane would vet the girls I brought home and either shake their heads or say, 'Maybe, Dad.' "

It was a happy day indeed when the one brought home for

the girls' inspection turned out to be Sue, a peaches-and-cream, blond, well-to-do farmer's daughter and self-confessed "country girl" who was then working in London, cooking Cordon Bleu lunches for city businessmen at the Bank of America's city headquarters. The Major's own daughters, delighted to see their father so happy, gave the couple their full blessing. Major Ferguson soon married his new Susan, who is fourteen years his junior, and to everyone's great joy they started a family: Andrew (now nine), Alice (now seven), and toddler Eliza.

The polo-crazy pair long for winter weekends, though, when Sarah may come to visit. Before her wedding, she was a frequent visitor, following a traditional pattern of the Sloane Square set, whose mass exodus to the country (frequently with a large bag of laundry in the trunk, to be thrown in the family washing machine) leaves certain residential areas of London like Pimlico, Chelsea, and Fulham as deserted as the Marie Celeste at weekends. Nowadays, Sarah's traded the load of laundry for a retinue of bodyguards who must be fed and housed. The Major is fiercely protective of his younger daughter's privacy and cloaks her visits in secrecy. Prince Andrew may sometimes come with her, but it doesn't faze the Fergusons.

The mood at Dummer Down Farm, even with the family's newest, blue-blooded addition, is "damned relaxed. We have dinner around the kitchen table," explains Major Ferguson. "We carry on normally. He is a hell of a good chap and he is fantastic for one's daughter." The house itself, set in flat Hampshire countryside (with a truly countryish smell of manure on the breeze) is secluded and immaculate; Sue Ferguson is compulsively tidy and the house is as neat as a new pin. The beautifully decorated interior is filled with antiques that have been handed down through the Ferguson family for generations. Among the monogrammed linens and ancestral portraits are charming touches that prove the Fergusons' sense of

humor—so evident in Sarah—prevails at her father's hom
too.

In the kitchen, guests can drink from a selection of doze
of china mugs—including some to commemorate the we
ding, with Sarah's smiling face on it. There are newspap
headlines pinned to the kitchen notice board, and a gue
hanging his coat may opt to use a giant coat hanger in th
shape of Sarah's head. Such cheap and amusing souven
make the Ferguson family smile. In the light and airy dini
room—where Susan Ferguson serves delicious English-sty
roasts and fresh soups—sits a royal wedding cake that mu
periodically be dusted off. And Susan cleverly had her daug
ter Alice's hoop and headdress, worn on the great day, r
created by florist Jane Packer in dried flowers as an everlasti
souvenir.

However often Sarah descends upon the elegant yet e
tremely comfortable red-brick Georgian farmhouse, thoug
it could never be often enough for her father. "We contin
to be very close," he told *People* magazine in a recent int
view. "Sarah is a very caring person, even about her geriat
old father! There can't be many daughters who ring up
radiophone on the night of their wedding, which she di
Funnily enough, I probably speak to her more now tha
before—about four or five times a week when she's not trav
ing."

Sarah or no Sarah, "It is a joy, an unbelievable relief to
at home weekends," says the Major. In complete contrast
the action-packed summer season, "I don't ride. I don't shoo
I don't hunt." Mrs. Ferguson forsakes the shopping and dus
ing, too, devoting the weekend to their children and to ea
other, the highlight a big roast for Sunday lunch, with hom
grown vegetables picked that morning from the garden, fo
lowed by a rich, sticky pudding like treacle tart. To walk off t
calories, the family go to feed their horses during the afte

noon. And Major Ferguson himself tucks the children up in bed, sending them off to sleep with a bedtime story.

It's clear as the freckles on her face that Sarah inherited her sandy, redheaded, rosy-cheeked coloring from her darling "Dads." But her willowy sister Jane has her mother's genes; straight dark hair frosted by the sun, long legs, and a quite different bone structure. The sisters grew very close when their mother left, but nowadays, Sarah's and Jane's lives are quite literally worlds apart. Jane fell in love with another polo dynamo, redheaded Australian Alex Makim, during her late teens. He went on to become one of Australia's top polo players but, at the time the couple met, was working at Dummer as a groom while learning about the sport. Jane took a Cordon Bleu cookery course, then worked both as a cook and an office assistant, but finally decided to take a trip and visit her handsome beau in his homeland. "I think if you love someone," she explains, "you want to see the way they live."

Passionately in love with her slim, blue-eyed boyfriend, Jane was undeterred by the lack of glamour offered by the life in the outback that beckoned. "I'm definitely a country person and I think that helped." So she opted for a total life change and arrived in Australia as an eighteen-year-old bride in 1975. Actually, Jane adapted to life in the outback faster than you can say Waltzing Matilda, setting up home with her new husband on his family's huge North Star Farm at Goondiwindi, seven hundred miles north of Sydney, a tiny town with a single store that sells everything from stamps to sewing notions. "Dummer is my home," she declared ten years later, "but this is my home too. I'm not really a homesick sort of person, but I suppose everyone goes through some bouts of homesickness," she admits wistfully. Now, that homesickness may be particularly intense, because late in 1988, the Makim marriage hit the rocks. Jane, unable to take her beloved children back to England without her husband's permission, has remained for now in Australia to ponder her future.

Perhaps the contrast became too much between her own life and her sister's. There were only occasional visitors to accommodate, who would arrive by air or by way of the endless, bumpy dirt road where signs caution you to beware of kangaroos. They were greeted, upon finally reaching North Star, by a sign that read, "Close the bloody gate" in Spanish.

While Sarah lived in splendor in some of the world's most famous stately homes, Jane's home was a tiny, wooden house, called Wilgawarinna (which means "house among the trees" in the language of the land's former aboriginal occupants), built by Jane's father-in-law, Wilko Makim, in 1936. Jane was the first to admit that "it's certainly no palace." The floors are covered in linoleum, the sitting-room wall is cracked. A VCR was the couple's only real luxury.

But for the years of her marriage, Jane Makim gave it her all, farming a thousand head of livestock, rounding them up on horseback, branding them, and working from dawn till dusk, while on the other side of the globe, Sarah was being whisked from one appointment to another in a purring limousine. While Sarah was zipped into designer dresses every morning of her life, stepping into shoes that someone else had polished, Jane slipped into cowboy boots, scruffy jeans, and a T-shirt (as well as a cast-off sweater of Sarah's on colder days), which are the only appropriate garb for riding tractors or horses across the arid, dusty landscape of Australia's interior. But for now, she has hung up her cowboy boots and is waiting to see what her future holds. Whatever she chooses, wherever she lives, it is certainly likely to be more glamorous than North Star Farm.

But a few years back, in happier times, Sarah's wanderlust led her to fly the thirteen-thousand miles to visit the farm her sister called home and spend a month at North Star. And the pair had frequent, long-distance chats on the crackly radiophone. She called her excitedly an hour before the royal engagement was announced to share the news with her, and misses her sister's children enormously. Jane's children are a boisterous boy and girl, little redheaded Seamus (who became famous Seamus when, as a pageboy, he yawned during the royal nuptials) and three-year-old Ayesha, a name that means "gift of God," and now poignantly reflects the Makims' joy at the time of her arrival, for she was born after Jane had heart-breakingly suffered two miscarriages. Fergie's not just Ayesha's aunt but her godmother, too; the Makims had their daughter christened in the United Kingdom at the pretty, medieval All Saints Church in Dummer (where they had been married ten years before) just before Sarah's royal wedding. The whole family was reunited for this special, nostalgic occasion, upon which Major Ferguson and his ex-wife stood together for the first time in years, their differences buried—though perhaps not forgotten. "Ayesha is a very special child," Jane Makim said shortly after her daughter's birth. "It's taken a long time to get her."

Few occasions in Goondiwindi's calendar would call upon Jane to wear the tamarillo-colored silk suit she chose for Sarah's wedding. (Before the wedding, when she had to send off her son's measurements for his page-boy suit, Jane slipped in the design for her own dress, with a color swatch, for Sarah's approval.) The Makims' life wasn't all down-home hillbilly farming, though. North Star has its own polo club, where Jane was secretary, and which enabled the couple to travel to major tournaments around Australia. But Australians are notoriously casual people, and Jane's dress hung unworn in the wardrobe (alongside the Bellville-Sassoon wedding gown designed for her own wedding, twelve years ago) for the most part. An exception was a rare day trip to that highlight of the Australian social calendar, Melbourne Cup Day. So keen are Australians on this day at the races that the date is a national holiday! Spotted early by the group of press and photographers covering the event, she got a taste of what life is like for her younger sister all year round. "I don't know how

Sarah manages to smile all the time," she commented. "It's so difficult to do all day!"

Except for the stack of files bursting at the seams with press clippings lovingly cut out by Sarah's big sister, there were scant reminders back at North Star that the Makims had become in-laws to the world's most famous family. The Makims were always very laid back about the royal connection and their front-row seats at the wedding, which most people only got to see on TV. "It doesn't really hit you at the time," Jane said recently. "You wish you could rewind it all and experience it again. It's maybe six months before you think to yourself, 'Hey, I was there, I met the Queen.' "

But little Seamus likes to remind visitors to the farm about his big day, proudly showing off silver cufflinks engraved with the royal crest and his own initials as well as the wonderful sailor suit, tailor-made by the Saville Row firm of Gieves and Hawkes, that he wore with a blunted miniature silver dagger. (As Seamus walked down the aisle, paired off with one of the bridesmaids, Mrs. Sue Ferguson apparently overheard Seamus whisper to the little girl, "If you laugh at me once more, I'll cut your finger off with my knife." Such a display of macho bravado, from a mere five-year-old, is the stuff of Australian legend.) For Seamus, having a royal for an auntie has definite advantages. During the arduous twenty-four-hour trip whisking Seamus and his family to England for the wedding, the little lad got the ultimate treat: he was invited onto the plane's flight deck. What fun for a chap who usually travels by Land Rover and school bus.

Like Major Ferguson, Jane Makim is highly protective of Sarah and hates to see her criticized in the press, which has been littered with accusations about Fergie's frumpy style and her ample figure. "When I read that she is being called the Duchess of Pork, I really bristle," she declared in an interview. "Like me, Sarah just can't resist cream buns and cakes, but I don't think she's overweight." It particularly rankles when comparisons are drawn between Sarah and her slender sister-in-law Diana. "You simply can't compare them because they have different personalities," she rationalized. "Sarah hasn't got Diana's model-girl figure and never will have. But she's beautiful in her own way." The differences in their life-styles may have contributed to her own marriage problems, but still Jane Makim wouldn't trade places for anything.

Is the same true in the Spencer sisters' households? Perhaps not, for there was a time, around 1978, when it looked as if another Spencer girl, Lady Sarah, might be picked by the Prince of Wales as his future bride. Flame-haired Sarah, eldest of Lord Spencer's three girls, had been escorted by Prince Charles to countless dances and dinners and was invited to join the heir apparent on his annual skiing holiday in the Swiss Alpine resort of Klosters. A fun-loving creature, Sarah had shown a wild, rebellious streak as a child and, after the messy divorce of her parents, proved too much of a handful for several nannies who were appointed to keep her and her siblings in order. "I can't remember exactly how many, but it was a lot," she recalls of the stream of uniformed nannies who flowed through Park House's nursery.

Sarah thrived under the media microscope, lapping up the attention, and she is reported to have subscribed to a press "cuttings service" so that she wouldn't miss a single column-inch of what had been written about her. It seems, though, that however sweet Charles was on the auburn, freckled beauty (whose coloring is so reminiscent of the Duchess of York's), on Sarah's side the relationship was merely platonic. Unexpectedly, Sarah broke the taboo that deters most girlfriends from revealing the secrets of their royal romances to the press, declaring in an interview: "Charles is fabulous as a person, but I am not in love with him." Instead, she explained, he was more like the big brother that she'd never had.

In a second interview, she was even more outspoken about herself. (It may well be that young Diana, a picture of discretion, learned from her elder sister's example to remain silent and smile sweetly when quizzed about her life or love.) This time, Sarah had announced to the world that she had suffered from the "slimmer's disease," anorexia nervosa, and a drinking problem, which may well have been provoked by unhappy events during her childhood. She confessed to a journalist that she had been expelled from West Heath School (where Diana boarded) for being drunk. Even though she was captain of the school swimming team—also playing lacrosse, tennis, netball, and even the odd game of cricket—she revealed that "I used to drink because I was bored. I would drink anything, whisky, Cointreau, sherry, or—most often—vodka, because the staff couldn't smell that on my breath." Her early brush with alcohol put her right off, though; now she can't even stand the smell.

Interestingly, it may well have been Sarah—who went on to marry Guard's Officer Neil McCorquodale and now lives at Stoke Rochford, Lincolnshire—who sagely stepped in to counsel her younger sister Diana when the weight started falling off *her*, remembering her own battle with anorexia. Twice, Diana has slimmed right down beyond the point of mere slenderness. Just before her wedding, for instance, a photograph of the princess-in-waiting on the steps of St. Paul's exhorted one Fleet Street paper to run the banner headline, "Don't Lose Another Pound, Di!" Again, after the birth of her son William, she dieted fanatically. Her rapid weight loss prompted the press to interview leading experts in the field of anorexia nervosa, with the suggestion that Diana had succumbed to the obsessive slimmer's disease just as her sister had done years before. Lady Sarah's measurements had plummeted from the fashion-model standard of 34-24-34 to a painfully thin 27-20-28, and it was only after she volunteered for treatment at a hospital, a few months after she began to date Prince Charles, that she could bear the idea of eating again.

Sarah Spencer had met Prince Charles at a Royal Ascot week houseparty in 1977—which seems a perfect place for Sarahs to encounter princes, since Sarah Ferguson first caught *her* prince's eye in identical circumstances eight years later! So often were Charles and Lady Spencer seen together in public that she was generally accepted as "number-one filly in Charles's string of thoroughbred beauties"! The romance cooled, though, once Sarah agreed to be interviewed by the press, having broken royal rule number one. Perhaps, in view of the fact she'd owned up to the fact she didn't love Charles, the breakup genuinely didn't bother Sarah. Nevertheless, it is a shadow that allegedly lies over her friendship with the woman who wooed and won the Prince's heart, her younger sister Diana. A family friend is reported to have said, "There will always be a jealousy problem between Sarah and the Princess, following Sarah's flirtation with Charles. There is an ever-present edge. That's why Diana was never keen to stay in the same ski chalet that Charles had shared with Sarah."

But Diana happily took Sarah along to a recent school reunion, and there's no question that Auntie Diana adores and spoils her sister's children, little Emily Jane and George McCorquodale. She sees less of Sarah's children, though, than she does of Jane's—her other sister's brood: Laura, Alexander, and Eleanor. They live literally a stone's throw from Diana's Kensington Palace door and make perfect playmates for Di's little princes.

Earl Spencer can be justly proud of the marriages his daughters have made. Unlike Sarah, her elder sister, dark-haired Jane was never a problem teenager, rarely putting a well-shod foot out of line. She was a quiet schoolgirl, far more studious than either of her sisters. Sarah got six "O" levels and Diana didn't get any, but Jane diligently worked to gain eleven; she was the family "swot." Ten years ago, Jane announced a most suitable match: she became betrothed to ex-

Etonian Robert Fellowes, a member of the royal household who was then assistant private secretary to the Queen.

Johnnie Spencer led his daughter up the aisle of the Guard's Chapel to meet a husband of whom everyone approved wholeheartedly, and Diana, dressed in a Laura Ashley-ish, flower-sprigged, flounced frock and carrying a pretty bouquet, was thrilled to be a bridesmaid for the very first time in her life. Little did the royal guests present—including the Queen Mother—realize that the tall, shy teenager who carefully rearranged her sister's train and held the bride's bouquet during the ceremony would one day be welcomed with unprecedented pageantry and pomp into their own family.

Jane and Diana share the same deep sense of duty combined with a feeling for the fun things in life, and they spend as much time together as their schedules and motherhood allow. Because of his royal job, Robert Fellowes has been granted a "grace and favor" apartment within the "royal ghetto" at Kensington Palace; indeed, because of her husband, Jane was able to play a major role in kindling her sister's royal romance. Robert was required to travel to Balmoral House during 1980 to carry out his duties during the Queen's annual sojourn—she is never able to switch off completely because there are daily red boxes of paperwork to attend to—and Diana tagged along with her elder sister to help with her new niece, Laura. Prince Charles was at Balmoral, too. And the rest is history.

Nobody could have been more excited about Diana's blossoming romance than her charming father, Lord Spencer, who knew how crucial it was to his daughter's well-being that she had love, affection, and a sense of security. Johnnie Spencer had done his best to give his children a warm and happy home after their mother left, making a special effort to do the school run and be around for nursery tea at Park House in the afternoons; indeed, it might be said that for a while, he sacrificed his own emotional needs to attend to theirs, keenly feeling the scars of his marital breakup. Then he inherited the

Spencer earldom on the death of his father, on June 9, 1975, which brought massive responsibilities, distractions, and massive death duties. It also brought new titles for his children; until their grandfather died, the girls had been the Misses Spencer. They were now the Ladies Sarah, Jane, and Diana, and their brother assumed Johnnie's former title, Viscount Althorp.

Park House had to be packed up and a move organized to the massive mansion that now became the family home. For the Spencer children, particularly the sensitive Diana, it was a dramatic upheaval. They had been happy in Norfolk, near to the beach and surrounded by childhood friends, even though they only had the chance to play with them during school vacations. Althorp was altogether more imposing and less cozy than Park House, and the children never felt it was home in quite the same way.

Their reticence to settle comfortably into Althorp may have had partly to do with the fact that their father had found a new love. His constant companion was Lady Dartmouth—ironically, the daughter of romantic novelist Barbara Cartland, whose bodice-rippers Diana had devoured at school, making no secret of the fact that Miss Cartland was her favorite author. Still, it was one thing having Barbara Cartland's books on the shelf, quite another having the novelist's daughter presiding over *their* home. Raine (nicknamed "Acid Raine" in some circles) had been married to the Hon. Gerald Legge at the age of eighteen; he later inherited the title Lord Lewisham and later still became Lord Dartmouth. They had four children and, to the outside world, nothing was amiss with the Dartmouth marriage. But in 1976, Raine met the still debonair and very lonely Lord Spencer when they found themselves on the same charity committee to protect the nation's heritage.

"My fault was that I fell madly in love when I was forty-five," she declared. From the moment they met, Johnnie and Raine were virtually inseparable, but the Spencer children initially gave her a frosty reception. She is an effusive and domineering woman who always looks impeccable (if sometimes somewhat overly made up). One of her friends once said, "Raine's not a person, she's an experience." After her wedding ceremony, on July 14, 1976, at Caxton Hall (with only two witnesses), the new Countess Spencer tried hard to become a second mother to the Spencer children, who were largely unreceptive to her overtures. In the end, the gaps between their trips home to Althorp grew longer. But of all the children, it is the Princess of Wales who most warmed to her stepmother.

Perhaps what the children resented even more than the fact that she had, as they saw it, stolen their father's affections, was the decorative influence she brought to bear on Lord Spencer's ancestral home. Changes most certainly had to be made to bring the house into the twentieth century, but Raine Spencer didn't stop with the installation of central heating and gas-log fires (after one weekend guest complained that the arctic conditions in her bedroom had led her to sleep in her mink coat). She drew up grand plans for the refurbishment of Althorp and encouraged Lord Spencer when he had to sell off family treasures, including works by the Dutch artist Van Dyck, to finance the changes and settle a staggering bill for £2.5 million in death duties.

To be bequeathed a grand house in the middle of the English countryside with more than enough bedrooms to entertain all your friends at once sounds like heaven. In fact, what today's aristocrats are inheriting is a round-the-clock nightmare. The Duke of Marlborough, who owns the Palladian masterpiece Blenheim Palace, once lamented to me, "Just imagine the problems the average householder has keeping a home warm, safe, and well decorated—and multiply them by a thousand. We've had scaffolding up at Blenheim for thirty years; as soon as the renovations are complete on one wing, another part is crying out for attention. And just when you think you can see the light at the end of the tunnel, they tell you the bloody sluice in the lake needs replacing—and bingo! There's another fifty grand down the plughole."

Johnnie Spencer understands the Duke's plight only too well. The prohibitive costs of running a stately home must somehow be offset if the house is to be preserved for the enjoyment of future generations rather than handed over to the National Trust (who maintain and refurbish many British architectural gems). Luckily for Althorp, Raine has a particularly commercial outlook on life—perhaps inherited from her prolific novelist mother, whose books have sold literally millions of copies around the world and been translated into virtually every language, including Chinese. Shortly after the royal wedding, they threw open the house to the public, who not surprisingly descended in droves to drink in the splendor of the future queen's ancestral abode.

Proceeds of guided tours and sales from the Althorp gift shop—where sticks of rock candy and bottles of homemade wine are snapped up by the visitors—are plowed into Althorp. There are also regular banquets for paying guests, and the stately home can be hired for official functions. "We've got to make this place pay," its owner rationalizes. "If this involves throwing a party for Tupperware manufacturers, why not?"

Lord Spencer is well aware that originally, Althorp—with its magnificent mahogany staircase, rich red walls, and solid gold artifacts—attracted mainly royal watchers. But the annual tally of visitors suggests that the word spread like wildfire that Althorp offered a truly magnificent day out.

It was in 1978 that Johnnie Spencer suffered his stroke and was at death's door for four months. "A lot of people," he observes, "come here because they know I've been ill, so they bring their husbands or their wives who have had the same trouble and they say, 'Here's Lord Spencer; *he* managed to get over it and you can do the same.' That's very nice, being an encouragement to other people. A lot of ladies bring their husbands here, and they look a great deal more decrepit than I am!"

It took the major family tragedy of Lord Spencer's stroke to help banish the children's image of "interloper" Raine as a wicked stepmother. Throughout her husband's illness, Raine was utterly devoted, barely leaving his side. The Spencer children warmed slowly to their father's wife in the light of the caring way in which she nursed him back to health, bossing him gently back to fitness. He had to learn to walk and to talk properly once more and had recovered enormously by the time he led Diana somewhat unsteadily down the aisle to meet Charles at the altar. These days, Lord Spencer is fitter still. But as the family was united in its distress, relations between Countess Spencer and her stepchildren improved enormously. Michael Shea, the royals' former press secretary, described their relationship thus: "Diana quite often goes to Althorp for weekends, or to have dinner, or her father and stepmother come to see her in London. So I wouldn't call it strained. I would just call it polite."

He added, "The Princess is, of course, very close to her father." And nevertheless, when he travels up to London to visit his darling Diana and princely grandchildren—he was the first honored visitor to her Kensington Palace home, signing the leather guest book "Earl Spencer (Daddy)"—Raine often stays behind, perhaps diplomatically not wishing to intrude on the intimate moments that her husband can share with his princess all too rarely these days.

Raine and Johnnie Spencer are utterly inseparable and still behave like a pair of lovestruck teenagers, holding hands in public and trying to organize their schedules so that they spend few nights apart. She publicly refers to him as "my heavenly man." They have worked together on two sumptuous coffee-table books, *Japan and the Far East* and *The Spencers on Spas*. Lady Spencer—who, when she published two short stories as a teenager, once looked set to follow her mother's literary example—is an unpaid but highly involved committee member of the British Tourist Authority.

She concedes that she has learned a lot from her cuddly second husband, and close friends testify to her more mellow outlook on life. "He's so wonderful with people," she declares of her sixty-four-year-old husband. "There's something special about those big blue eyes that makes people stand up and tell him all their problems, and he's taught me to see that everyone has their interesting side—which before . . . well, it wasn't that I wasn't interested, but I sometimes felt I didn't have the time." Nevertheless, she declares, she regards "John" (as she prefers to call him) as "my husband, my lover, and my best friend. I sometimes say to him, 'I'm so busy I never see any friends,' and he says, 'I'm your best friend.' "

While entertaining Lynn Barber of the *Sunday Express* magazine, an award-winning London journalist, to tea recently, Raine Spencer pointed at a delightful painting of her husband as a small boy standing somewhat forlornly on a beach. "I always think he looks rather a sad and lonely little boy. I don't think that living in a big house particularly brings happiness. People tend to forget the loneliness you may suffer if you're a child."

It may well be that Diana's younger brother Charles understands only too well the poignant truth of her stepmother's remarks. Currently, he enjoys the title Viscount Althorp, which he will keep until Lord Spencer's death. Then he will become the ninth Earl Spencer, master of the grand Northamptonshire family seat, full of priceless silver, glistening candelabra, corridors of ancestral portraits, and eight thousand acres of land, including flower-filled gardens tended by a team of full-time horticulturalists. Customarily, upon his father's death, the estate should pass to his heir to minimize possible death duties, but interestingly, Charles is on record as saying, "I can't see my stepmother handing it over." Nevertheless, one day Althorp *will* belong to its present viscount, and now that the royal princes are all but married off, Charles is in fact one of Britain's most elegible bachelors, a tall and strikingly handsome young man with a rosy complexion and piercing blue eyes. Once plagued by puppy fat, he is now slender, and those chubby cheeks have slimmed down to reveal an aristocratic bone structure just like his sister Diana's.

In the early days of Diana's romance, however, "the other Charles" proved to be something of a royal headache. Young and impressionable and with any teenager's desire to let the good times roll at the drop of a top hat, party-loving Charles was dubbed "Champagne Charlie" by the press—and also labeled arrogant, pompous, and spoiled. There was a time when Charles Edward Maurice Althorp's name was never mentioned save in connection with allegations that he'd gate-crashed a party, been seen with a harem of gorgeous girls, or had drunk himself into oblivion at a charity ball. He was branded a "Hooray Henry," the label given to bread-roll throwing, devil-may-care aristobrats who live in London all week (working as real estate agents or commodity brokers) and descend on their parents' country homes at weekends to drink the cellars dry of vintage claret.

But his Champagne Charlie phase turned out—no doubt to the intense relief of the royals—to be blessedly short-lived; anyway, the pranks had been exaggerated out of all proportion and were probably the symptom of nothing but harmless adolescent exuberance. His worst "crimes" were to be banned from a nightclub for being "rude and obnoxious" and being present in a Kensington restaurant while a group of chums tried to "de-bag" (or forcibly take the pants off) a British disc jockey. The cross that Charles Althorp had to bear was that, unlike his friends and contemporaries, he couldn't let his red hair down without making front-page headlines. Added to which, it must be slightly irksome when your big sister—the awkward, shy teenager whom you once teased mercilessly, but who acted as almost a surrogate mother when your own did a disappearing act—suddenly becomes the most famous woman in the world, who can no longer come out to play as and when you'd like.

Old Etonian Charles—who had coedited the *Eton Chronicle*, his school magazine, turned out to be the brains of the Spencer family. He got good grades in three "A" levels (short for advanced levels, the exam taken in specialist subjects by eighteen-year-olds in the United Kingdom—and distinctly more taxing intellectually than the "O" levels, which were all his sisters managed to gain for their resumes) and won a place at Oxford University. He resisted temptation to lie back and do nothing during the year before he "went up" to Oxford, despite the fact that a generous family trust fund could have enabled him to safari in Kenya, soak up the sun on Bondi beach, or simply twiddle his thumbs and be a party animal for a spell. Instead, he took a series of odd jobs to gain an insight into the real world, quite different from life at Althorp, which is so filled with antiques it's like living in a museum, and where there are servants to polish the shoes, make the beds, and do the dishes.

"I wanted to get some experience in the nine months before going up to Oxford," he explained of his decision to work as an errand boy for the Queen's stockbrokers, Rowe and Pitman, and his stint as a trainee quality controller in a food factory. He also signed on as a £200-a-day extra on *Another Country*, a film whose theme—homosexuality in an English public school—once more plunged Charles into a controversy. However, Charles's eye for beautiful blondes has firmly silenced anyone who dares to insinuate that his first film role in any way reflected his own predilections.

Once at Oxford, he foreswore partying for the pursuit of serious study. He chose as his subject history—appropriate for a man who will one day find himself surrounded by it and who hails from a family that can be traced back through the records to the year 1330. He passed his exams with flying colors and learned to keep a lower profile, although the press was still eager to catch him out. Charles had to keep his college bedroom door locked after one reporter burst in, no doubt hoping to catch the future queen's younger brother "in flagrante" with his latest blonde.

And the partying days weren't *quite* a thing of the past; at the age of twenty-one he came into much of his fortune and was able to splash out a staggering £100,000 on a never-to-be-forgotten party at Spencer House (another family home) in St. James's, a sixty-room mansion valued at about $12 million—which will, one day, also be his. There, a thousand bottles of vintage champagne flowed in rivers; there was also a satellite link-up with Los Angeles which enabled U.S. chanteuse Phyllis Nelson to sing a chorus of "Happy Birthday" from thirteen thousand miles away. The cabaret was performed by a team of four scantily clad dancers, which allegedly prompted Diana to cover her sapphire-blue eyes and declare, "This looks as if it were for men only. . . ." Prince Charles, the Princess of Wales, and the Princess's sisters enjoyed every moment, dancing to the disco beat into the small hours alongside 320 other members of the British upper crust, political figures, and television personalities. When Charlie Althorp emerged to the strains of the dawn chorus at around 4 A.M., he blinked, saying, "It's been a wonderful night, and it's a wonderful morning."

Charles, something of a daredevil, learned to fly (and was nicknamed "Biggles" by his friends after a fictional British pilot) and to parachute; he completed a jump for charity. Indeed, during his time at Oxford, Charles revealed a philanthropic side to his nature infinitely more in keeping with his elevated station in life than the endless round of partygoing in which he used to indulge. One cause particularly close to his heart, and for which he helps with fund-raising events, is the Royal Marsden Hospital specializing in the treatment of cancer. Charles and Diana's own cousin, Conway Seymour, was a patient of the hospital before he finally succumbed to leukemia in 1981. Neither Charles nor his sister has forgotten the hospital's valuable work or how they helped Conway during his battle for life.

During the long college vacations, Charles was also able to work on the ten-room falconer's cottage home, which his dad gave him on the grounds of Althorp. (In London he has another home, a white stucco-fronted Victorian house in South Kensington. To help pay the overhead and keep burglars and prying reporters at bay, he has tenants in his basement— friends who can be relied on for discretion.) Charles got a good degree from Oxford and went out in the world proud of the fact that he'd be the first member of the Spencer family to work for his living.

A keen cook, Charles cherished ambitions of opening his own restaurant. As he once told journalist Richard Compton Miller in an exclusive interview, "I try to be vaguely original when planning a dinner party—like beginning with gulls' or quails' eggs. I then do a delicious guinea fowl or salmon, which my mother sends down from Scotland." But as fate would have it, Charles got a taste for a quite different career— as a television announcer. The wedding of Sarah Ferguson and his sister's brother-in-law opened the door and gave Charles his big break: NBC, looking for London commentators who could offer an insight into the royal nuptials, took something of a gamble and recruited the inexperienced Viscount to conduct interviews and comment on the procession's progress. So impressed were the network's bosses with Charles's savoir faire and flair that they offered him a permanent job, reporting on the cultural and social scene in London.

When he isn't filming for NBC, Charles tries to schedule a lunch with his sister at a quiet Italian trattoria like La Nassa. He also makes a point of popping in to Kensington Palace to play with his nephews, the little princes. Although showing no sign of settling down yet, he has expressed a desire for a large family, "more than three children, anyway."

I was recently at a gala charity soiree to mark Chanel's relaunch of their legendary perfume, Chanel No. 5, an event that coincided with an exhibition of exclusive clothes and costume jewelry dating back to Coco Chanel's first designs. Rising head and shoulders above the tuxedoed gentlemen and couture-clad ladies, the piercing blue eyes of a strikingly handsome young man caught and held my eyes for several delicious, heart-stopping moments. And it dawned on me that the future Countess Spencer will be one lucky lady.

3

Fine Romances

The Queen must have been worried. In the late seventies, with Britain's supply of virgins running out, her eldest son—the future king—was in his thirties and still a lonely bachelor. She knew from personal experience that a monarch needs someone to lean on, someone to crack jokes with when the crown becomes—literally and metaphorically— too heavy, and someone to give you a loving hug rather than a bow or a curtsey. And if matters didn't improve soon, it looked as if the world's most eligible bachelor—known as "action man" for daring deeds including diving under the polar ice cap, parachuting, and playing polo—might remain eligible unto his grave.

There had been a string of beautiful girls to party and play with such as the Duke of Wellington's brunette daughter Lady Jane Wellesley, who, at one point in 1971, looked destined to walk up the aisle with Charles. But he was carving out a career in the forces and the couple decided to "wait and see." Evidently, absence didn't make the heart grow fonder, and they drifted apart. Sabrina Guiness (heiress to a banking fortune) had a life-style considered too racy for a future queen; she loved to hang out with movie stars and dance the night away at showbiz parties; she had worked as a nanny to hell-raising Hollywood star Ryan O'Neal and to David Bowie and she recently proved to have exerted a fatal attraction over heart-throb Michael Douglas. There had been a volatile blonde called Anna Wallace—known to her circle as "Whiplash," supposedly because of her great love of fox hunting—whom Prince Charles is reputed to have been keen to wed. She'd even been given the "royal once-over," invited to Balmoral for the Queen to pass judgment. Supposedly, Miss Wallace—rather stunned—turned down the prince's proposal, knowing better than anyone that her former romances ruled her out as a perfect match. Eventually, at a party for the Queen Mother's eightieth birthday, the split came; she felt Charles was ignoring her all evening and the two had a blistering row before she stormed out of his life forever.

And so the list grew. He must have danced with a thousand blondes and dated hundreds of lovely ladies. Only the Prince—plus his valet and detectives, who for reasons of security always remained nearby—know how many of those he made love to. Women have always been seduced by power—and Charles, as future king of England, had plenty. He may not have had Redford or Newman's drop-dead gorgeousness, but he was a *prince*, and many young women could guess at and dream of the life of luxury, international travel, and glamorous clothes and jewels that the Princess of Wales now revels in. Privately and publicly, women literally threw themselves at him; on royal "walkabouts," girls would appear from nowhere and plant great, wet, smacking kisses on the Prince's lips—to the horror of his detectives and bodyguards, who fretted that if lusty young women could break through his defenses, so could a gun-wielding terrorist.

Decorum demanded, however, that Prince Charles be introduced to his future bride under more conventional circumstances—whatever the fantasies of would-be queens like the slender blonde who saw Prince Charles going for a swim in Australia and promptly dove into the ocean to try to get to know him better. Many of the European royalty and nobility were ruled out because they are Catholic, and Charles—who will one day be head of the Protestant Church of England—would (like any other member of his family) have had to give up his right to the throne to marry a girl from a different religion.

The list of suitable virgins had been narrowed down to half a dozen or so. She *had* to be sexually unsullied because the royal family could not take the chance that some former paramour, in a fit of pique, might reveal embarrassing details of a heretofore private liaison. By the age of nineteen, most young British women had had some sexual experience, and Charles was getting older every year. (Ironically, in the late eighties, the moral tide has turned—and virgins in their twenties are once again not so hard to find.)

Meanwhile, flame-haired Lady Sarah Spencer may well have blown her chances as future Princess of Wales by revealing to a women's magazine that she'd once had a drinking problem and was also anorexic, but she and the Prince had maintained their "platonic" friendship, and the two still saw plenty of one another. In fact, Sarah unwittingly engineered the first meeting between Charles and the woman who would become his wife when, in 1977, she invited Charles on a shoot at the family seat of Althorp, where he was introduced to Lady Diana in the middle of a muddy plowed field. Both Charles and Diana have claimed on occasion that they can't remember the moment—but it's easier to believe Charles than the woman who is now his princess. If you were sixteen years old and home from school for the weekend, wouldn't meeting the Prince of Wales stick in *your* memory forever? In fact, insiders say that Diana was quite, quite crazy about the Prince throughout her adolescence. While her school friends at West Heath decorated their walls with posters of pop stars and Hollywood actors, Diana cherished secret thoughts of Prince Charles. It may well be that the real reason she had no romantic skeletons in her closet was because she was already in love with him.

The leggy but still plump Lady Diana got the chance to know her prince better a couple of years later when the Queen invited Lady Sarah to bring her younger sister along for company at a houseparty one weekend at Sandringham. Diana leapt at the chance to be near her favorite former home—and her pinup prince. Another sister helped Cupid along when she invited Diana to join her at Balmoral (where Lady Jane and her new baby were spending a Scottish summer, accompanying her husband, Robert Fellowes, while he performed his royal duties).

Soon after, Diana learned to expect occasional phone calls inviting her to join Charles when he assembled a group of friends for a night on the town. At that time, it wasn't romance but companionship he sought; Anna Wallace had only recently flounced out of his life—and his heart. But Charles began to feel deeply attracted to Diana's unaffected charm. He found her great fun, always quick to laugh, and irreverent. Her then-curvy shape appealed to him too—typically, he had always liked his women with a bit of "meat" on them. Above all, she wasn't fazed by being around royalty, and never sycophantic. She made him feel, well, normal.

She was the girl next door, to begin with, but with certain natural attributes that qualified her to be included on the list of possible brides. The optimum time for a woman to conceive and produce healthy children is during her early twenties, so Diana's prime childbearing years were still ahead of her. Her love of children was obvious; she helped out part time at the Young England Kindergarten School in Pimlico and had formerly worked as a nanny for a little American boy, Patrick Robertson, whose father was an oil-company executive. Indeed, at her first official photo session, Diana posed in the nursery school garden with one little girl perched on her hip and another holding her hand. Like it or not, the most crucial role of any woman Charles chose as his wife would be to produce an heir to the throne.

The future king had to be logical and pragmatic when it came to finding Miss, or Lady, or Princess Right. He once said, "If I'm deciding on whom I want to live for the next fifty years—well, that's the last decision in which I'd want my head to be ruled entirely by my heart. You have to remember that when you marry in my position, you're going to marry someone who, perhaps, is one day going to be queen. You've got to choose somebody very carefully, I think, who could fulfill this particular role, and it has got to be pretty unusual." He couldn't risk making a mistake: It had to be right first time.

It was no "grand passion," but Charles, still licking his wounds from Miss Wallace, knew how exhausting *that* emotional merry-go-round could be. Diana, meanwhile, was utterly lovestruck. Friends have said she followed him "like a little lamb." But if Prince Charles wasn't head over heels in love, then at least one of the pair was positively swooning with delight. She found him thoughtful, caring, and considerate, and the fact that he was a real-life prince made it doubly thrilling. But she wore her infatuation well. Having seen firsthand how her sister blew it, she vowed to avoid Lady Sarah's mistakes.

Being wooed by a prince is enough to turn any young woman's head; something to tell future grandchildren even if it doesn't "work out." Prince Charles, by all accounts, is a romantic soul. As a suitor, he is given to quoting poetry and has a well-used account at a florist's, so his young ladies found themselves royally romanced in more than one sense. On the occasions when he'd take his companions dancing, there would be a discreet table in a dimly lit corner of Annabel's with a bottle of fine champagne chilling nicely. But before you swoon at the very thought of all this princely attention, it must be remembered that Prince Charles grew up surrounded by security men and servants. He may barely notice their presence, but hovering acolytes have put the damper on his dates' ardor on occasion.

It may indeed have been her immaculate, always-polite behavior toward the press (who began to dog her everywhere) that prompted Charles to see Lady Di in a new light—as perfect marriage material. Charles was prepared for a barrage of press attention and speculation at every new romance. He may, in fact, have depended on the press to sniff around in the young ladies' pasts and reveal anything untoward. Of course, the yellow press needed no prompting, but try as they might, they could find no dirt on Di. Things were looking up.

Rumors of a blossoming romance were fueled when long-stemmed roses began arriving regularly at Lady Diana's door. She had bought the apartment with trust money that matured on her eighteenth birthday and shared it with three roommates, Anne Bolton, Carolyn Pride, and Virginia Pitman. At the first whispers of the royal romance, Coleherne Court—to the irritation of the other residents in this luxury Earl's Court mansion block—was besieged by waiting reporters. Madcap dashes across the country at breakneck speed were made by the "royal Rat Pack" (as the group of journalists preoccupied with royal affairs is known) at the merest hint that Charles and Diana were enjoying a secluded tête-à-tête together or were on the guest list at some top nob's houseparty.

Other women would have freaked out at the invasion of their privacy, but Diana hid behind her bangs and demurely smiled her way through the siege. Her roommates were positive souls of discretion, sworn to secrecy and under pain of death not to talk to a soul about her rendezvous with the prince. They helped put journalists off the trail and generally maintained a veil of secrecy over their friend's love affair, only too happy to see her with a boyfriend, and *what* a boyfriend, at last.

Charles started truly to love her for the way she rose to the occasion. And though thwarted in their search for a scoop by her Mona Lisa smile and politely dismissive remarks, the press, whose hearts she won just as effectively as the Prince's, loved her too. (One journalist is alleged to have secretly counseled Her Ladyship *not* to give him the exclusive interview his editor was hassling for, in case this might jeopardize her marriage prospects.) Charles's mother and grandmother were particularly delighted, and the rapturous public just *longed* for him to make the whole thing official. "We want a wedding" went the rallying cry.

Having weighed the evidence and found it in Diana's favor—his only worry was the age gap, unavoidable if he was to marry a virgin, or at least one who didn't look like the back end of a smashup—Charles finally popped the question on February 5, 1981. Nobody can say he didn't warn Diana as best he could about what she was letting herself in for. He knew firsthand about the total lack of privacy permitted to royalty and about the demands of the job. He painstakingly explained them for the umpteenth time to Diana, insisting that she must wait as long as she wanted before honoring him with a reply.

Charles planned to let her mull it all over while she spent a holiday on her mother's Australian sheep farm. (By then, he'd realized he was going to miss her cheerful, smiling face and their private jokes; maybe he even fretted that if he didn't propose, she'd fall for some rugged Australian.) "I wanted to give her a chance to think about it," he has said. "To think if it was all going to be too awful. She'd planned to go to Australia with her mother quite a long time before anyway, and I thought, 'Well, I'll ask her then so that she'll have a chance of thinking it over while she's away, so she can decide if she can bear the whole idea—or not, as the case may be.'"

As we all know, love is blind—and deaf, too. Diana didn't need asking twice before she accepted the proposal which, for her, was the culmination of years spent dreaming of just such a moment. But if she had been more worldly, more experienced, and less in love, would her answer still have been, "It's what I want"?

She had seemed to cope like a natural with the pressures right up until the moment of her engagement announcement at Buckingham Palace—the first time that the clever royal couple (who had successfully evaded press attempts to snap them together) were photographed in public. But not the last, oh *no*. The world became desperate for Di. She rapidly became one of the most talked about, photographed, and pursued women in history.

The few months between her engagement announcement and the big day itself were frenzied. Where did the romance go, she must have wondered, as she was whisked from dress fitting to hair appointment, met with equerries and royal staff to learn the rules she must obey during her future life: whom to curtsey to, not to giggle when women curtsied to her (as they all should when Diana approaches), and how officially to refer to her mother-in-law. She had to bid farewell to casualness and play down her friendly nature. She would have to be referred to, from her marriage on, as Your Royal Highness. (Despite Diana and Sarah's friendliness and approachability, if you dare to refer to them to their faces as Fergie and Di, you'll be met with a most frosty reception. Protocol is still the absolute order of the day when royals are present. Physical contact is to be avoided at all costs, with the exception of shaking the royal hand, which must only be lightly touched, not stroked or squeezed.)

There were rooms full of new clothes, but no more carefree shopping expeditions. She couldn't set foot in public without a Scotland Yard officer in watchful attendance. Even when she went to the bathroom, there was someone keeping guard. So many lessons to learn and so little time to herself. But that, alas, is a princess's lot.

She had meetings with Dudley Poplak to pore over endless wallpaper samples and fabric swatches for her new homes. Now that she had been well and truly welcomed into her husband's family, she and Charles each spent more time with the other royals and had to snatch precious moments to be alone together. They were showered with official invitations as every good cause and charity—not to mention private hosts and hostesses—clamored for their presence. Whatever happened to dinner for two?

Having left behind her loyal roommates when she moved into Clarence House, Diana had also bidden farewell to early-morning tea and the sharing of secrets at the cozy Coleherne Court apartment. There were still thrilling moments—like the time she went home to Althorp and got the chance to flaunt her valuable engagement ring as any excited bride-to-be would, allowing her awestruck women friends to try the bauble on for size. But for much of the time, the fairytale princess-to-be found herself virtually imprisoned—if not in a castle, then at least in the royal palace of Clarence House (although as the wedding day approached, Diana was allowed to move into a small apartment inside Buckingham Palace, next door to her fiancé's suite, enabling them to live practically as man and wife). There was so much to do before the wedding deadline that there barely seemed to be a moment to share with her father, family, and friends, making her feel increasingly isolated. The family member she saw most of was her maternal grandmother Ruth Fermoy, still the Queen Mother's lady-in-waiting. But when it came to choosing the princess's own retinue of attendants, she had to go along with the upscale trio who had met with the Queen's approval: Anne Beckwith-Smith, Lavinia Baring, and Hazel West. (Rumor has it that Diana actually wanted Sarah Ferguson on the list, but her friend was vetoed through lack of experience.) It must slowly have dawned on Diana that for the foreseeable future, not Prince Charles, not Di herself, but Her Majesty the Queen would rule the royal couple's roost.

As any bride knows, there are inevitable arguments between the bride's family and the groom's over wedding plans; these can create friction between the supposedly happy couple to the extent that every engaged woman occasionally wonders if she's made a dreadful mistake. Diana can have been no exception. But with a royal wedding, the family and royal staff take over almost completely; it's the Queen's wishes—not the bride's—that are pandered to on all but a few counts. All the bride has to do is show up and look stunning. Diana had barely even heard of, let alone met, most of the people who were on the invitation list to her own wedding. Heads of state, international dignitaries, presidents, and politicians all had to take precedence over names that Diana would sentimentally have liked to include.

And everywhere that Diana went, the press was sure to go. This, above all, took its toll on the by now fragile emotions of the bride-to-be. Her temper was undoubtedly made still shorter by the fact that she'd been on a drastic diet. Diana had been deeply unhappy about the first pictures of her that had appeared; the famous back-lit shot of her in a flimsy cotton skirt made her legs "look like a grand piano's." Her husband may have loved her early voluptuousness, but Diana was determined that not an extra pound would mar her enjoyment in flicking back through her wedding photos—and even Charles couldn't complain at the metamorphosis taking place before his very eyes. Di had never been an ugly duckling, but few could have suspected that beneath the heavy bangs, blunt-cut hairstyle, and loose casual clothes lurked a rare bird of paradise.

Diana was well aware that television gives the illusion that one is ten pounds heavier than in real life; knowing that her ceremony would be flashed around the world via satellite, she exercised, skipped meals, and half starved herself to fashion-model slenderness. The new clothes from top designers were constantly having to go back to the seamstresses to be nipped and tucked. Pre-wedding nerves did whatever else was necessary to reduce her once hearty appetite. It had, of course, to end in tears. And it did, shortly before the wedding, during a polo match she had loyally attended to watch her horseman husband-to-be play a chukka or two. The crowds at polo matches are notoriously civilized and well behaved. In their desperation to see Lady Diana, Superstar, this mob behaved more like a rugby scrum, almost crushing the unprepared princess-to-be. She fled in floods of tears; then she spent a few minutes collecting herself, blew her nose and wiped her mascara, and bravely reemerged to face her public.

The media circus could reasonably have been expected to calm down after that wedding of the century. But it never has. Diana is the most photographed woman in the world, the ultimate cover girl. Even now, when the leading British weekly magazines *Woman* and *Woman's Own* emblazon Diana across their covers, they are guaranteed a sellout issue. Nobody—except someone with a crystal ball and strong psychic powers—could have predicted that, eight years after she stepped into the glass carriage to be slowly transported down The Mall to meet her groom, she would still be living her daily life in a goldfish bowl. In some respects, Diana couldn't have known what her life would be like, because her international, transglobal popularity was unprecedented. But if she hadn't been so swept off her feet, so utterly in love both with her prince and the idea of being in love itself, if she had just been a bit more experienced, then Lady Diana Spencer could have "read the runes" and taken a cold, hard look at her future life. A more worldly person might never have leaped at the opportunity. But then, a more worldly person would never have been offered it.

By the time Prince Andrew started dating Sarah Ferguson,

with whom the Princess of Wales had spent many hours chatting on the sidelines at polo matches, the inevitable had happened. The first flush of young love shared by any young couple was now merely a memory for Diana and Charles. Married life, as it must, had become routine. Diana had fulfilled her most important duty and produced two heirs to the throne, shaken millions of hands, and learned all about life inside a gilded cage. She may wistfully have looked at her still-single girlfriends and realized just how innocent she'd been when she accepted Charles's proposal. She'd barely had a boyfriend and may well never even have been kissed by another man. The very words that had so delighted her—"It was for life, forever"—were now engraved on her heart as a reminder of what that really meant. It was too late; there was no turning back. And forever is a very long time.

The arrival of Diana's little princes had liberated Charles's younger brother basically to marry whomever he pleased—within reason. But he was under no pressure to settle down just yet and could play the field and enjoy the freedom that came from being relegated to fourth in line to the throne (after Charles and his sons, William and Harry). He once told journalists, "I'll know there and then if I do find somebody. Then it's going to come like a lightning bolt." While he was waiting for this anticipated *coup de foudre,* his young free-and-single life-style earned him the reputation of a Lothario and the nickname "Randy Andy."

His long list of conquests may have caused his mother a good few sleepless nights. Unlike Charles, he generally spurned aristocratic company, preferring beauty queens, calendar girls, and actresses. He felt that as just reward for long hours and brave deeds as a naval officer—he served during the Falklands crisis as helicopter pilot, having signed up with the navy in 1979 on a twelve-year commission—he was entitled to play hard off duty. The list of conquests grew ever longer: ballerina and model Clare Park (whose beautiful face endorsed Oil of Olay in the United Kingdom); onetime beauty queen Carolyn Seaward; actresses Finola Hughes (who starred opposite John Travolta in *Staying Alive*) and Katie Rabett (who later had a role in a James Bond movie); and ex-model Vicki Hodge (who was several years older than the prince and who later sold the salacious inside story of a trip to Mustique with Andrew and a group of friends to a British Sunday newspaper). Andrew, a keen photographer, actually published a book, prior to his engagement, featuring ethereal shots of many of the women who'd drifted in and out of his life. If he'd chosen to do a calendar, he could have gone from January through to December without once repeating his models.

But the girl who first stole Prince Andrew's heart was an American-born actress, Koo Stark, also his senior by three years. If her resume had included nothing more risque than bikini shots from a Bond movie, then there is a good chance that Kathleen Dee-Anne Stark might now be the Duchess of York. The couple had met in 1982 on the after-dark circuit of London's nightclubs, of which the Prince was a habitue. Soon after, Argentina invaded the Falkland Islands in the South Atlantic, and the British armed forces—with whom the Prince was serving as a navy pilot aboard the HMS *Invincible*—found themselves embroiled in a bloody conflict. Separated by thousands of miles of ocean and unable to make contact except by radio, both Andrew and Koo's hearts grew fonder.

But meanwhile, the press were, as usual, digging around in the new royal girlfriend's past for morsels with which to delight their prurient readers. This time, they uncovered a biggie: that she'd played the title role in a mildly titillating soft-porn movie called *The Awakening of Emily*, made by the Earl of Pembroke (whose family tree links him with both Sarah Ferguson and the Princess of Wales). There's no doubt the Queen was aware of Koo's history, but she wisely decided to turn a blind eye, hoping, no doubt, that the passion between Andrew and Koo would burn itself out.

Oh, to have been a fly on the royal wall the weekend Koo spent at Balmoral House that September! Shortly after that, a battle-weary Prince Andrew whisked Miss Stark off to sojourn at his Aunt Margaret's home on the famous paradise island of Mustique. With a party of friends, they traveled together as Mr. and Mrs. Cambridge, but the vacation turned out to be anything but a secluded idyll. Newsmen with telephoto lenses lurked behind palm trees and aboard speedboats in the lagoon, hoping, no doubt, to catch a frolicsome Ms. Stark reenacting certain moments of her film career. It was all too much, and after just a week, the not-so-happy couple jetted off in different directions to cool it for a while.

But it was not yet over; the Queen invited her beloved middle son's somewhat unsuitable companion to Balmoral once again during the next summer. Perhaps the romance was already fizzling out, because by the end of the year it was curtains for Koo. She is said to have been utterly crushed at the breakup and only recently admitted in an interview that she is not the type to bounce back. "If something hits you, it hits you. I just go to bed, pull the covers over my head, lie there in a state of shock. Then, gradually, my fingers begin to tingle. I begin to realize that I'm still here, that I'm hungry, that I'm going to have to get up and make something to eat." There can be few people who doubted that she was thinking back to the sad aftermath of her royal romance.

Andrew was extremely upset. But he wasn't the only person present who was nursing a broken heart when he met up with Sarah Ferguson at Ascot that summer. Indeed, at the very time she was invited by Diana to join the royal party for the racing season's most glittering week, Sarah had hoped to be married to someone else. Unlike her future sister-in-law, when Sarah started to date her own prince she was very much a woman of today—a woman of experience.

Her first boyfriend, whom she'd originally met while rough-ing it in South America with her friend Charlotte, had been Old Etonian Kim Smith-Bingham, a debonair Sloane who ran a ski equipment business in the top Alpine resort of Verbier, where Sarah notched up the countless hours on the slopes that have enabled her to become a black-run expert skier. Smith-Bingham would invite her out to the winter wonderland for a month at a time, where, he recalls, "She spoke French when necessary and mixed with the large international crowd there." When the snow melted each spring, Smith-Bingham would return to England to spend the summer season. There, their life was much like any other courting couple's: trips to restaurants with friends and to the theater (they saw the circus musical *Barnum* together). "I usually paid," he recalls, "al-though after we'd been going out for three years we occasion-ally went Dutch. She loved giving small dinner parties." (Fergie, however, maintains that she can barely boil an egg—despite the diploma in cooking which her father shelled out for.) Sometimes Smith-Bingham would return the culinary favor, preparing for Fergie his best dish—spaghetti bolo-gnese.

But after Smith-Bingham and Sarah drifted amicably apart, she fell hook, line, and sinker for jet-set playboy Paddy McNally—to whom, ironically, she was introduced on one of her skiing jaunts to see Smith-Bingham. At forty-four, he was exactly twice her age, a man very recently widowed with two growing sons to raise. However, Smith-Bingham and his wife Twist were already living apart before she died of cancer. (Her bizarre nickname is alleged to have sprung from the fact that "she always gets her knickers in a twist"!) McNally had been enjoying bachelor life full tilt once more when Twist died, much to the chagrin of Twist's father, millionaire Ken Down-ing, who felt that McNally should have "held Twist's hand" during her fatal illness. But he gave up his newly rediscovered liberty overnight to assume total responsibility for Sean and

Rollo, who were then eight and eleven years of age. McNally had long mixed in the fast-moving, high-living world of Formula One Grand Prix racing; he'd been manager to onetime world champion Niki Lauda and, at the time of his wife's tragic death, was roommate to British racing driver John Watson.

McNally was no oil painting, but attractive nonetheless: smooth, suave, a man of the world, rich—and unlike many wealthy men, given to spend, spend, spending. Fergie frequently found herself back in Verbier, staying at Les Gais Lutins, McNally's eight-bedroom mountain chalet (also known as "The Gay Gnomes" or The Castle), where the social après-ski whirl is a higher priority to most tourists than life on the piste. (So popular is the resort with a certain sector of London society that, for the entire month of February, it's hard to hear a word of French for the babble of English laughter.) For the Sloane Square set, sloping off to Verbier consumed maybe one or two weeks of their year; for the zesty redhead, it became a sophisticated way of life. She loved the skiing by day but never took to the hard-drinking evenings; her family, like Andrew's, is almost all teetotal.

Thanks to McNally's job, there were frequent trips to Grand Prix events, where she spent deafening stints in the pits, contrasting serenely with the typical frosted-blond circuit groupies with their skintight jeans and glossed lips. Sarah is a one-man woman with a deeply faithful nature; she found it hard to come to terms with McNally's habitual but innocent flirting, often making certain that the leggy object of his attention knew exactly where she stood. She would introduce herself in the friendliest way to such a woman with a "Hello, I'm Fergie," or "How long have you known Paddy?"—subtly staking her claim and marking out her territory.

She grew to love not just McNally but his two sons, who spent much of the year at their Roman Catholic boarding school. They soon returned her affection (having overcome initial resistance to the flame-haired lovely who stepped so capably into their mother's shoes). Major Ferguson wasn't doing cartwheels with joy over his younger daughter's love match, but Fergie was a grown and responsible woman who knew what she was doing. Nevertheless, she certainly wasn't always happy. Ingrid Seward, editor of royalty watchers' magazine *Majesty* (who knew Fergie well in her McNally days), recalls walking into the bedroom at a party to find the usually bubbling redhead in floods of tears. "I put a comforting arm around her and asked what the problem was. 'Oh, nothing,' she replied. 'It's just me being stupid.' " On another occasion, she's supposed to have stormed out of Drones, an upscale Belgravia watering hole, in tears.

In three years, Sarah and Paddy McNally never actually lived together; indeed, there were frequent absences as his business interests took him all over the world, where Sarah, who had her own job, couldn't always follow. The partings from Smith-Bingham and McNally throughout these relationships gave Sarah the perfect emotional training for her future as a royal bride, who would have to endure long separations while her husband served in the Royal Navy. As her stepmother has said, "Both relationships were always terribly tricky—full of good-byes—so Sarah is used to 'getting on with it' on her own."

But deep down, Sarah yearned to set up home with McNally. He, meanwhile, never seemed to come any closer to naming the day and making their relationship official. Indeed, with two teenage sons, he was reluctant to start again with diapers, 3 A.M. feedings, and a home full of Fisher-Price toys. With a strength and courage many women of her age lack (often staying in dead-end relationships for years rather than risking being alone), Sarah gave him an ultimatum: marry her or say good-bye—this time, forever.

McNally's silence on the subject said everything. Sarah had her answer, even though the final curtain had not yet fallen on their affair. So by the time her friend the Princess of Wales issued an invitation to join the royal party at Ascot, she had courageously vowed not to invest any more time in the dead-end relationship. She had, at least, the prospect of some new frocks, fun, and frivolity to look forward to. McNally even drove her to Windsor Castle to meet her royal chum, little realizing that he was delivering her direct to the doorstep of her future husband.

Nobody quite knows to what extent the Princess schemed to match her redheaded pal with her brother-in-law. Certainly by the time Sarah arrived on the scene, Diana was beginning to feel increasingly lonely. She had her beloved sons to play with, but there were increasingly frequent chunks of time spent apart from her husband.

She may well have felt that a new sister-in-law would ease the loneliness when her husband disappeared across the London skies in his red helicopter. Or, perhaps she simply wanted company during Ascot week, knowing that all around her her royal in-laws would be studying form, peering through binoculars at Thoroughbreds, and shaking hands with the jockeys. Diana prefers to use her gut instinct when it comes to choosing winners, and the best bit about Ascot for her is bumping into old friends and admiring (or poking fun at) other women's clothes. She is definitely more interested in the silks worn by women than those on the backs of jockeys.

At lunch during Ascot, Prince Andrew sat next to the bubbly, vivacious redhead he'd known casually all his life yet had never really spent much time with. She was so different from the bevy of Barbie-doll beauties he'd loved and left or loved and lost. During lunch, he playfully coaxed her to tuck into the dessert she was served. "He made me eat chocolate profiteroles, which I didn't want to eat at all. I was meant to be on a diet," Sarah recalled. Andrew insisted—so he later confessed—"I got hit!" (Secretly, Fergie—who may enviously have admired the size 8 figures of other girls on the racing circuit or in the skiing resorts, and may have been told by former boyfriends that she'd look better if she shed a few pounds—probably warmed to the Prince on the spot for his very insistence that she eat her dessert. Here at last was someone who didn't seem to want to change her.) Later during the week, the pair could be spotted holding hands when they thought nobody was looking. The Queen, meanwhile, smiled to herself and kept her eyes on the racetrack.

And so the love affair began. They started to snatch as much time together as his naval career allowed, and it gave Fergie the huge boost in confidence she so desperately needed. She and McNally finally called it a day, and instead of seeing her mope, her friends were surprised to find Sarah inexplicably suffused with happiness. As a friend of Sarah's said, "I knew something was up. I had gone round to Clapham to cheer her up, expecting to find her in tears about Paddy, but there was a light in her eye and she was full of sparkle." Meanwhile, she stopped seeing so much of those friends in her set who couldn't be relied on and began counting on others to maintain secrecy.

On the home front, she had no worries; her roommate in the pretty Edwardian red-brick house was Carolyn Beckwith-Smith, whose cousin is Princess Diana's lady-in-waiting. Carolyn was accustomed to remaining tight-lipped on royal matters. The two girls got on like a house on fire, gleefully referring to themselves as "the Lavender Hill Mob" (after a team of crooks in a movie comedy, "Lavender Hill" designating the South London suburb they lived in). Carolyn would even stand in as a decoy, emerging with her head down and driving off in Sarah's BMW. A few minutes after the platoon of reporters sped off on a wild goose chase in pursuit, a laughing Sarah would slip out unnoticed.

The press had already begun their relentless speculation that here was "the one," but Sarah had spent three years as a personal assistant in a public relations firm and had learned how to handle reporters and photographers with tact and charm. She was a dream for them; unlike Lady Di, who'd kept her head bowed so that photographers shot off roll after roll of her then-mousy bangs, Sarah stared straight into their lenses, flashed a smile worthy of a toothpaste commercial, and even wound down the window of her car so that they could get a clearer shot. The Rat Pack never rattled her.

In any case, Andrew was only fourth in line to the throne, and press interest, though intense, never rose to the frenzy of that endured by the woman who would one day be queen. That same person, in fact, the Princess of Wales, had given Sarah an insight into what the pressure might be like. Sarah knew far better than the Princess what she was letting herself in for—and it was a small price to pay for love. Besides, for Sarah, being in the spotlight made a delightful change. When a royal photographer from Rupert Murdoch's tabloid *The Sun* "doorstepped" Fergie—who without thinking opened her front door to his rat-tat-tat—he asked her how she was coping with all the fuss. "I'm loving every minute," she declared. Arthur Edwards then suggested that the Princess of Wales had been imparting wise advice. "Well, I must say, she has given me a few tips," laughed Sarah.

The Duchess's confident air belies her inner insecurities. She is always the first to poke fun at herself, protesting (inaccurately) that she's not bright or beautiful. "What, with my behind?" she jokes. She's always been sensitive about her weight, and being surrounded at school by slender, fashion-model types compounded the feeling that she was lumpy and unattractive.

But when an eligible young man, a *prince* no less, began to court her, it did wonders for her self-esteem. All those photographers had their Nikons pointed in *her* direction. The snack bar opposite the office where she worked by day (for a Mayfair art book publisher) did a roaring trade in cappuccino and has since, in grateful tribute to the boost to business, changed its name to the Royal Snack Bar! And when Sarah would arrive home at night to find another bouquet of roses or a love note signed, discreetly "A," it thrilled her to the core.

She loved their rendezvous, for dinner or a visit to the movies, and was overjoyed when the Prince gave her a mascot for her car: a silver owl, which reminded him of her wide-eyed expression. (These car mascots are a royal trademark. Prince Charles has a Welsh dragon on his Jaguar and a polo pony on his Ford. He gave Diana a frog for her own car—referring to their private joke that she kissed one and it turned into a prince! Even the Queen's Rolls Royce is adorned with a solid silver horseman.) Sarah blossomed like a spring flower and became visibly more glowing day by day. The royal wooing did more for her spirits and her looks than a month at a health spa ever could.

The royal romance had an unexpected, welcome spin-off: the boost it gave Prince Andrew's tarnished image. It's unlikely that even if the royal family had roped in the world's most expensive public relations outfit to work on Andrew, they could have improved his popularity the way Sarah did. As oil magnate Armand Hammer (a close friend of Prince Charles's) described it, "She's a great influence on Prince Andrew. He was getting a little too wild and out of control. I think she's terrific," he added.

Until he started to date the effervescent, sparkling Miss Ferguson, the press found Andrew egocentric, arrogant, and too much of a prankster—the last straw had been when, on a fund-raising official visit to Hollywood, he was handed a paint-filled spray gun and couldn't resist turning it on the posse of journalists covering the event. Now, suddenly, he was metamorphosed into charm personified, as polite and courteous as a prince should be, and everyone was keeping their fingers crossed that the romance with flame-haired Fergie would last forever.

Aware of what a tough task Sarah would be taking on by signing on as a royal—having seen the toll it occasionally took on his elder brother's young wife—Andrew had to do some last-minute soul-searching before he took the romance one stage further. So he retreated to the Caribbean again, to a villa in the Bahamas belonging to the family of a naval colleague—and this time he was alone with only his thoughts for company under the blazing tropical sun. "I needed time to think and to sort myself out," he declared. "In my heart I knew that Sarah was the right girl for me. But I had to get away from everyone and have a serious talk with myself." In the understatement of the century, he continued: "I had such good fun being a bachelor. Before Sarah came along I thought marriage was a long way off. I also had to make the crucial decision—would she be able to cope as my wife?"

Experienced, capable, very mature—and a bundle of fun—Andrew rapidly reached the conclusion that the woman who had won his heart slowly but surely, their love blossoming out of a friendship in the healthiest way, would cope handsomely. For Christmas—which she spent with her family—he gave her jewelry. It's always a sign that a man is interested, but the royals don't throw it around carelessly! She was delighted with her heart-shaped gold earrings, and from then on they always graced her ears.

In early 1986, Sarah took the press by surprise. The infamous Rat Pack had already flown off to Switzerland to await the arrival of Prince Charles and Diana in Klosters for their annual skiing holiday when Sarah arrived (wearing a borrowed black-and-white suit Diana had reached into her own wardrobe for) to accompany the Princess and mischievous Prince William on a visit to Prince Andrew's ship, HMS *Brazen*. And next day, when the royal couple finally did hit Klosters, Sarah was with them, fueling rumors that an engagement was imminent. But when persistent photographers asked outright if she would marry Andrew, she did a fine imitation of a Cockney accent, laughing: "Cor, blimey, you must be joking," before whizzing off down the slopes too fast for all but the most expert of skiers to follow.

A couple of weeks later, the couple were invited by the Duke and Duchess of Roxburghe to their stately home of Floors, set in sixty thousand acres of countryside on the borders of Scotland and England; it was used as a setting for the Tarzan film *Greystoke*. The treasure-filled castle's owners are close friends of royalty, and Prince Charles has been on the guest list. Ironically, Floors had been the location of an earlier tryst, when Andrew rendezvoused there with Koo Stark. It's one of the United Kingdom's most magnificent homes, but its northerly location makes it drafty, and visitors are advised to pack thermal underwear. This weekend, the last in February, the weather was as foul, wet, and windy as can be. Wellington boots and umbrellas were necessary for walking by the River Tweed, which runs through Floors's acreage.

Sarah flew up alone, using the alias "Miss Amwell" to put the press off the trail and little guessing that this romantic weekend would change her life forever. She was totally taken aback when Prince Andrew fell to his knees in this most romantic of settings—a drawing room hung with priceless tapestries and filled with elegant French furniture—and proposed. He was equally surprised when she said yes. But just to make sure that she wasn't having her leg pulled, she added: "If you wish, when you wake up tomorrow morning you can tell me it's all a huge joke," and that she wouldn't mind.

To her great delight, the following day brought no retraction. In fact, Andrew recently declared it to be "the best decision of my life." Unlike most grooms, he had to get his mother's approval, but the Queen was overjoyed, "over the moon," in fact. She had taken instantly to her middle son's warmhearted, well-mannered, natural girlfriend, whom she knew to be emotionally well equipped for the rigors of the job. There was the formality of asking Major Ferguson for his daughter's hand in marriage, an experience that Andrew concedes was "fairly nerve-wracking."

Only then, Sarah and Andrew, able to spend a night together at Kensington Palace at the Prince and Princess of Wales's invitation, were able to discuss designs for "the ring" and plan an announcement to a waiting, watching, and hoping world. (Prince Andrew, mindful that his old flame Koo Stark shouldn't be shocked and distressed at the news, allegedly phoned the young woman in advance. Friends, however, declare that Koo—whose own marriage to Green Shield stamps heir Tim Jeffries, was just hitting the rocks—was quite inconsolable.)

Meanwhile, Sarah packed her bags, walked past the assembled press corps with an inscrutable smile, and said good-bye to her roommating days. The day before the press were to be summoned to Buckingham Palace, Sarah slipped into a fashion show given by rising British designer Alastair Blair (for whom her friend Susannah Constantine, a girlfriend of Andrew's cousin Viscount Linley, works as a personal assistant) and picked out a navy blue belted suit that showed off her hourglass-shaped (but generous) figure and extremely well-turned ankles to perfection.

On the chilly morning of March 19, photographers had little doubt why they were being summoned to the lawns behind Buckingham Palace. They—and the crowds who'd been waiting with expectation—weren't disappointed when, at 10 A.M. (an hour earlier than anticipated), an announcement was pinned to the palace's wrought-iron gates proclaiming: "It is with the greatest of pleasure that the Queen and the Duke of Edinburgh announce the betrothal of their beloved son the Prince Andrew and Miss Sarah Ferguson, daughter of Major Ronald Ferguson and Mrs. Hector Barrantes."

The happy couple sealed the declaration with a memorable kiss. "Let's make it a smacker!" laughed Sarah, to her future groom's embarrassment. "Once is enough," he declared, before leading his bride-to-be back into the palace for a celebratory lunch. Later, they conducted a very laid-back TV interview. When asked what had attracted them to one another, Sarah declared in her relaxed style: "Wit, charm, and good looks," and Andrew, eyes sparkling, added: ". . . and red hair." They agreed wholeheartedly that they were "good friends" and that their happiness was shared by the rest of his family, including a "delighted" Prince of Wales. Princess Anne went so far as to say, "I think my brother is an extremely lucky man." And Sarah's beaming father, Major Ferguson, let slip that "I don't think any father is satisfied with a daughter's boyfriend. But I am now."

It was a far cry from the rather stiff interview given by the Prince and Princess of Wales half a decade before. When asked if they were in love, Diana had nodded yes, but Charles seemed compelled to add, "Whatever that means."

In Paddy McNally's words, "Sarah is a highly intelligent, level-headed girl and I think she can handle any situation with great ease and with a great deal of charm. She's a girl in a million. Any man would be lucky to go out with her, let alone marry her. She is a marvelous lady, an outstanding woman." When Diana's own announcement had been made, there was no romantic figure from her past to make such a fond declaration. A thought which, now that it's too late, may haunt her always.

4

The Princes Charming

Both Diana and Sarah discovered that love and marriage went together like a horse and carriage. Indeed, *in* a horse and carriage, the gilded glass carriage that traditionally transports fiancées to their royal grooms. But what are they like, these modern-day princes who've chosen them as friends, lovers, consorts for life?

Very different, that's for certain. For a start, they're virtually a generation apart. Prince Charles is twelve years older than his younger brother, who arrived in the Queen's "second batch" of children. Charles was already away at prep school when Andrew made his debut, on February 19, 1960, at 4:15 P.M.—an Aquarius. Andrew was positively pampered compared to Charles, who'd been born soon after the end of the war, when Britain was on a conservation drive and shortages were rife across England. The heating, for instance, was kept turned down very low. His nanny, Helen Lightbody, was such a firm believer in the benefits of fresh air that, come hail or shine, Charles would be pushed in his pram around the gardens of Buckingham Palace, or left outdoors on the terrace to sleep and to fill his young lungs with crisp, cold air. The baby Prince Charles's face would occasionally turn purple with cold—but it doesn't seem to have done him any harm; Charles rarely comes down with a cold.

There were, supposedly, icy showers, too—which prepared Charles for the tough approach of Gordonstoun, the Scottish school attended by all three princes. There was even a nation-wide shortage of soap, and the thrifty queen encouraged her children to do the daily rounds with the palace maids, sticking scraps of soap together. Meals were basic and clothes were darned and mended, even though the billionairess queen could have afforded to give her children mink underwear. This scrimping and saving may sound eccentric, but Queen Elizabeth simply likes to lead by example. At a time when even the most basic daily necessities were scarce, she felt it was irresponsible to flaunt extravagance and wealth.

There's no doubt that Charles learned a lot from that; he, too, has a thrifty streak. Charles is the only major royal *not* to receive an income from the state, but this prince is no pauper. Nevertheless, despite being valued recently by a British financial magazine at approximately $600 million, with an annual income of at least £1.7 million from his Duchy of Cornwall estates in the West Country and several lucrative areas of Southwest London, the future king keeps an eagle eye on every penny spent on his household, trying to cut back where possible. He must roll his eyes skyward at Diana's dress bills—even though, in the back of his mind, he knows that the silks and satins are a small price to pay for the great boost she's given to the royals' image.

Charles and his sister Anne had to contend with the fact that for much of their childhood, their mother was away on business. Their grandfather, George VI, died of lung cancer in 1952, and suddenly Mummy wasn't just Mummy anymore. She was Queen of England. It may be about then that his own fate began to dawn on four-year-old Charles, casting a shadow over an otherwise idyllic childhood. He couldn't choose to become a railroad engineer, a businessman, or a musician; his role and responsibilities were carved out from the moment he was conceived. He couldn't even entertain fantasies about enjoying a quiet retirement one day. Being king or queen of England is like a life sentence; you're signed up from day one and the contract expires only when you do. Small wonder, then, that he grew up a serious, thoughtful, and quiet child. He was always energetic—courtiers remember him as a terrible fidget, a trait that it's clear (from constant tie-straightening and stroking of his nose) Charles has never shaken off—but as a child he was never as boisterous or troublemaking as his sister Anne or little brother Andrew.

It's also hardly surprising that Charles was always very mature. He hardly ever mixed with playmates of his own age and unlike his sons William and Harry later on, he wasn't thrust into a class of screaming four-year-olds to fend for himself. Lessons (which started just two weeks after his mother's coronation) were taken at home, in a room known as the small schoolroom at the front of Buckingham Palace, boasting a magnificent view of London's loveliest parks and the soldiers guarding home, sweet home, who eternally fascinated Charles.

From the cradle, Charles was being groomed for the ultimate hot seat, the throne. With Andrew, the Queen, having settled into the role, could afford to be a more laid-back mother. She devoted more time to Andrew than she'd been able to give Anne or Charles. In addition, attitudes toward child rearing were changing, and Andrew got the full benefit of the notion that mothers should bond more with their babies. (In Charles's babyhood, it was absolutely acceptable among the English upper classes that children might be seen for an hour or two at teatime and cared for by staff the rest of the time.) The Queen would play with Andrew after breakfast, at coffee time, and depending on her schedule, would herself wheel Andrew around the romantic, flower-filled Buckingham Palace grounds in the afternoon. She even cleared out papers from one drawer of her desk and kept it full of Andrew's toys, so that while she did her endless paperwork he could play at her feet. For six months, the Queen scrapped evening dates whenever possible so as to bathe and feed her baby boy before dinner.

Today's child-care professionals agree that the more time a mother is able to spend with her infant, the more confident and secure he'll grow up to be. If you contrast reserved Prince Charles with his boisterous brother, the evidence seems to back the experts up. Interestingly, Andrew, who'd been kept out of the public eye (except for official portraits) until he was almost a year and a half old, became the most extroverted of the royal children. Prince Charles and Princess Anne, both subjected to the spotlight during their early childhoods, have never seemed as comfortable in the glare. Andrew was outgoing, fun-loving, and occasionally naughty. There are shades of his uncle Andrew in young William, in fact—who once tied together the bootlaces of the palace sentries, supposedly liberally laced the palace swimming pool with liquid soap, and terrorized the family dogs (the Queen's much-loved corgis). Unlike Charles, he wouldn't be forced to endure the worst ravages of the British climate; wet and windy days meant a game of indoor football in the palace corridors. He once conceded that "every now and then, a pane of glass got broken. But I don't think we ever broke a piece of Meissen, or anything like that."

Even the clothes that Andrew and Charles wore were different, thanks to changing fashions. Charles was kept in short pants until late in his childhood, while for all but the most formal occasions, Andrew kept snug in long pants. It's just more evidence of how, thanks to changing times, Andrew was raised more liberally and leniently. He is also secure in the knowledge that, barring a tragedy, he will never have to shoulder the burden of kingship. Again, fate was on Andrew's side when it came to playmates. His aunt, Margaret, had young children with whom he could play, and the Queen, perhaps sensing just how lonely her eldest son had been, invited other wellborn children into the schoolroom to share in Andrew's early formal lessons. (From the age of two, though, she'd been teaching him the alphabet, how to count and tell the time—no doubt wishing that when her son and heir had been small, she hadn't been so distracted by the pressures of her new royal role.) Andrew was also encouraged to mix with children from less privileged backgrounds, and he joined a London group of Cub Scouts.

This liberal outlook showed up later on, of course, in his choice of girlfriends. Unlike Charles (who always had to bear in mind the prospect of finding a suitable bride), Andrew dated girls from every social stratum.

The choice of prep schools for the princes was different, too. Prince Charles was sent as a boarder to Cheam School, Prince Andrew to Heatherdown—both of them in Berkshire and almost a stone's throw from the Queen's favorite weekend retreat, Windsor Castle. Later, though, Charles and Andrew both went to the same public school, Gordonstoun, where their father, Prince Philip, had reveled in his schooldays. Set in the bleak Scottish countryside and famous for its "outward bound" approach and emphasis on physical fitness, it's been described as "a gymnasium of morale and muscles," and Andrew and Charles have duly become fanatical about the outdoor life. Charles (once known as "action man" for his daredevil life-style) has a passion for polo, hunting, shooting, wind-surfing, fishing, skiing. "I am a hopeless individual," he's said, "because I happen to enjoy an element of danger. I think that if you occasionally live dangerously it helps you appreciate life." This philosophy seems unutterably poignant in the light of Charles's very close shave in spring 1988 in an

Alpine avalanche, which killed a close friend and critically injured another. The experience devastated Charles, who blamed himself for egging the skiing party on to tackle the perilous path down the mountain despite avalanche warnings.

Except for polo, Andrew enjoys all those pursuits and more. At Gordonstoun, he was able to indulge his great love of the sea (shared with Prince Philip) with regular sailing lessons. In 1983, Andrew would crew aboard one of the challenge yachts in the America's Cup Trials. He also became a keen canoeist. Not long after they were married, he was to introduce his go-for-it bride to the sport on a canoeing trip in the Canadian wilderness. In order to keep up, the detectives—never far from their charges' side—had to be in peak fitness themselves.

Andrew and Charles both spent stints abroad (part of the school's curriculum), and both still have a soft spot for the countries of their carefree exile. For Andrew, this was Canada, while Charles attended Timbertop School in the Australian outback, where the boys had to "muck in" with the natives and were afforded no special privileges. It was a rare taste for Andrew and Charles of what life is like for everyday folk, and it's not surprising they cherish such fond memories.

Ever anxious to please, Charles kept a low profile at school and was diligent and studious; he was rewarded by being named "head of school." But by all accounts he never enjoyed remote Gordonstoun as much as did Andrew, who's been described as "a bit of a handful." From Gordonstoun came the first whispers of Andrew's arrogance, amid suggestions that he pulled royal rank at times.

Careers in the armed forces beckoned both princes, and they both signed up for the Royal Navy—after Charles, who'd worked hard to pass his exams, had earned a second-class degree in history from the ultraselective Cambridge University, where Britain's elite scramble for places. It was no mean feat. He was the first heir apparent ever to graduate with a degree and was justly proud of his achievement.

Other than a career in the forces, what else is a prince to do? The answer, of course, has lately come from Andrew and Charles's "baby brother" Edward, the first star-struck royal. Having signed up with the tough-as-nails Royal Marines, Edward quit after just a few months of training (and a furious row with Prince Philip, who felt his younger son was being wimpish and letting the side down badly). Soon after, he organized a TV pageant to raise funds for charity and acted in a stage production.

Outshone, perhaps, by his two dashing older brothers, Edward has decided to try to become a star in his own right, and the commercially minded Andrew Lloyd Webber (creator of phenomenally successful musicals like *The Phantom of the Opera, Cats,* and *Evita*) was quick to sign him up as a production assistant. For the moment, Edward is a glorified "gofer." But there can be little doubt that he wouldn't mind seeing his own name in lights in London's theater district, and his bizarre career choice has shocked not only the royal family but also the British public. It is somehow "not the done thing" for princes to be fetching coffee for musical millionaires.

Sarah and Diana have both married men of the sea, because when Charles and Andrew made *their* career choice, the armed forces seemed the only option. Perhaps Charles, who was a leading light in his university college's drama society, might himself have wistfully dreamed of a career on the stage. He would rapidly have been brought down to earth by the reality of his position in life, however. Instead, he took up a career in the navy, rising through the ranks to command his own minesweeper, the HMS *Bronnington,* where he shared cramped below-deck quarters with ordinary seamen from all over the British Isles and enjoyed the freedom—for once—of life unshadowed by his bodyguard. After all, the heir to the throne had an entire platoon to defend him!

But the time came when Charles had to leave the seafaring life and throw himself into royal duties full time. Andrew, however, who joined the navy in 1979 (two years after Charles had left), doesn't have that pressure, and he's made it clear that the navy's a full-time job. It certainly allows Andrew to indulge his love of flying. By the time he enlisted for a twelve-year stint (first command: "Get your hair cut"), he'd had flying lessons at RAF Benson (where the Duchess of York later learned to wield a joystick), flown solo, and parachuted from the skies. In the navy, where he told bawdy jokes below deck and gained a reputation for being fairly brash, he earned his wings faster than expected and began his helicopter pilot's training. Sarah and Andrew endlessly compare notes on flying, and he was hugely touched by her keenness to take to the skies and share one of his greatest passions.

In fact, Sarah Ferguson married a war hero, for Andrew—just twenty-two at the time—saw active service during the Falklands conflict between Britain and Argentina. Based aboard the aircraft carrier *Invincible,* he had several close shaves while carrying out daring missions at the helm of a Sea King helicopter, rescuing survivors from sinking battleships. Being lonely, frightened, and several thousands of miles from home marked the dawning of Andrew's (perhaps belated) maturity; bearing the emotional scars of any serviceman who's seen colleagues killed and injured, he returned to England a changed man. Argentina's surrender coincided with another momentous event—the birth of his nephew William. Andrew reportedly let out a yelp of delight and ordered drinks all around in the officers' mess. A colleague asked Andrew how come he was so delighted, since William's birth had edged him down the royal line of succession. "That's exactly why," beamed the prince. "Now I'll be able to have more privacy."

He was wrong, of course, because just a few months later, press and photgraphers would force "the Robert Redford of the family" (as his brother Charles once dubbed him) to cut short a sojourn on Mustique with Koo Stark. But William's birth did at least free him from the awesome prospect that he might become king. Now only third in line to the throne, Randy Andy was free to play the playboy—which he did with gusto. The press soon forgot the heroic aspects of his character and took a dislike to the Queen's second son, feeling him to be cocky and arrogant, not to mention immature, too fond of practical jokes, and uncaring of protocol.

Even Prince Philip is supposed to have had harsh words with his son, ordering him to "pull his finger out and be a gentleman, otherwise he wasn't fit to be a prince." Andrew seemed to have degenerated into a bread-roll, cream-cake-throwing sort of "Hooray Henry," with a soul as shallow as a champagne goblet. His seduction technique was no more mature. One sophisticated Londoner who encountered Andrew at a weekend houseparty claimed afterward, "He tells stupid jokes and cracks you on the shoulder, roaring with laughter. His bodyguard hoots, and you're left sort of smiling thinly. And his idea of a really hot-shot chat-up line is to push you into a strawberry bed while you're concentrating on a croquet shot."

Thus the press set about painting an unflattering picture of Andrew at every opportunity and made life fairly miserable for every new girl who entered the marriage stakes. Andrew got his revenge when he was able to paint *them,* literally. While in Los Angeles on a fund-raising mission for the British Olympic Association and for his old school, he visited a shelter housing project in the black suburb of Watts, where his guide took time to demonstrate a new kind of spray gun. The temptation for Andrew to point it at the assembled press corps was irresistible; white paint splattered thousands of dollars' worth of camera equipment (which was later replaced, apologetically, by Buckingham Palace).

Nobody knows whether or not the gun just "went off by accident," but if it was deliberate, who can blame Andrew? He thought the heat would be off when little Wills arrived, but instead, now that older brother Charles was married, everyone seemed to want to know the ins and outs of his romantic life. He searched high and low (and often *very* low) for the girl of his dreams and, by the time Sarah came on the scene, had earned a lusty reputation.

One thing Diana and Sarah can be sure of is that each of their princes was more than ready to settle down. Eventually, the merry-go-round of maidens had begun to tire even "Randy Andy," and he fell hook, line, and sinker for the first truly outdoorsy type he'd ever dated. (Earlier girlfriends felt more at home in glamorous restaurants than traipsing across a grouse moor or shouldering the burden of a heavy knapsack.) And the arrival of Sarah Ferguson upon the scene appears to have induced a personality change in her once-brash beau. Gone is the rudeness and the egotism, replaced by a new, caring attitude in a prince who is as excited as his wife is at the prospect of parenthood—sleepless nights and all.

Of course, only two years after their marriage, they are still getting to know each other, and they're probably well aware that frequent absences *do* make the heart grow fonder. As yet, Sarah and Andrew have hardly had time to slip into a daily routine together. When they reunite after a few days, a week, or even a month apart, there is so much to talk about—their new house, their new baby. And it's obvious to everyone that Sarah and Andrew share a very passionate physical relationship. They're exceptionally affectionate in public and in private and constantly tease one another, which psychologists agree to be the sign of a healthy relationship. As one insider puts it, "They try hard to behave in front of the cameras or during their royal duties, but it's clear to see that it's a struggle. As soon as the spotlight is switched off, they're literally all over each other, practically *pawing*. Obviously, they have a very passionate relationship behind closed doors. It's written all over them."

Diana's scheme to pair her pal Sarah up with Andrew may, ironically, have sown seeds of discontent in her own marriage, sparking off a "seven-year itch" just a fraction early. Before her very eyes, she saw a love affair blossom that painfully contrasted with her own. Charles, dignity always in the forefront of his mind, has never been particularly affectionate toward his wife in public, occasionally kissing her hand or cheek. It was almost invariably a somewhat giggly Diana who prompted the early, playful caresses exchanged between her and Charles. Theirs has never been the sort of match that prompted people's eyes to mist over as they wistfully thought, "Ain't love grand."

But in history, the marriage of heirs to the throne has rarely been a matter simply of love, sweet love. The exception is the case of Edward VIII, who gave up his throne for Wallis Simpson and showered her with millions of pounds worth of fabulous diamonds, sapphires, rubies, and emeralds as consolation for the fact she'd never be allowed to wear what he craved for her: the crown jewels. Diana and Charles's match was a matter of practicality first and love second. Diana grew up with the goal of marrying well, and the blunt truth is that Charles had to find a young, wellborn woman (who happened to be a virgin) with whom he could coexist for the rest of his life and who would continue the royal line. They struck a deal; there could be no looking back, and each will have to live with the consequences forever.

Diana and Charles are certainly no Romeo and Juliet or Antony and Cleopatra. They are no Edward and Mrs. Simpson, either; the history books will not record theirs as one of the world's most romantic love matches. Much has been made of the fact that their passions and interests are almost poles apart. There *is*, certainly, almost a generation between them. And it was inevitable that a young woman who relinquished her freedom, her youth, and the usual pleasures of growing up to settle down with a man much older than she, from whom she could never divorce, would get itchy feet.

Diana could never have foreseen quite how her life would

be transformed for the worse. She must have imagined, with the rosy, dreamy outlook of the teenager she was, that only happiness lay ahead. "Ah, but she knew what she was letting herself in for," British people are fond of declaring. She didn't. She *couldn't,* because, quite simply, she stepped out of St. Paul's Cathedral straight into a spotlight that nobody has switched off for one moment. Nobody could have foreseen that every moment of Diana's life would be watched, followed, and reported on, because this development was unprecedented. No member of the royal family had ever been subjected to such pressures. Diana broke new ground. It was bound to put a strain on the young, inexperienced ingenue and prompted Michael Shea, the Queen's private press secretary, to declare that "the Princess of Wales feels totally beleaguered. The people who love and care for her are anxious at the effect it is having."

If, in public, Diana was having to cope with sudden superstardom, then behind closed doors she must have been aware that the generation gap was growing increasingly apparent in her marriage. Charles is a serious soul, given to deep philosophical thought and almost obsessed with the problems of the nation he will one day rule. He is supremely anxious to carve out a useful role for himself in society, worrying about inner-city decay and pollution; he has begun converting his Gloucestershire farm into an entirely organic enterprise, growing spring beans, wheat, and oats without the use of chemicals.

Charles is deeply concerned with the meaning of life. Diana prefers to get on and *live* it. His bookshelves are lined with volumes on philosophy, homeopathy (a longtime interest of many royals, some of whom successfully turned to homeopathic medicine for help with minor ailments), Zen Buddhism, psychology. He has apparently consulted Dr. Winifred Rushforth, a Jungian psychologist, to try to unravel the meaning of his dreams, and is particularly interested, having read Jung's entire works, in the phenomenon of coincidence. Diana swoops with delight, instead, on the latest romantic blockbuster by longtime favorites Barbara Cartland (who is actually her stepgrandmother, mother of Countess Spencer) or Danielle Steel. "I enjoy her books," Diana once said to a bedridden patient during a hospital visit, "but my husband disapproves. He doesn't like me reading light novels."

Their circles of friends are quite different. He surrounds himself with wise, older counselors like explorer Sir Laurens van der Post or philanthropist Armand Hammer, men from whom he feels he has a great deal to learn. Diana, by contrast, likes to spend her free time kicking her heels and partying with faithful younger pals from her carefree single days, going to their dinner parties and lunching with them. She is never overawed by *their* intelligence or made to feel intellectually inferior in their company. While Diana was busy earning her party-girl reputation, Charles was carving out a niche for himself as the royal family's resident eccentric. It's doubtful that either was exactly overjoyed about the other's changing image.

Diana has one passion which the Prince does his damnedest to share—pop music. But never does Prince Charles look quite so ill at ease as when he's standing beside his wife at a fund-raising rock concert (like the Live Aid concert, organized by Bob Geldof, or the annual star-studded event organized for his own charity, the Prince's Trust). While Diana claps and sings along and generally has a ball, Charles (who an observer described to me as having "absolutely no sense of rhythm") can be seen tapping a foot and trying to disguise the fact that he'd rather be almost anywhere on earth. When it comes to pop music, Diana is like an overgrown teenager. Belatedly, she's enjoying the adolescence she never really had.

Remember, her idol was Prince Charles when her schoolmates were swooning over David Bowie, Mick Jagger, and Bryan Ferry. And unlike the average teenager, she has the power to be introduced to her pop music heroes—with whom, I am reliably informed, she proceeds to flirt fairly shamelessly. Behind the scenes, minutes before the Band-Aid concert, while Charles and Diana were introduced to the day's star-studded lineup, an insider informs me, "She batted her eyelids and looked up from under those bangs of hers at Phil Collins and made absolutely no secret of the fact that she thought him highly attractive. Geldof got the same treatment." Because Charles can only be dragged out for charity rock concerts, Diana takes a party of friends to see idols like Collins or Elton John perform and likes nothing better than slipping backstage for a chat after the curtain falls. "It's as if she's decided that becoming a 'royal groupie' is her perk for all the hard work she puts in."

But if Charles has trouble getting down and getting funky to his wife's chart-topping favorites, there is at least one musical passion they share. Diana took piano lessons from an early age, and Charles is a mean cellist. And the Princess—she of the zero "O" levels—surprised everyone when, during a television interview last year, she confessed that far from being addicted to pop, she plays classical music endlessly at home: Grieg, Rachmaninoff, Schumann. Diana keeps a stash of classical cassettes in her car to while away long journeys. And the evidence was there for all to see when, on the Australian tour early last year, she was cajoled by the music teacher at a school the royal pair were visiting to tinkle the ivories. Without sheet music, a very embarrassed Diana performed a Rachmaninoff piece (once used as the theme music for the film *Brief Encounter*). Before scuttling away, red-faced, the Princess earned thunderous applause and a pat on the rump from her husband!

It wasn't her only public performance. At the British Embassy in Bonn last year, after a professional pianist had just finished playing, Diana calmly strode across to the piano and, without being asked, while everyone else was sipping brandies and coffees, gave a perfect rendition of a complicated Beethoven sonata. "To say we were amazed is putting it mildly," declared an embassy official afterward. "We just couldn't believe our eyes. Not just because the Princess played faultlessly. But because it takes guts to sit down at a piano when a professional has just finished. She could have fluffed a few notes and looked very silly in front of all those guests." The only person present who didn't look surprised was Charles, for whom she plays regularly in private; he "acted as though it was the most natural thing in the world." Piano playing is also her annual Christmas party piece for the assembled family at Windsor Castle—although her songs are reputed to be very much less bawdy than those belted out by Charles's Aunt Margaret.

For every one of those jaunts to rock concerts, there is also a trip to Covent Garden's Royal Opera House (where Diana also catches performances of the Royal Ballet when she can). Originally, Diana professed herself to be bored stiff by Charles's love of opera, but in time it has seduced her. Opera lovers have even been treated to the sight of a delighted Diana leaping to her feet to applaud a performance by Luciano Pavarotti.

But a mutual admiration for Mozart is not enough to make a marriage happy. And in 1987, Diana and Charles spent so much time apart that rumors spread like wildfire that a rift as wide as the Grand Canyon had opened up between the heir to the throne and his beautiful wife. For thirty-seven days, they didn't spend a night under the same roof. They hadn't even scheduled a day to be together to share a celebration of their sixth wedding anniversary. Diana tried to explain it away by saying, "My husband and I get around two thousand invitations to visit different places every six months. We couldn't possibly get through many if we did them all together. So we have decided to accept as many as we can separately. This means we can get to twice as many places and twice as many people."

While an increasingly pensive and reclusive Prince Charles was tramping over grouse moors and contemplating the future by the swift-flowing Dee, Diana fulfilled no less than twenty-seven engagements in London. As any member of the royal household will tell you, Diana has become a career princess. She has, in the last couple of years, become acutely aware of the good that she can do—fund raising, counseling the sick and bereaved, and spearheading charities. Initially seduced by the glamour of the job—which turned out to be as illusory as a cardboard Hollywood film set—she has wholeheartedly thrown herself into her work, discovering that the cloud at least has a silver lining. (It has also provided her with a greater understanding of her husband's role and position.) Staying behind in her lovely home at Kensington Palace, where she could see her friends, fulfill her duties, have time for shopping (apart from newspapers and candy, there's practically nothing to buy for miles around Balmoral) and, most importantly, be near to William and Harry, who are now at school, seemed infinitely preferable and much less boring than spending what turned out to be a particularly damp and overcast autumn with Charles and some of his family at the drafty castle she's said to loathe.

It was inevitable that if they continued to lead separate lives, sooner or later their names would be linked romantically with others, even if the press could not agree on the identities of the people supposedly enraptured by the royal duo. Prince Charles was reported to be seeing Lady Tryon, the effervescent blonde he calls Kanga (short for Kangaroo, after her Australian heritage), a longtime friend from his single days, whom he used regularly to join on summer fishing holidays in Iceland. Undoubtedly, Dale Tryon is Charles's closest female confidante (after Diana), and he once wistfully declared, "She's the only woman who ever understood me." But at the time of their alleged week-long tryst, Dale was 120 miles away on the other side of Scotland, with her husband Anthony,

Lord Tryon, and their four delightful children. In reality, Dale and Anthony Tryon have an extremely happy marriage; she is a successful dress designer whose notable clients include none other than the Princess of Wales, with whom she regularly lunches near her Beauchamp Place shop.

Further afield, outrageous rumors suggested that Charles was secretly dating beautiful Italian noblewoman Fiametta Frescobaldi, whose parents own the sumptuous hillside villa where he's several times stayed during his solo Tuscan painting holidays. Later, the press attempted to suggest that it was not Fiametta but her slender, attractive, fifty-year-old mother who was Charles's clandestine paramour.

But the most scandalous stories to emerge concerned the Princess herself. She was linked with handsome city businessman Philip Dunne—actually the boyfriend of socialite Katya Grenfell (one of the Duchess of York's close confidantes), who had in reality been appointed as one of Diana's "walkers" to escort her to events that Charles could not (or didn't want to) attend. Her manner toward Dunne was certainly playful and flirtatious, but as any man who's had the pleasure of Diana's company will confirm, that's her style; it is an integral part of her charm. She flirts with everyone, male, female, age five or eighty-five, four- or two-legged.

Most damning of all, however, was the suggestion that she had dined *à quatre* at the Chelsea home of media kingpin David Frost and his wife Lady Carina Fitzalan-Howard—that her companion had been a tall, dark, handsome, and unidentified stranger. They reportedly bade each other a lingering farewell on the doorstep of the Frost residence, gazing into each other's eyes before kissing on both cheeks and embracing.

Meanwhile, the Palace did nothing to allay the whispers, growing increasingly loud, that there was trouble afoot. "They both refuse to dignify the rubbish that is printed about them by commenting on it," one insider declared. But silence, this time, only served to fuel the rumors, even though it's royal style to rise above the press and public speculation whenever possible, adopting the attitude that if a matter is ignored enough, journalists will eventually get bored and go off to pester Elizabeth Taylor or Joan Collins instead. This one, however, didn't seem to want to lie down and go away. And when floods engulfed Charles's Wales, the Queen Mother's brainwave to pack the pair off for a visit together to the stricken region backfired since, just hours later, the seemingly unhappy couple jetted off in separate directions yet again.

A palace aide dismissed it by announcing that "this couple plan their schedule half a year in advance. Diana knew as long ago as the previous spring that her husband would be in Scotland during October. She didn't expect him to rush back to her side simply because some malicious gossips thought he should." However, the papers had a field day. Experts in body language were summoned to examine videos of the flying Welsh visit and report on the health of the royal marriage; they declared that Charles's constant fiddling with his necktie, scratching of his nose, and nervous hand movements showed him to be anxious, uncomfortable, or nervous. Diana, meanwhile, turned her body away from her husband's at every opportunity, "expressing a subconscious desire to avoid the risk of even a casual brushing contact." The psychologist's unnerving conclusion? "This isn't normal behavior for people in love. The emotional temperature is very, very cold."

A close contact of the royal couple, who sees them socially both in public and in private, told me at the time that she believed the psychologist was accurate in his diagnosis. "Charles appears to be bored with, and by, Diana. And she, in turn, seems no longer to be physically attracted to him. They seem to be happiest apart." But another reliable insider believes that fears about a rift surfaced, ironically, just when Charles and Diana had reached a contented status quo in their relationship.

"Given the chance, many modern couples would choose to spend more time apart—only for most of them, it isn't a workable solution; they have nine-to-five lives and must coexist under the same roof. Charles and Diana have the option *not* to live in each other's pocket. There's a quaint old English saying, 'a hedge in between keeps the grass green.' That seems to be the tack that the royal couple have taken." In other words, they have discovered—perhaps like Andrew and Sarah—that absence does make the heart grow fonder. By allowing one another to pursue individual interests, they banish feelings of frustration. Each understands exactly the pressures that the other must endure. Basically, Charles has a penchant for hunting, shooting, fishing, and the arts; he likes to stay home during precious time off. Diana leans toward rock concerts, nightclubs, shopping, sunbathing, and eating out. But they also have some important things in common: their love of two boisterous boys, a passion for gardening, opera—and, very importantly, eight years of shared history under their belts.

Insiders suggest that, in fact, far from yawning ever wider, the age gap between Charles and Diana is beginning to shrink again. Theirs was not so much a seven-year itch as a six-year hitch. In common with many couples, they have discovered that marriage is a matter of give and take. Charles—set in his ways and accustomed for years to a fixed itinerary that accommodated all his favorite pastimes, from Sandringham for New Year, Switzerland in February, fishing (with the Tryons) in August, followed by a couple of months at Balmoral—has discovered that to get the best out of his wife, he'll just have to pack the sunscreen and a sun hat and tag along on the family summer holiday that Diana has added to the agenda—staying with the Spanish royal family and frolicking in the Mediterranean sunshine—even though he's no great fan of the heat. Then Diana will smilingly indulge his yearning to "get away from it all" on painting holidays, returning with skilled vignettes of the landscape as souvenirs for his wife. And since his painting is accomplished enough to earn a place in the Royal Academy Summer Exhibition, Diana's delighted with the miniature paintings—and to have the occasional week on her own.

At home, the couple still refer to each other invariably as Darling. Charles also affectionately calls his wife Duch (short for Duchess—apparently a childhood nickname Diana earned from her friends because of her impeccable, grand manners). They still exchange gifts and love tokens, and Diana has a leaning toward humorous greeting cards, with a smiling face beside her signature.

Nobody could deny that on the Australian visit early in 1988, the couple had their old smiles back. And they certainly seemed genuine. Diana and Charles laughed at each other's jokes, reached for one another affectionately in public, twirled at a breakneck pace around the dance floor, and appeared to the world like a young couple whose marriage—now that their sons are growing up (and indeed, now that the bride *herself* has done some maturing)—has a new lease on life. Mopping his brow after jiving alone to "In the Mood," Charles announced that "dancing with a princess can be dangerous." But he was obviously thrilled to be out with a wife who only had eyes for him. Despite countless cameras and two hundred paying guests, they still managed to convey the romance of an intimate moment. "I've never seen them look happier," pronounced royal watcher and leader of the Rat Pack James Whitaker, astonished. "Diana was *flirting* with Charles."

Charles seemed less self-absorbed and weighed down by the responsibilities of his role than in years. When a member of the crowd shouted out, "Give us a smile!" Diana was able to answer truthfully, "But I haven't stopped smiling all day!" She appeared, once more, to be truly happy—and let's all hope that's the case. Because for Charles and Diana to live a public lie condemns them to the unhappiest of futures. And

Cinderella could wake up each morning of her life with the realization that, far from living a fairy tale, she is trapped in a nightmare—imprisoned forever in a gilded cage of her own choosing.

Why didn't the Queen intervene when the going got rough and the press's pressure to know the truth about rumors of a rift was making life almost unbearable for Diana and Charles? They were finding it hard enough to deal with their own problems, let alone the pain of having every gesture, every word, pored over by "experts." An insider tells me that Her Majesty did stamp the royal foot and furiously told the feuding duo to shape up at one point, formally ordering them to spend more time together. But Diana and Charles were too wrapped up in their own Windsor war, for once, to heed the matriarchal dictate. And the Queen, highly indulgent of her elder son, decided that if she stayed tight-lipped in future, the couple might resolve their differences of their own accord. At least, she may have reasoned, with Andrew ecstatically married to Sarah, there was *one* idyllic love affair in the family.

A divorce is out of the question, even though, on paper, it's a possibility. Nothing in the Constitution states that Charles *couldn't* divorce. But it's unlikely that Charles or Diana would feel that the raging controversy that a divorce would spark off, and the subsequent damage it would do to the royal family's standing—not to mention the disillusionment felt by their subjects—could possibly justify the split. The monarchy's credibility could be permanently, irrevocably damaged by it. Better then to come to an arrangement whereby Charles and Diana could lead separate lives—fulfilling duties at the other ends of the earth, if necessary—while remaining married.

The two strongest reasons why Charles and Diana will never divorce are William and Harry. The couple are united in their belief that children should have *two* parents and as happy and untraumatic an upbringing as possible. Diana knows only too well the pain endured by the child victims left behind when a marriage crumbles. In the event of a split, there is no doubt that the Queen would do everything in her power to deny Diana custody, since the little princes must be raised and educated for the unique future that lies ahead of them. Everyone around the Princess knows that they are the apples of her eye. Diana, who has wanted children all her life, would therefore never dream of leaving them behind in the Kensington Palace nursery and moving out herself—which is what would happen—simply so that she could recapture the freedom she willingly relinquished when she "signed up."

Besides, if Charles were to decide on a divorce, he'd be opting for a very lonely future indeed. As Queen, Elizabeth is head of the Church of England, and Charles will one day step into those shoes. If he divorced, he would have two options; never to remarry or to stand down as head of the church if he should fall in love and wish to tie the knot again. In order to do that, he would probably have to abdicate in favor of William. For Charles, who has trained and worked all his life toward the moment when he will be king, it is an action as unthinkable as, for Diana, flying the coop would be.

5

Dressed to Thrill

*A*h, the clothes, the clothes. Closets and closets full of satins and silks, fit—fitted—for a princess. In her self-appointed role as royal clotheshorse, Diana certainly gets a huge kick out of this aspect of royal life, showing off top designers' latest creations to perfection. She is their ideal model, five feet, ten inches tall and with the proportions of the top model she could well have become if marriage, motherhood, and royal duties hadn't come first.

Not everyone realizes that Diana's image was carefully molded by experts in the early days of her love affair. The nineteen-year-old ingenue was sartorially innocent and favored the classic, slightly dull clothes her friends wore: striped shirts (worn with the collar turned up), dirndl skirts, flat pumps, sweaters from Benetton, and a warm navy blue cashmere-and-wool coat to keep the winter winds smartly at bay. Fine for a nursery-school teacher but hardly fitting for a princess-in-waiting. The stiffly formal royal blue suit she aptly chose off the rack from Cojana at Harrods—price £310—for the photo session marking the announcement of her betrothal was matronly, almost middle-aged. Diana's sole fashion adviser at that time is believed to have been her lady-in-waiting. So, following her engagement in February 1981, at the suggestion of her sister Lady Jane Fellowes, who once worked as an editorial assistant at *British Vogue*, Diana was introduced to two of the magazine's experienced fashion and beauty experts, Anna Harvey and Felicity Clark.

Diana's impending arrival at Vogue House in Hanover Square prompted a flurry of activity. One young woman who worked at Vogue at the time recalls, "They even scrubbed the graffiti off the lift and cleaned the windows." Lady Di arrived and was ushered into the editor's office—Vogue's long-term doyenne Beatrix Miller had vacated it especially for the occasion. (On this and subsequent visits, the editor could be spotted in the adjoining secretary's office tapping her fingers while waiting for Anna Harvey and her colleague to finish the consultation.)

Clothes were summoned from designers' showrooms all over the West End garment district of London for the future queen to inspect. To Diana, it was like being ushered into an Aladdin's cave filled with jewel-colored clothes in fabulous fabrics. Previously, she'd shown no particular interest in her wardrobe, but those visits to Vogue House sparked off an enduring delight in designer clothes. Harvey and Clark would spend hours closeted away with the princess, occasionally being brought tea and biscuits by Vogue minions. One of the latter recalls, humorously, "I had to take in a groaning tray of refreshments to our VIP visitor. We'd been told to curtsey to her whenever we saw her, but here I was with cups full to the brim with tea and I was already shaking with nerves. I had to choose: no curtsey, or the tea slopping in the saucers. I cut the curtsey and Lady Di gave me a big smile." When Diana had made her selection, the younger Vogue assistants would have to pack every garment with countless layers of tissue paper and have the packages delivered to Her Ladyship's home.

Vogue staff *still* keep the princess abreast of new styles they think she might like, but the visits to Vogue House were canceled for security reasons. And after Anna Harvey and Felicity Clark made the initial overtures to Britain's top designers, Diana met with them all in person to make her selection or to commission unique designs for her wardrobe. They often go for appointments and fittings at Kensington Palace, but Diana still loves to visit their showrooms, just as she did during her engagement, to see sketches in progress, sift through the racks herself, and soak up the pally, "rag trade" ambience.

The handful of British designers whose clothes she selected in the privacy of Beatrix Miller's office still supply the mainstays of Diana's royal wardrobe. But she puts together her selections with her own newly developed taste and style—won partly by scrutinizing photographs of her public appearances and formulating a list of "Di Dos and Don'ts." Elizabeth Emanuel (who designed her wedding dress) declares: "Her look is a lot more sophisticated than it was. Now she knows what suits her." Although she is said to be influenced by Richard Dalton, her hairdresser, she learns by her own fashion mistakes; would that we all had a posse of photographers on hand who would capture ours forever on celluloid, that we might never repeat such errors in the future. But then again, imagine the horror of coming face-to-face with your fashion faux pas every time you open a magazine.

Not that Di's wardrobe *is* totally without fault, the experts agree; but there are some who feel it's improved out of all recognition, including Richard Blackwell, the caustic compiler of the annual Worst-Dressed List, who declared that "Diana has improved beyond measure in the last year—she often looks darn good."

When the new Princess of Wales arrived on the scene, the British fashion industry was in the doldrums. For years, the fashion focus had been elsewhere: Paris, Milan, New York. Nobody had looked to London to set trends since the days of Carnaby Street, bell-bottomed trousers, the Beatles. And then along came savior Di. Whether or not it would have been her initial choice to "Buy British," it was made clear to Diana that she had to wave the flag, and she has rarely wavered from that fashion path in public (except for occasions when it would be more diplomatic to do otherwise, like her choice of German designer Escada's giant yellow-and-black checked overcoat, which she wore on an official visit to that country late last year). She is a traveling ambassadress for British designers. It's all a far cry from Queen Victoria's remark, made during the last century, "Fashionable dressing? Anything but that."

But no outfit she has ever worn ever knocked 'em dead like the black strapless taffeta evening gown chosen from designers Elizabeth and David Emanuel (who would go on to create her world-famous wedding dress). The date was March 1981, the occasion a recital to raise money for a new extension to London's Royal Opera House. "That'll give them something to look at," quipped her future husband, who couldn't keep his eyes off his suddenly ravishing bride-to-be, declaring to waiting reporters as he alighted from the royal limousine, "Just wait till you see what's coming next."

Charles wasn't the only one who couldn't believe his fiancée's magical metamorphosis. Tina Brown (now editor-in-chief of *Vanity Fair* but then writing in British *Tatler* magazine), declared: "It was the greatest moment of sexual theater since Cinderella leapt out of her scullery clogs and into her glass slippers. She was saying, 'I'm not just suitable, I'm gorgeous, as well.'" Alighting from her limousine, however, Diana bent so low to collect her rustling skirts that papers next morning printed closeups of her décolletage, leaving readers to make up their prurient minds about whether or not the shadow of a soon-to-be-royal nipple had been revealed. Rumor has it that the Queen Mother—whose house guest she then was—

delicately pointed out that the dress was an unsuitable choice. Whether or not it had been cut too low, whether or not Di *had* unwittingly flashed a nipple, black is taboo for royal wear except during periods of mourning (though, as we shall see, this is one dictate which her sister-in-law seems to have got away with flouting). For whatever reason, the memorable gown, alas, now gathers dust under cellophane in the royal closet.

Gone, these days, are the white pie-frilled collars and demure droopy frocks that represented Di's first flirtation with designer dressing, at a time when she was still flushed with romance. Indeed, she had little time to settle into her style before her first pregnancy, when everything had to be let out at the seams to fit her swelling stomach. Still, Diana gave maternity wear a new lease on life; before Diana, maternity clothes were middle-aged and matronly. Suddenly, the manufacturers woke up to the fact that mothers-to-be, like Diana, didn't want to look as if their dresses had once had tent pegs attached; motherhood and style were no longer mutually exclusive. The British fashion elite were only too thrilled to rise to the challenge of producing the first real designer pregnancy wear. (Although, like most new mothers, she probably wanted to make a funeral pyre of the whole lot after her babies were born, and she will certainly want to forget the emerald-green tent she wore leaving St. Mary's, Paddington, with her first-born, which made her look positively mountainous.) For the most part, Diana was pure swelegance.

Since the birth of her sons, the romantic, floaty clothes have been, for the most part, banished. Unlike continental princesses, who will patronize perhaps a handful of couture houses, the Princess does the rounds and has been seen in designs by no less than thirty fashion houses—some of whom have admitted to providing fifty outfits! Proud of her new figure, she has opted for a flattering, body-skimming style that shows it off to stunning effect. Diana's new look has been dubbed POW-er dressing (since she's known privately among her staff as POW—short for Princess of Wales). She's been wrongly accused of being interested in nothing *but* what she wears—any glance down the list of good causes she devotes her time to should quash that—but she insists publicly, "My clothes are not my priority. I enjoy bright colors and my husband likes to see me look smart, presentable, but fashion isn't my thing at all." But surely, Diana, thou dost protest too much. And if she *is* as clothes crazy as insiders suggest, then perhaps she's simply remembering the compliment paid by her husband, who once said, "You know, I like seeing a lady well dressed. It was one of the things I noticed about her before we got married. She had, I thought, a very good sense of style and design."

So who are the designers whose talents transformed the boringly dressed Lady Diana Spencer into an international style leader? The list reads like a who's who of British style. Early favorites were Dutch emigré Jan Vanvelden; Arabella Pollen—who began by making clothes for friends when she was trying to support herself while writing a film script; and, of course, the Emanuels. She made David and Elizabeth Emanuel famous with that daring low-cut black dress but gave their careers the biggest possible boost when she selected them from dozens of hopefuls to design her ivory silk wedding gown. The Princess owns a dizzying one hundred dazzling evening gowns, several of them supplied by the Emanuels— who were the first married couple ever to have been admitted to the prestigious Royal College of Art—including the striking black-and-white dress gathered into a giant striped bow at the hip, in which she upstaged the sheikhs on her Middle Eastern trip in 1986.

Jasper Conran is another lingering favorite from the early days, designing timeless suits in fine wools—updated classics perfect for day wear. (She was also spotted last year at the film premiere of Harrison Ford's *Mosquito Coast* in Conran's daring duchesse satin evening separates: a cropped orange satin jacket and black, frill-tailed, and bustled skirt.) Formerly British Designer of the Year, twenty-seven-year-old Conran (who is the talented son of design supremo and Conran boss Sir Terence Conran and his ex-wife, best-selling novelist Shirley Conran) studied at the Parsons School of Design in New York and briefly worked for Fiorucci before setting up his own label (with the help of a large bank loan). No handouts for *this* Conran; he's made it on his own (and now has a shop on the Princess's favorite shopping boulevard, Beauchamp Place, where she may nip in after lunch).

There is an amusing tale about the Princess of Wales's fittings with Conran—who rarely ventures out without his small and extremely affectionate dog. The highly sexed puppy apparently clung to the Princess's leg with great ardor, to her amusement and Conran's mortification; when Diana was out of earshot, a furious Conran handed the pup to his assistant with the command, "Get this dog *done.*" The dog didn't reform one bit, although he looked cuter than ever, and one day, Conran (who had read about "residual hormones" after a dog is neutered) turned to his assistant and said, "Just *who* is the vet who's supposed to have done the dog?" "Vet?" asked his bemused assistant. "We thought you wanted us to send him to the poodle parlor." Conran now goes on his sorties to see the Princess without his four-legged friend, and the amusing experience doesn't seem to have dimmed her affection for his stylish, silk-lined separates.

Dressmaker Catherine Walker of the Chelsea Design Company has long been a favorite of the Princess's style counselor Anna Harvey, from *Vogue;* lately, Walker has been supplying the Princess with more and more chic day wear. For the stiflingly hot tour of Australia early last year, Diana's suitcase was brimful of cool numbers from Walker—including the strapless sarong-style evening gown the Princess wore to lead the dancing with her husband, frock 'n' rolling new life into her marriage for all the world to see. It may well be Di's dedicated patronage that prompted this French-born, Anglicized, long-haired brunette to expand from maternity wear, Sloane-set taffeta ballgowns, and children's wear into simple, structured separates. (Di still shops direct from Miss Walker's Fulham Road emporium, however, housed in a former conservatory, where she can select little sailor suits for her sons from Chelsea Design's elite children's line.) "Clothes should be fun," declares Catherine Walker, and nobody agrees more than the POW.

For a dinner to promote British fashion to the Spanish in Madrid, Diana chose another rising star, Rifat Ozbek, in a turquoise watered silk-taffeta suit, richly embroidered with crescent-moon symbols influenced by the designer's Turkish heritage. A former architecture student, Ozbek describes his clothes as having "the classic continental cut with the British wit." They are certainly show-business favorites; Whitney Houston wears them, as do Tina Chow, top model Marie Helvin, and countless other celebrities; the fashion tribe fight for front-row seats at his twice-yearly shows, which are fashion extravaganzas in celebration of each new collection's theme: La Dolce Vita, the Ballet Look, or lately, Mexican Fiesta, a carnival of paintbox colors with sombreros, flounced skirts, and Carmen Miranda headgear piled high with imitation oranges and bananas (although somehow, despite what she's achieved to boost the British millinery industry, I can't see the Princess in anything like *that*).

Diana (and her sister-in-law) both steer clear of the catwalk shows, but they love to watch the reruns on a VCR tape, which will be rushed around to the palace soon after the show. The Princess and the Duchess can then get a flavor of the collection, picking out a few possibles before an appointment with the designer himself. They may select styles "off the peg" or have couture items created especially; a "toile" will then be made (a pattern cut from a heavy muslinlike fabric), which will be fitted precisely to the wearer's figure and altered to suit, so that the finished garment fits like a glove. One of the Princess's hat makers reports that she had to trundle back and forth to Kensington Palace for no less than *four* fittings for a single hat, a clue to Diana's perfectionism. Imagine how long it takes to get a *dress* "just so."

Practical considerations are paramount. "I can't always wear what I'd like to an engagement because it's just not practical. There is only one golden rule," insists Princess Di. "Clothes are for the job. They've *got* to be practical." Which usually rules out linen, for instance, because it creases too badly. Even the most crisply starched linen frock looks like you've slept in it by the time you slink out of a limo; also wraparound, sarong-style skirts won't do, since a wayward gust of wind can whip them open to reveal the royal unmentionables—as Fergie found to her embarrassment on stepping off a plane in Mauritius.

Some of the Princess's grandest entrances have been carried off in exotic exclusives from the South Kensington couture studio of Victor Edelstein. He also made the black-and-white spotted, ruffled dress she wore to the races for Derby Day in 1986, outglitzing even *Dynasty*'s Joan Collins. Edelstein once had a ready-to-wear business, but he is far keener on creating elegant and unique clothes for ravishing women; other royal devotees are Princess Margaret's daughter Lady Sarah Armstrong-Jones and Princess Michael of Kent. He explains his philosophy thus: "You mustn't make a person feel like a cabaret when they go out. You must bring fantasy and invention to clothes, but not so that they're demanding to wear. When a woman puts a dress on, it's got to make her *feel* wonderful." So every dress is fitted to perfection, lined with silk and interlined with floaty organza so that not one stitch of the hem shows. Of the Princess, Edelstein says, "She likes body-conscious clothes, and why not? She's got the figure."

Another designer whose flattering, feminine creations have recently joined the royal wardrobe is Anouska Hempel (who, married to millionaire businessman Mark Weinberg, is also known in social circles as Lady Weinberg). Her austere, pale-pink duchesse satin shawl-collared dress received the accolade of being chosen for the official portrait of Diana and Charles to mark their tour of Australia early last year—appropriately enough, since this multitalented blonde originally hails from the land of Oz. She finds time, too, to run an interior decoration business and a top hotel, Blakes, in South Kensington (a favorite of movie stars and tennis players like John McEnroe). Her womblike showroom (with black windows, for the utmost discretion) is decorated in dark, somber shades, and here Miss Hempel provides a highly personal service for her elite clientele, like the Princess. Anouska explains: "There is great value in one woman telling another what to wear, if she's honest," continuing, "I never let a woman out of here looking dreadful. There's no point having a fantasy if you can't fulfill it." With prices of her exclusive evening wear soaring into the thousands, one sincerely hopes not.

Longtime society favorites Bellville Sassoon, who created a wedding dress for Jane Makim (Fergie's sister) a dozen years ago, have notched up over fifty outfits for the Princess, and partner David Sassoon (who teamed up with Belinda Bellville to create both couture and ready-to-wear-collections) calls Diana a "miracle worker" for the boost she's given British fashion. "She has achieved the best image we could possibly hope to have in this country. We are lucky to have someone as glamorous and pretty as she is," he eulogizes.

Bruce Oldfield, who creates slinky day wear and even sexier evening clothes, concedes that the exposure the Princess has given him "has definitely helped my career." Soap-opera stars are big fans of Oldfield's theatrical clothes, the ultimate in body-conscious dressing; breathtaking dresses the Princess has worn include a royal-blue, crushed velvet off-the-shoulder number and a stunning, white sequined gown. Other evening-wear designers whose clothes are infiltrating the royal ward-robe in increasing numbers are Murray Arbeid, who created a stunner in ivory lace; and Casablancan emigré Jacques Azagury, who declares, "I always imagine my clothes on the most beautiful women, and I haven't been disappointed yet."

Single-handedly, the Princess was responsible for breathing new life into the pantyhose industry. Aware of criticism that she was a shopaholic clotheshorse, she learned to deploy new accessories to distract fashion watchers from the fact that some of her clothes had been worn on quite a few occasions. Her hose were lacy, seamed, patterned, studded with dia-manté or with tassels or bows, drawing the eye to her ex-tremely shapely legs. Indeed, Diana went through a period of setting a new style every time she set foot outdoors, and with every new look, her imitators swooped upon the hosiery coun-ters in department stores.

Though the Princess is seen more and more without a hat adorning her platinum crop, hats are still de rigueur for more formal occasions (like church), and it can be no coincidence that since the Princess arrived on the scene, it's been boom-town for hat makers, who love the challenge of creating some-thing contemporary. As Graham Smith from Kangol, who supplies hats to the Princess and her sister-in-law, explains: "When she was first married and so young and attractive, I think she inspired a lot more conventional young women who wanted to dress up for weddings, christenings, and special occasions. She brought back formality and it was the begin-ning of a big interest in hats. Sales boomed."

Others who benefited from the need to cover the royal heads include John Boyd, Viv Knowland, Marina Killery, Freddie Fox, Stephen Jones, and Kirsten Woodward, the tal-ented young designer whom Karl Lagerfeld plucked from ob-scurity to create the hats for his many fashion shows, including Chanel in Paris and Fendi in Rome. The Princess doesn't always insist on an exclusive design. Indeed, for Sarah Ferguson's wedding, I was delighted to see that she had commissioned a turquoise-and-black straw hat from Kirsten Woodward which was the same shape as one I'd bought from Woodward a year before!

Actually, the Princess's burgeoning wardrobe is something of a royal headache. It's been estimated that, at last count, she was the proud owner of at least eighty suits, one hundred ball gowns, fifty day dresses, and countless blouses. There are matching accessories for almost every outfit; court shoes with high heels—which Di wears when her husband isn't around to be dwarfed by her height—and dozens of pairs of flats. Storing her hats alone is a huge challenge: she has literally hundreds, which must be boxed up to keep them undamaged for their next outing.

Her wardrobe is planned weeks in advance to avoid the last minute panic the rest of us have to endure when we realize that the outfit we'd decided to wear is actually hanging in the dry cleaner's! Only drastic changes in the weather—or the delivery of a frock the Princess is particularly dying to slip into—throws off the schedule. It's the arduous task of her two full-time dressers, Fay Marshalsea and Evelyn Dagley, to catalogue the Princess's finery, meticulously recording what was worn where.

Diana's relationship with Fay Marshalsea is particularly poignant. Just a few weeks before Miss Marshalsea's recent wedding to RAF officer Stephen Appleby, a troublesome lump under her tongue was found to be malignant. The bride-to-be, who'd worked for the Princess for three years, bravely fought back the tears and went ahead with her big day while also having to endure daily radiotherapy for her cancer. To the congregation's great delight, Diana graced what should have been the happiest day of Fay's life with her presence, but the young woman had barely been back at work a month when she became too ill to work. Diana instantly stepped in to offer whatever support Fay needed, allowing her to stay on in the Kensington Palace apartment because it was closer to the hospital where she had daily appointments. Diana would regularly drop by for cups of tea and to let Fay know of her concern, even, on one occasion, accompanying her ailing aide for treatment. "She just wanted to be there to support me," recalls Marshalsea, who, doctors hope, will make a full recovery. "When I was ill, she was always either seeing me or asking after me. She is a lovely person to work for, and very special to me."

Marshalsea has now happily resumed her role as the woman who ensures that Diana looks every inch "princess perfect" around the clock, nary a stray thread or an unraveling hem sullying her perfection. When Diana undresses, her clothes are checked to see whether a visit to the cleaners or the laundry is in order or whether the clothes can be brushed down and aired before being hung on a satin-padded hanger, slipped inside a monogrammed cover, and returned to the capacious closets. Her dressers also pack for her, calculating how many trunks and suitcases are called for. They're giant, aluminum valises in which the clothes can hang, so that only the lightest pressing is called for before the Princess can sashay forth looking immaculate. One report claims that for her tour of Australia in 1983, ninety trunks were packed!

Only when she's off duty does the Princess get free rein. And the results sometimes have the designers, who take such pains to ensure she looks stunning, rolling their eyes skyward in horror. (They prefer to remain nameless for fear of being banished to the Tower—or at the very least, losing their star customer.) It has been taken for granted that the "princess of style" has innate good taste, but she often gets it quite wrong. For formal and official occasions, she has the cream of couturiers queueing at the gates of Kensington Palace to swathe her immaculate figure in their creations. But left to her own devices (with the equivalent of a diamond-encrusted American

Express card with which to indulge her fancy), the Princess can look like a refugee from a cheap chain store.

In the short space of twenty-four hours, the Princess of Wales, designers' darling (and patron saint of the British hosiery industry) can deserve a place on both the world's "best-" and "worst-" dressed lists, as we witnessed last year. One night, she wore breathtaking flamenco flounces with wittily mismatched evening gloves—one red, one black—which displayed the stroke of originality we have come to expect from the Princess. But how easily Diana's well-intentioned fashion twists turn into catastrophes—like the night *before* the red-and-black triumph, when she made an impromptu appearance, notching up her *third* visit to *The Phantom of the Opera,* clad in a hideously uncoordinated combination of black satin bomber jacket, demure ruffled blouse, and red leather trousers worn with high heels. The overall effect was a bizarre mixture of Margaret Thatcher and a roadie from a Whitesnake tour, and the Princess's off-duty wear sometimes gives the impression that she's played blindman's buff in her closet, simply grabbing the first three garments which came to hand.

Often her fashion mistakes are hideously expensive. And the newfound passion for leather (which she shares with the Duchess of York) is more the taste we have come to expect from TV soap stars than a British blueblood who is to become queen of England. The aristocracy has long believed that leather is suitable only for handbags or saddlery, and even the very finest, softest, and most expensive skins look more at home on the thighs and behinds of a racing driver's girlfriend or the lead singer of a group like Fleetwood Mac.

Unlike the rest of us, however, Diana does not have the chance to meander freely through department stores at her leisure, putting her looks together. And she was, after all, raised to dress in classic cashmere, skirts from Laura Ashley, and the odd taffeta ball gown, like the ranks of Sloane clones from whom she rose to enter the royal dynasty. At least she's left *those* behind. It must be difficult, too, when your much older husband occasionally exhorts you to "grow up"—not to kick your heels and dress up like something out of *Peggy Sue Got Married*. But Diana has assumed the role of British fashion ambassadress and, as such, her casual clothes should be assembled with the same critical eye as her official wardrobe. Because otherwise, the end result, alas, is to appear to fashion pundits as if she's given *both* her dressers the same night off! What a Di-saster!

Of course, Diana's sister-in-law loves clothes too—perhaps not, however, with Diana's passion. Sarah resisted the temptation to undergo a royal "makeover" and, as a result, she too has suffered vicious attacks from fashion editors. (She did, for a brief spell, have the help of a magazine editor from *Brides* named Lucy Dickens to do some of the laborious legwork of matching accessories, etc.) To my mind, however, much of this criticism is quite unjustified. It is rarely addressed to her clothes themselves, but to her shape—and whether or not the garments she's selected are right for womanly curves. Where does it say in the royal rulebook that a princess has to look like Jerry Hall, Paulina Porizkova, Christie Brinkley—or an ironing board? Fergie's hearty lust for life includes a healthy appetite, and she is simply not concerned enough about having hip bones that stick out and a tummy as flat as a pancake to starve herself. It is hard enough to make it through the day without a rumbling tummy and a hunger headache.

Having once been editor-in-chief of two British fashion magazines, I support her decision *not* to try to achieve the "ideal" model shape, which her bone structure (heavier than her sister-in-law's) isn't anatomically suited for anyhow. When Diana was at her slenderest—prompting rumors that she herself was suffering from anorexia nervosa—I lost count of the number of letters we got from women with totally distorted body images who were half starving themselves to death in the hope of emulating Di's model measurements.

Fergie's fashion sense has been crucified in the press at times. The man behind the Worst-Dressed List (who was less scathing, for once, about the POW) dismissed the Duchess by saying, "She looks as though she should be in the running to be queen of a country fair." But most damning was the attack launched by British "W" magazine, which recently left the Duchess off a list of the fifty most stylish women in Britain today. "When we were introduced to Andrew's bouncy fiancée," they wrote, "she was prettily scruffy, delightfully dressed-down, with the potential for glorious glamor." More than a year and a half later, they claim, she gets it wrong more often than she gets it right. "W" writes: "Rumor has it that part of the problem is that Sarah won't accept the advice and guidance of the designers and experts." Too often, they claimed, her clothes seem chosen to highlight her weaknesses rather than flatter her curves. "At her worst, in droopy flower-print dresses, she is uncannily reminiscent of a char-lady"—the English slang for "cleaning woman."

I disagree with "W"'s verdict; unlike the Princess, Sarah never set herself up as a fashion icon, with the hope of revital-izing the fortunes of the garment industry. In fact, she has opted for a quite different tack, and one that may make her sister-in-law green with envy. When Diana decided to "buy British," she achieved her goal of breathing new life into Britain's flagging fashion fortunes, and the style world sud-denly turned to London for leadership. Overseas buyers flooded the city, stocking their stores with British designs, reminded by the Princess of Wales of how London can get it right. But it's a fickle business, and though for a while the young British designers were innovative and bold, there had to come a time when the focus switched to another city on the international design circuit of Milan, Tokyo, New York, Paris.

Suddenly, Paris was in the spotlight. Christian Lacroix emerged, Karl Lagerfeld left the couture house Chloe and not only started his own label but also stepped into Coco Chanel's shoes and revitalized Chanel. Just in time, in fact, for Fergie's first shopping spree. Diana has on more than one occasion hinted that she'd love to parade in Italian and French designs but is obliged to fly the flag.

Free of her sister-in-law's sartorial burden of being dressed exclusively by British designers, Sarah was able to dash across the English Channel and straight into Chanel, emerging—having shed twenty pounds—svelte, chic, and, some calculate, £20,000 poorer. (This fueled gossip that the Queen had given the Duchess a generous dress allowance to supplement the Yorks' earnings: £18,000 from Andrew's navy job, £20,000 salary from her work for the Swiss-based publisher, plus £50,000 per annum from the Civil List he then received, paid for out of British taxes—though this spring he was awarded a generous 73 percent raise.) In fact, it's rumored that the Duchess came to "an agreement" with the couture houses in question, being offered a hefty discount—though the royals aren't allowed to accept clothes as gifts. Fergie probably paid cost price for her creations, which Saint Laurent in London won't confirm or deny—although they *have* said, cryptically, "You'll just have to read between the lines." Diana, meanwhile, is obliged to pay nearly full price for her outfits.

To begin with, Fergie had been only too glad to snap up some of her friend the Princess's cast-offs: a black-and-white checked Chelsea Design Company coatdress that she slipped on to see Andrew aboard HMS *Brazen* or a blue chiffon dress she wore to Ascot, which Sarah had revamped from a two-piece first seen on Diana (when she was still plain old Lady Di) at the trooping of the colors for the Queen's official birthday.

The era of happy hand-me-downs was short-lived. Fergie's transformation began with the purchase of her little blue engagement suit from Alastair Blair's ready-to-wear collection. (Interestingly, Blair used to work with Parisian designer Karl Lagerfeld, where one of his favorite customers was Audrey Hepburn. Could it be that he pointed Sarah in the direction of his former mentor?) But Sarah got the opportunity to wear her £500 suit six months before any of Blair's other customers. The day before the Buckingham Palace photo session, her friend Susannah Constantine—who'd long been dating Prince Andrew's cousin, Viscount Linley—invited Sarah to join press, buyers, and a select group of customers at the quiet Scotsman's first London fashion show. (Susannah still works for Blair, and the leggy, long-haired royal girlfriend is seen everywhere in his creations.)

With only twenty-four hours to go before the announcement, Blair was asked to tailor the deep hyacinth-blue suit to Sarah's shape; she wore it tightly belted to emphasize her narrow waist. "She suits simple clothes," he declares—and the suit, classic and timeless, fastened with pewter buttons, was just that. Of course, Blair met the royal deadline and got international publicity on a scale that's every designer's dream. Overnight, the Duchess's patronage made Blair a design star; she soon commissioned a tight-bodiced, tiered, black, cream, and royal-blue off-the-shoulder evening gown in (how appropriate) duchesse satin, which set off to great effect her ivory skin and delicate new sapphire necklace. Visitors to Madame Tussaud's famous museum can actually see an identical dress, worn by her waxwork double. For Fergie, it was the equivalent of Diana's strapless black taffeta number, proclaiming to the world that she, too, could be gorgeous. If the Princess was POW-ing them, then Fergie was WOW-ing them! And she was so happy with the Blair evening gown that she ordered yet another for the Tiffany Ball, strapless powder-blue with big black-velvet bows.

Blair says of the Duchess, "The return to the curvaceous figure is the big swing in fashion—women shaped like women, and the Duchess has been very influential in that way." Like most women, he maintains, "She needs clear lines, silhouette, and proportion." Full-figured Sarah has learned about Hollywood actresses' favorite optical illusion: that shoulder pads in her clothes will draw attention away from her wide hips. Out went dirndls; in came skirts cut sexily short and tailored, showing off a pair of shapely legs. It was farewell to big, baggy jackets and hello to shapes, tailored again, that accentuate her curves rather than disguising or flattening them.

Sarah still shops off the rack from the London branch of Ralph Lauren; he's a long-term favorite of Sarah and her mother, Susan Barrantes, who, in her chambray separates with long, flowing hair, could have stepped straight from the pages of one of Lauren's advertisements. Ironically, she could have done just that—rumor has it that Señora Barrantes so typified the Lauren look that Ralph wanted to sign her up for a campaign! Several of the New York–based designer's flowered, pastel crepe de chine dresses were picked out for her overseas tour to the idyllic island paradise of Mauritius in 1987, and Sarah found the featherweight silk perfect to combat sizzling heat.

Sarah's former roommate, Carolyn Beckwith-Smith, had once helped out in the King's Road corner shop occupied by ex-model and designer Edina Ronay, whose Fair Isle and fine-knit patterned sweaters sell for hundreds of dollars in top shops like Bergdorf's or on Rodeo Drive (she has also signed a licensing deal to open twenty-eight shops across Japan). Thanks to the success of her knitwear, former actress and model Ronay expanded into classy separates, and the Duchess decided they were just perfect. Last winter, she was often seen in Ronay's Russian-style red jacket with decorative military-style frogging across the bosom and a matching Cossack-style hat. "There are certain parts of the collection where I'll think, 'The Duchess of York would look nice in that,'" declares Ronay, who then steers Sarah toward pieces she knows will flatter her. As Edina explains, "Men designers are great on fantasy because they don't actually wear the clothes—well, I know a few who do—but they don't understand that women don't like certain things. You've got to be careful around the hip and stomach area because most women haven't got fab figures."

Perhaps that lack of feminine insight was the problem with another commission (allegedly for twenty-five outfits, though most have never seen the light of day) that went to young designer Paul Golding, a twenty-eight-year-old graduate of Oxford University's languages department. It was Golding's designs that elicited some of the harshest criticism from fashion pundits, who pointed out that a princess's clothes mustn't just look good in the flesh—they have to photograph well, too. One of Golding's least flattering designs for the Duchess was the pale-blue gingham-checked dress she wore to Ascot in June 1987; its wide horizontal bands completely cut her in half and made her look as if she'd high-stepped from the chorus of a Rogers and Hammerstein musical.

She loves to gear her wardrobe to mark a special occasion. When she earned her flying wings, Fergie amused all and sundry by arriving in a sheepskin flying jacket and white polo-neck shirt, her wayward locks secured with a pair of especially commissioned biplane hairclips and a white chiffon Red Baron scarf tossed casually over her shoulders—prompting the comment, "Crikey, it's Biggles!" Barrettes often replace hats, but she made famous a Davy Crockett–style headband with a fur tassel down the back—now copied all over the slopes of Europe—when she wore it in Klosters (she opted for the real thing, in raccoon, on her Canadian hike). She also goes to her mother's favorite hat maker, Freddy Fox, who declares, "Luckily, she likes hats altogether, especially with wide brims . . . . she must reconcile herself to wearing more hats in the future."

As for the more formal Paris wardrobe, Sarah went straight to the top: to Yves Saint Laurent and Karl Lagerfeld, at Chanel. (She also ordered a Karl Lagerfeld suit from his Bond Street shop, putting in a special request for it to be made up in navy, not the black that they had in stock.) Her sensational

Saint Laurent wardrobe includes an electric-blue suede suit encrusted with diamanté bows, which she wore to a London fashion auction hosted by Christie's to raise money for AIDS. It was there that I saw her bid against pop singer Boy George for a huge orange-and-black picture hat by the historic Parisian designer Hubert de Givenchy—Boy George beat her to it! Incidentally, a highly embarrassing situation was avoided that evening thanks to the Duchess's sense of humor. Prince Andrew's ex, Koo Stark, had also been invited and was mistakenly ushered to the front-row seats set aside for the Duchess. When Sarah turned up, she was warned of the faux pas, so she decided, instead, to grab the nearest seats at the back of the room rather than create a scene. She thoroughly enjoyed herself and gaily laughed the incident off with her friends.

Another Parisian suit is in rich, dark velvet with gold braid etching out a bow across the front. Karl Lagerfeld actually relaunched the bow when he took up residence at Chanel, but by wearing it in her hair, embroidered on her clothes, and decorating bustles and shoulders, the Duchess has made it her distinctive trademark. The Princess, by contrast, loyally sticks with her husband's symbol, the Prince of Wales's feathers.

At last, Sarah is learning to turn her back on wishy-washy pastels and go for bold brights—red, emerald, royal blue—which contrast flatteringly with her hair. And for the Manhattan premiere of the Andrew Lloyd Webber musical *The Phantom of the Opera*, when she was dubbed Duchess of New York by a rapturous crowd, she dazzled in another Saint Laurent creation, with a giant frill of black netting at the shoulder and cuff. Interestingly, whereas the Princess of Wales was politely counseled that she shouldn't wear black except for mourning, the Duchess has inexplicably broken this royal rule on many occasions; she is the proud owner of a perfect little gilt-buttoned Chanel suit in black (the lucky lady also has a fine-checked, Nehru-collared Chanel suit) and several more black numbers.

To the great astonishment of the fashion establishment, Sarah even looked as though she was thinking of augmenting her burgeoning wardrobe with the outrageous designs of Paris's enfant terrible Jean-Paul Gaultier, since she summoned his collection to Buckingham Palace and told the London shops stocking Gaultier's garb that she would "let them know." Perhaps the realization that she was pregnant prevented Sarah from placing an order, or maybe, common sense prevailed: Gaultier's spring collection was full of breastplates, bras on show, cycling pants, and even ballet dancers' codpieces. But her very desire to see Gaultier's avant-garde collection was further evidence that there is one royal rule for the woman who will be queen but another for her sassy sister-in-law.

The Duchess has been introduced by her sister-in-law to Catherine Walker of the Chelsea Design Company (having first learned to love her creations by wearing Di's secondhand numbers), and she patronizes another British designer, Gina Fratini, who's long been dressing up debutantes in delicate silks and lace. Sarah's favorite is a mauve shot-silk ball gown which, like many of her clothes, is cut to cling to every curve. (Since her pregnancy, there are a few more curves to cling to, and—having never been slender—Fergie's had to work doubly hard to get her shape back. She must envy Diana's ability to slim back to her prepregnancy shape in just a month.)

The Duchess's choice, however, of a French team to fashion a new image for her has put many British designers' noses out of joint. But Sarah seems immune to controversy. Although the Queen, Queen Mother, and Princess Margaret like to wear fur to stay warm and toasty—mink wraps to slip over their evening wear—the younger royals have never before opted to drape themselves in animal fur. There is a fervent antifur feeling among many Britons (who are traditionally animal crazy), but the Duchess flew in the face of convention—and set the establishment fur flying—when she gladly accepted the

Looking more relaxed and restored than any mother of a three-week-old baby has a right to—the coiffeurs and makeup artists prepared Diana for a portrait with her redheaded son Harry. (Snowdon/Camera Press/Photo Trends)

Sarah, aged six, with her favorite teddy bear, poses on the staircase before the ritual bedtime story read by Major Ronald. (Alpha/Globe Photos)

From the Ferguson family album, Daddy's little baby girl, bonny Sarah, aged ten months, already had the bright red crowning glory that would catch her prince's eye. (Alpha/Globe Photos)

The bad old Di's classic style (or lack of it). The floaty skirt, ruffled blouse, and sleeveless anorak, which was almost a uniform and once favored by thousands of identical contemporaries. (Syndication International/Photo Trends)

So in love–Diana and Charles hold hands on their Scottish honeymoon. Nowadays, Diana's known to be restless when she has to spend too long a time at the slow-paced Balmoral royal retreat. (Ferguson/ Camera Press/Photo Trends)

The bride wears the famous Spencer tiara. Her father, sensibly, gave his daughter an empty jewel box as one of her wedding gifts. (Litchfield/Camera Press/Photo Trends)

The future King and Queen. (Snowdon/Camera Press/Photo Trends)

An official, yet relaxed family portrait to mark the birth of the boy who's second in line to the throne, William Arthur Philip Louis, born the twenty-first of June, 1982. Or, to his dad, just plain "Wills the Wombat." (Pictorial Parade)

The official portrait of Charles's and Diana's glittering wedding, taken by royal cousin the Earl of Lichfield. Attendants included Princess Anne's son Peter Phillips, Princess Margaret's daughter Lady Sarah Armstrong-Jones, and little Clementine Churchill, Winston's great-granddaughter. (Syndication International/Photo Trends)

The sprawling lineup smiles for Scottish fashion photographer Albert Watson (a favorite of *Vogue* magazine, chosen by Sarah and Andrew). Sarah's and Andrew's wedding was very much a relaxed family affair, unlike Diana's and Charles's majestic wedding in St. Paul's Cathedral. To the disappointment of the British public, however, it wasn't declared a national holiday. (Albert Watson/Camera Press/Photo Trends)

At Westminster Abbey it seems as if practically everyone in the wedding party from the Queen to the humblest pageboy was allowed to sign the marriage certificate declaring the Duke and Duchess of York officially man and wife. (Syndication International/Photo Trends)

That kiss–the lingering royal smacker that the world waited for, and which made Charles's and Di's, five years earlier, look chaste by comparison. (Harvey/Camera Press/Photo Trends)

An official engagement portrait, taken in the Blue Drawing Room at Buckingham Palace, with Sarah in the tricolor Alastair Blair dress her doppleganger wears in London's Wax Musueum. (Donovan/Camera Press/Photo Trends)

The honeymooning couple take off for the sun-drenched Azores, the first of many overseas trips enjoyed by the globe-trotting Duke and Duchess: Mauritius, Switzerland, America, Australia. And the list grows. (Harvey/Camera Press/Photo Trends)

Biggles gets her wings–in an aviator jacket and silk scarf. She was known affectionately as "Chatterbox One", and describes flying as "a great challenge." (Syndication International/Photo Trends)

March 19, 1986–speculation ends as Prince Andrew announces his engagement to publishing assistant Miss Sarah Ferguson. (Photo Trends)

Nautical but nice–a seafaring flavor for husband and wife (in a Catherine Walker for Chelsea Design Company) on an official visit to Italy. (Syndication International/Photo Trends)

For every gala, for every dance with Travolta, there are a hundred factory visits and a thousand strange hands to shake. Here, visiting a smelting works in Australia, in headgear less glamorous than usual. (Syndication International/Photo Trends)

Rocking and rolling in her most famous rocks–the emerald bracelet a sunburned Diana decided to wear Hiawatha-style while touring Australia. (Syndication International/Photo Trends)

Bonne-Di! Diana, in flirtatious mood, poses with the somewhat underdressed lifeguard team at Terrigal Beach in Sydney, where she presented a trophy named in her honor.
(Camera Press/Photo Trends)

British royalty meets the uncrowned Queen of Soaps–Joan Collins–and out-chics her, in a polka-dot Saint Laurent. Another star-studded gala to gossip to her faithful friends about.
(Syndication International/PhotoTrends)

Sarah's a firm favorite of the Prince of Wales—and she's seen here giving the future king a playful kiss on the sidelines at a polo match. Her father is the Prince's polo manager.
(Syndication International/Photo Trends)

It's official—soon after the long-awaited announcement that Fergie's a mum-to-be. One possible reason f the delayed tidings is that the Duchess is rumored to have lost an earlier baby.
(Colton/Camera Press/Photo Trends)

Sarah—with her grandmother, the Hon. Mrs. Wright—greets her new baby half-sister Alice, firstborn of her father's second family. Twenty-one years divide the girls, but they share an excellent relationship, and Alice was a natural choice as Sarah's bridesmaid. (Alpha/Globe Photos)

Watching Daddy at the polo–the future King William, less boisterous than usual, sits on his mother's lap at Windsor Great Park, where the royal couple are often to be found off-duty during the summer months. (Rex Features/RDR Productions, 1987)

A freshly coiffed and visibly radiant Diana shows her second son, Prince Henry Charles Albert David, to the world, on the steps of St. Mary's Hospital Lindo Wing. (Syndication International/Photo Trends)

Prince William cradles baby Harry in a charming pose captured by
Princess Margaret's ex-husband Lord Snowdon–still very much a
family favorite, despite the rift.
(Syndication International/Photo Trends)

Even in the plumed uniform of a Knight of the Garter, traveling by open coach in Windsor, Prince Charles can't upstage his shining wife, whose wide-brimmed hat outglitzes his velvet bonnet.
(Syndication International/Photo Trends)

The Lady in Blue—ravishing for the official royal portrait in an off-the-shoulder dress by Bruce Oldfield, increasingly one of her favorite British designers. He also dresses Joan Collins. (Photo Trends)

gift of a fox fur coat from a Canadian dignitary in 1987. (Andrew got one, too, but he appeared less than bowled over.) Her husband also commissioned a fur coat to be tailor-made for his wife—before feelings back home boiled over into a raging controversy and he was forced to cancel the order. The royal household's explanation for the acceptance of the brace of fur coats was that "it would look downright rude to return them." But Sarah's been spotted sloping round Alpine villages in hers and would almost certainly like to feel free to sport her fur back home, if it wouldn't ruffle quite so many feathers.

But unlike the rest of us, Diana and Sarah aren't allowed to forget their less-than-flattering fashion failures, their bulges, or their secret desire to slink around in mink. Their clothes are scrutinized with more fascination than almost anyone in the world's and every British-designed creation is worth millions of pounds in export orders. Each time they make a public appearance, from the Sydney Opera House to the White House (and a thousand less glamorous venues), the eyes and cameras of the entire world are focused on their clothes, to be discussed, praised, or damned. They have assembled wardrobes that cost a king's ransom in order to fulfill the role in which they've been cast, that of traveling fashion ambassadors. But what woman alive wouldn't leap at the chance to *frock around the clock* like Di and Fergie?

6

By Royal Beauty Appointment...

Princesses have to be beautiful. We expect it, demand it, a legacy from reading too many tales by Hans Christian Andersen. Fortunately, Diana and Sarah don't let us down—high cheekbones, big eyes, glossy hair. But they know better than anyone that beauty doesn't come effortlessly; the bad news for couch potatoes everywhere is that Di and Fergie diet and exercise as conscientiously as any *Vogue* model.

There's another reason for keeping fit: to cope with the strenuous schedule of tours, charity events (lots of late nights), and official engagements. Diana has never canceled an engagement in all her years as a princess, mostly because she takes care of her health.

The princesses are fitness fanatics—and happily, they have a pool at their disposal. On most mornings, after William and Harry are safely delivered to school, Diana is driven to Buckingham Palace to do her ritual twenty laps in the heated pool. Fergie swims there, too; the pair will occasionally race together. They protect their hair from the chlorine by pinning it up or wearing rubber bathing caps, since the chemicals could alter the color, giving the royal hairdressers apoplexy. Diana also plows up and down the pool each weekend morning at her country hideaway of Highgrove, and hosts on royal tours are often requested to put a pool at her disposal. It energizes her for the rigors of the day ahead.

Diana's theme tune, though, should be "Dance, little lady, dance." Once upon a time, she wanted to become a professional ballerina, but she grew too tall; she now tops five feet, ten inches and is still self-conscious about her height (especially since she's only an inch shorter than her husband). That accounts for her stooping posture; but in the privacy of her workout room at Kensington Palace, it's a different story. (In the early days of her courtship, staff at Buckingham Palace regularly saw the Princess, wearing a Walkman, dancing away down the corridors, lost in a world of her own, listening to the pop music she loves.) Now, for a couple of hours at least twice a week, private teachers put Diana through her paces with a combination of ballet, jazz, and tap exercises. She is skillful enough on the dance floor to have been twirled expertly around by John Travolta at a White House dinner and was deeply upset that she never got the chance to boogie with Mikhail Baryshnikov, her ballet hero, who had to sit and watch, nursing an injured leg.

Diana has also, lately, begun to enjoy horseback riding again. A bad experience as a child terrified the life out of her; at the age of nine, she fell from her pony Romany and, after her fright, would think of any excuse not to ride out with her family. But when she joined the royal ranks, the fact that she didn't ride made her an instant outsider. Her husband is a top polo player; her sister-in-law won an Olympic equestrian medal; her father-in-law drives horse-drawn carriages; and the head of the household, Her Majesty the Queen, can safely be described as being obsessed with the four-legged creatures. Diana's reluctance to saddle up was considered wimpish, to say the least, and heavy hints were dropped that if she expected to be totally accepted by the family, she'd better pull on her jodhpurs and mount up.

Pregnancy early in her marriage gave her the perfect excuse to stay at home while the rest of the royals braved the elements to go riding in even the foulest weather. But ironically, it was the birth of her two boys, who seem to have inherited the Windsor horse-loving gene, that encouraged Diana to have another try. After a few private lessons, she found she quite enjoyed the exercise—great for the thighs and the tummy—and loved being able to trot along beside her little princes.

Sarah has never needed asking twice to leap into the saddle. From an early age, she was winning rosettes and cups at Pony Club events, and as Major Ferguson's daughter, a love of horses had been practically bred into her. (The daughters of the English upper and upper-middle classes are traditionally crazy about ponies. It usually lasts until about the age of thirteen, when they discover boys instead. In Sarah's case, the passion still endures.) It was Sarah's professed affection for riding that so endeared her to her future mother-in-law, and their friendship was forged on rides together. It is a closeness that has always been denied Diana.

Apart from swimming and riding, both girls like to get in a good game of tennis. Diana's mother was a champion tennis player and, to improve her own game, Diana has signed up with the exclusive Vanderbilt Racquet Club ($700 a year membership fee) in West London, about a mile and a half from the palace. She's a strong player and finds that thrashing the hell out of a tennis ball is the best way to ease the day's tension. She also has an exercise bike in her Kensington Palace gym and got into the habit of doing sit-ups after her sons were born. According to British "W" magazine, she could use some extra exercise designed to define her slim legs; the slenderest in the royal family, they're described as "elegantly turned and just strong enough not to snap in a southwesterly gale." They are displayed to perfection in the season's short skirts and suits. But she lost out in the "shapeliest royal legs for generations" to her sister-in-law Sarah. Though it's perhaps not surprising, really, that the Windsor wives have great legs, since they're constantly exercised on walkabouts in teetering high heels.

Annual skiing holidays, staying with friends in the exclusive Swiss resort of Klosters, are great exercise for both the Duchess and the Princess—skiing uses up hundreds of calories an hour. Diana, however, will never be the expert, daredevil skier that Sarah is, thanks to those many months spent with Kim Smith-Bingham and Paddy McNally in Verbier. She likes to ski fast, straight downhill, whereas Diana descends at a tamer pace. Sarah so loves to ski that while Andrew is away, she'll try to fit in a couple more trips to the slopes. She was enjoying a solo sojourn on the slopes early last year when news of her pregnancy leaked out.

Falling in love is traditionally the best diet there is, and the pounds melted away when Diana and Sarah met their princes. Butterflies in the stomach are a better appetite suppressant than Dexedrine could ever be. In Diana's case, she became dangerously thin and sparked off rumors that she might be anorexic. She hates to eat in public and pushes her food around her plate, slightly shy of being seen eating. It's a far cry from her adolescent days, when she craved gooey chocolate-cream eggs and would wolf down huge cooked breakfasts. Staff at Kensington Palace know now to prepare a light meal, perhaps salad, for the Princess when she's eating at home alone. Skipping meals altogether is a royal no-no; it's just too embarrassing to pass out with hunger in front of a crowd. She's not wild about foreign food, preferring baked potatoes, Cheddar cheese, and fresh fruit. Her weakness is the occasional bar of chocolate, which she once claimed "gives me energy." (Kit-Kats are supposed to be a favorite.) Perhaps, she's been reaching for those candy bars more regularly in the last year because there's no doubt that her dress size has gone up from an 8 to a 10, and the Princess is curvier than she has been since the early days of her engagement; she now weighs around 135 pounds. Her measurements have apparently increased from a too-thin 32-22-34 to 36-27-37.

Or maybe she's just taken the words of her new sister-in-law to heart. When Sarah arrived on the scene, she gaily announced that "women should be round." She has never been skinny; she has a hearty appetite and sees no reason why she should starve herself simply to conform to an unrealistic ideal. Fergie's figure is hourglass shaped: broad, childbearing hips, a small waist, and a generous bosom. It's a typically English shape, but apparently, she finds her voluptuousness a problem, for it's been reported that she told dress designers assembling her wardrobe for a recent royal tour that "I look so busty, nothing seems to suit me. It's these bloody melons I've got!" Her prepregnancy size fluctuated around 38-26-39.

Her weight zoomed upward when she gave up smoking some years before she met Andrew (although she would, occasionally, have a puff on someone else's—until her fiancé made his disapproval felt). And she does have a tendency to pile on the pounds if she isn't careful. Sarah doesn't need too much coaxing to tuck into sweet, sticky foods, as Andrew discovered that first day he tempted her with a cream-filled, chocolate-covered profiterole at Ascot. Her weight now hovers around the 140-pound mark—she's five feet, eight inches tall. Before her pregnancy, she'd slimmed down to take a size 12 dress; sometimes, jubilantly, a 10.

Sarah has married into a family of teetotalers, and her reputation as a champagne lover is quite ill-founded. Neither Diana nor Sarah drink more than a few sips anymore. When Diana and Sarah were criticized in the British press for "high-living high jinks"—amid claims that the Duchess had introduced the Princess to the bottle—Diana set the record straight publicly, declaring (in one of her first major speeches, when she accepted the Freedom award of the City of London), "Contrary to recent reports in some of our more sensational Sunday papers, I have not been drinking and I am not, I can assure you, about to become an alcoholic." Both princesses realize that, quite apart from the calorie content of alcohol, there's nothing worse than doing the royal round of handshaking with a crushing hangover. Instead, hosts are known to lay on plenty of Malvern water and sparkling Perrier—wonderfully, blissfully calorie-free—for the equally effervescent duo.

Before her wedding, Sarah signed up with Body's gym in the famous King's Road, where she followed a routine of aerobics and endless pedaling on the exercise bikes, plus the occasional stint on a Nautilus machine for spot treatment. She can reward herself with a sauna or a massage—which she finds hugely relaxing—afterward. Some of the weight Sarah initially lost has crept back on—perhaps with encouragement from her husband, who can't disguise his approval of Sarah's shape. (It's had diet doctors singing a hallelujah chorus. Having grown used to seeing half-starved dieting casualties who'd tried to emulate size-6 mannequins, they feel that Sarah is a healthier role model for young women than her sister-in-law was.) She tries to stick to baked potatoes and fish and avoid red meat. On a skiing trip to Switzerland in January, however, she was seen tucking into a huge plate of french fries—just as well, perhaps, that skiing burns so many calories.

Because they're two of the most photographed creatures in the world, Diana and Sarah got expert makeup tuition early on. They had to learn techniques that would ensure they didn't look washed out under strong lighting and could withstand the incessant popping of flashbulbs wherever they go, yet they must never look over-made-up or cheap. The professional who helped Diana was Barbara Daly (who later did the makeup for her wedding), who taught her to blend in a little pale foundation, blotting this with translucent powder, and to do her eye makeup: a fine shading of gray eye shadow, thin black kohl line, and mascara to show off her long eyelashes. She never wears blusher because even now, when anyone makes a risque remark or pays her a particularly fulsome compliment, she flushes. For her lips, she sticks to pale pink lipsticks and a slick of clear lip gloss. She has delicate, dry English skin and tries to stick to hypoallergenic cosmetics that don't make her complexion flare up—even princesses get the odd zit (carefully disguised with pale concealer).

Both the Princess and the Duchess like to soak up a tan—though their English rose complexions burn easily (like the occasion when Diana got so sunburned on her neck that she had to wear her necklace Hiawatha-style). The Princess is particularly keen to get her legs evenly tanned; she is the first royal to go without pantyhose in public, and if the weather doesn't oblige, she's been known to reach for the fake tan. Sarah's red hair means she's especially susceptible to sunburn. Sensibly, on her holiday with Florence Belmondo shortly before her marriage, the Duchess wore a big straw hat and a cotton cover-up—plus a sunscreen. She also paid several visits to a Mayfair tanning parlor to make sure she wasn't totally lily-white when she arrived in the Caribbean. Sarah repeated this experience before last year's trip to Los Angeles; she was furnished with a note from her physician giving the mum-to-be the necessary go-ahead. She keeps her face out of the sun as much as possible, hating the freckles that multiply across her nose and cheeks if she's not careful. But it's impossible not to get at least a healthy, rosy glow from the burning sun, and both the Princess and the Duchess find that the natural, healthy look cuts their makeup routine in half.

Fergie was taught to improve *her* makeup technique by Denise McAdam of Michaeljohn, the Mayfair hairdressers, whose other royal customers include Princess Anne and Princess Alexandra (although top session artist Teresa Fairminer, who works on commercials and fashion spreads for glossy magazines, did her wedding makeup). Soon, however, Fergie was a dab hand with the blue kohl pencil she uses to outline her eyes (sometimes worn with matching cobalt mascara; she likes mauve lashes, too, and is never seen without mascara because her own eyelashes are naturally fair). Like many redheads, she has a high natural color. She's freckled and doesn't need to wear base or powder during the day; but after dark, she goes in for a more heavily made-up look, with ivory foundation, gold eye shadow, and a light dusting of pale powder. She accentuates her high cheekbones with a bronzy shade of blusher.

Her makeup consultant is a great fan of the flame-colored locks that so appealed to Prince Andrew. Ironically, she was teased mercilessly about her "carrot" color at school. Little did she realize that her red hair would one day be her crowning glory—almost literally! Now the Duchess has made flame-red hair fashionable for the first time in years; her husband lovingly refers to it as "her magnificent titian mane." Instead of going blonde, many young women with mousy hair are having henna treatments or red rinses, to head-turning effect.

"The Duchess has the best hair any hairdresser could want," Denise McAdam announced recently. "It's thick but not too thick. It has curl but you can brush it straight. The color changes from deep red to nearly blonde—yes, it really does." And, she revealed, "I do trim her hair but I never cut it—it would be sacrilege." Indeed, "If she decides to have it shorter, it won't be my scissors doing it!" The creative talents of Miss McAdam have now been admired around the world—and she has to work amazingly fast. "Sarah's a rusher. She's usually got about fifteen minutes, an hour if you're really lucky."

If Sarah's diary is packed with official functions, McAdam (whose success has now enabled her to set up a salon to rival Michaeljohn) may be summoned two or three times a week to fix the Duchess's hair. (Sarah used to go to another West End salon, Leonard, but changed at the suggestion of Princess Alexandra, her husband's godmother.) McAdam keeps an eagle eye open for new hair accessories and brings a kit bag packed with ribbons, combs, and clips so as to be able to confect something original. McAdam's creations include the corkscrew curls for Sarah's wedding, a straight and shiny ponytail (with the help of a hairpiece pinned onto the Duchess's own), pincurls, French pleats, or hair held back in a net snood, a style Sarah has single-handedly revived. McAdam also weaves fresh flowers into the royal coiffure; they are wired onto combs by florist Jane Packer, who did the royal bouquet and flowers for Westminster Abbey. McAdam confesses, "The Duchess never quite knows what I am going to do—even I never know *exactly* how her hair will look until it's done." In Los Angeles recently, she wowed them with a halo of fresh roses in her hair, perfectly offsetting the rose-trimmed dress made by Lindka Cierach, creator of Sarah's wedding dress. Between visits, the Duchess is under strict instructions to use a deep conditioning treatment on her flowing tresses, so as to balance the drying effect of heated rollers, tongs, and blow-dryers.

Andrew has always been a fan of long nails, and McAdam also gives the Duchess regular manicures and pedicures; Sarah has beautiful hands with slender fingers and long, strong nails she keeps glossed or varnished. By contrast, her sister-in-law hates her hands; she used to bite her nails from nerves and tries to hide them for photographs, believing them to be her worst feature. That's one reason she favors long evening gloves. One indulgence the royal pair find irresistible is perfume: Diana wafts around in a cloud of Nina Ricci's L'Air du Temps, while Sarah prefers Madame Rochas.

The man who transformed Diana from meek mouse to stunning blonde was hairdresser Kevin Shanley, a partner in the Headlines salon. As Paula Yates, Bob Geldof's wife, wrote in her book *Blondes,* "Ever since Diana first ventured shyly out of Coleherne Court completely upholstered in Laura Ashley, her streaks have got steadily wider and wider until now there are no brown bits in between." Shanley also transformed Diana's boring page-boy bob into something altogether more alluring, sweeping her fringe back so that the world could see her aristocratic bone structure (emerging from beneath her puppy fat), prompting thousands of women all over the world to pitch up at their local hair salon with a clipping for their own stylists to re-create. Diana also persuaded her husband to allow Shanley to give him a more up-to-date image.

Shanley would arrive at Kensington Palace to dry and style Diana's hair after her swim, and he was invited along to ensure that the Princess's coiffure was always immaculate on overseas tours. Like Denise McAdam, Shanley had to develop a style for his client that would show off her tiaras in all their sparkling glory. But in 1984, a newly confident Diana swapped stylists when Shanley protested that her hair was far too short to sweep up into the severe style she wanted to try for the State Opening of Parliament. The press declared it a Di-saster, but the Princess had already decided to go with the talents of Kevin Shanley's partner in Headlines, Richard Dalton, who soon quit the salon (where, after the changeover, you could cut the atmosphere with a pair of styling scissors). Shanley blew his royal blow-drying chances once and for all when he offered Sunday newspaper reporters inside gossip about life at Kensington Palace.

Meanwhile, Richard Dalton is now freelance, able to follow the Princess wherever she ventures, and it's said she turns to him for advice on her total look. One insider declares that it's Dalton's love of theater that has influenced the Princess to go for the high-gloss, *Dynasty*-style look she's developing.

Dalton now visits the Princess at home several times a week to wash and style her thick, shiny hair while they listen to the radio, and Diana uses this enforced relaxation to catch up with the latest fashion magazines. She has her hair frosted every three weeks or so; usually, Dalton just does a "half head"— that is, the parting and the face-framing halo—but every three months or so the whole of Diana's hair is highlighted with a combination of peroxide bleach and a blond tint, solving any regrowth problems. Someone once said that blond is a state of mind, not a hair color. But if the platinum Princess—with the help of Richard Dalton—has become the ultimate blond bombshell, then her sister-in-law is surely a real red devil.

7

Career Princesses

There can be few more delightful twists to the story of these modern-day Cinderellas than to discover that one of them actually *was* a maid. Yet at the beginning of last year, that's exactly what Diana revealed when she met a woman for whom she'd once done housecleaning. At a charity event, Diana was reintroduced to Lucinda Craig Harvey, a theatrical producer. "Oh, we already know each other," giggled Diana. "I used to be her cleaner!" "And very good at it she was, too," replied thirty-two-year-old Lucinda, who once shared a Chelsea apartment with Diana's elder sister Sarah and used to pay Diana to come in and keep the place clean and tidy. It may well have been the last time that Diana ever had to flick a duster.

Diana—unlike her friend Sarah—never really had a "career." She'd helped out at a ballet school and made sticky paper collages with under-fives at the Pimlico kindergarten, but then along came Prince Charles with the glass slipper and rescued her from that. What Diana took on, however, is a role shared by many women married to top executives all over the world who have had to put their own careers—to a certain extent, their own lives—on a back burner. Diana is the ultimate company wife. Any suggestion of Diana pursuing a career of her own—however much, secretly, she might perhaps yearn to use her fashion expertise to design clothes herself, or take a job with a publishing company, as Sarah had—would be unthinkable.

She declares, "I feel my role is supporting my husband whenever I can and always being behind him, encouraging him. And also, most important, being a mother and a wife. And that's what I try to achieve." With a dash of honesty, she adds, "Whether I do is another thing, but I do try." And in addition to being a solid rock for Charles to lean on, Diana, like many an executive's wife, has her charity interests.

Diana is deluged by requests from charitable trusts, arts groups, and community ventures all over the United Kingdom who clamor for her royal patronage. When word of her love of dancing leaked out, ballet companies all over Britain immediately dispatched entreating letters to Kensington Palace. Diana is well aware what becoming a figurehead can do for flagging fortunes and weighs carefully with her advisers—in particular, her private secretary—which invitations to accept. She has to make sure that other royals—including her husband and other close members of the family—don't have "rival" charity interests on *their* lists. As one charity representative who recently signed up a young royal as its patron explained in an interview in the *London Times,* "It has taken us years. You have to write to his or her private secretary and, although you always get an acknowledgment, it can take ages for a decision to be made. And if the answer is no, only then can you write to someone else. You are never allowed to send off a whole batch of letters at one time, to see whether one bears fruit."

Occasionally, though, boldness pays swift dividends—reflecting, perhaps, a secret royal yearning to be as impulsive as you or I at times. Twenty-six-year-old Actor Kenneth Branagh, for instance, enlisted the patronage of Diana's husband for his theater group Renaissance without having to endure the regulation royal red tape. "It all happened so quickly," explained Branagh, star of films like *A Month in the Country*, "that you could have knocked me down with a feather. A Prince of Wales feather!"

The London City Ballet didn't have to wait too long for Diana's go-ahead, either. First off, they wrote to her private secretary; then, after an initial acknowledgment, they wrote a couple of newsy letters to let her know how their work was progressing. Only then did they again ask to be considered for the Princess's ever-longer list of patronages. To their great delight, the answer this time was yes—and the Princess, it appears, was equally thrilled. Possibly she is still disappointed that she grew too tall to dance professionally, so she takes the opportunity to pop in informally—often unannounced—and watch the dancers go through their rehearsal paces. Such visits must surely be enough to put even Mikhail Baryshnikov off his arabesques.

Diana still has a long way to go before she rivals the Queen, however. At the last count, her mother-in-law was president or patron of a staggering 174 charitable organizations; the litany encompasses the well known, like the Girl Guides, and the obscure, such as the Soldiers' and Airmen's Scripture Readers Association. Diana, so far, has notched up twenty, but she's already overtaken Charles's sister Anne, the Princess Royal.

The Princess of Wales's list is a personal one, mirroring her own interests, particularly in children. It includes the Pre-School Playgroups Association, the Malcolm Sargent Cancer Fund for Children, Dr. Barnardo's (who provide homes for orphans or children whose parents can no longer care for them), the Royal Academy of Music, and her particular pet charity, Birthright. The royals are supposed to keep quiet about which groups most interest them, but she devotes endless time and energy to Birthright, which raises funds for gynecological research into miscarriage and childbirth problems. In fact, the Princess recently wrote the foreword to a Birthright book entitled *What Every Woman Needs to Know.* Diana understands only too well what it is like to yearn for a baby and has heartfelt sympathy for women who have not enjoyed her good fortune. She also has a soft spot for Dr. Barnardo's Children's Homes, explaining: "I've got very healthy, strong boys, and I realize how lucky I am. I don't know how I could cope if I had a child who was handicapped or mentally handicapped in some way. So I'm going out there to meet these children and trying desperately to understand how they cope."

The charities for which the royal sisters-in-law have agreed to work are keen to point out that the women take their duties seriously. There are lunches to attend, new buildings to lay foundation stones for, speeches to make, and letters of appeal to write. It isn't simply a matter of turning up to cut ceremonial ribbons, plant trees, or accept bouquets and smile prettily—or of accepting the best seats at charity film premieres. Their unpaid involvement goes much further than lending their royal names to be emblazoned across charity notepaper prefixed by the word "Patron." As Diana pointed out in a television news interview with Alastair Burnet (which also helped raise money, through book sales, this time for the Prince of Wales Charities Trust), "I don't want to dive into something without being able to follow it up. Nothing would upset me more than just being a name on top of a piece of paper and not showing any interest at all." To wit, Diana and Sarah read every report on the charities they front. The Princess even learned sign language to help her communicate with the deaf, as part of her work for the British Deaf Association, picking it up impressively quickly from videotapes.

The Duchess of York, three years into her marriage, already receives ten written requests each week for official help. So far, the Duchess has said yes to Action Research for the Crippled Child, the Chemical Dependency Society, the National Flower Arrangements Society, and the Tate Gallery Foundation, among others. But she was particularly delighted to spearhead Search '88, a year-long program of money-raising events staged by Britain's four main cancer research organizations.

In addition to full-time commitments to a select few charities, the Princess and the Duchess make occasional appearances to launch hospital appeals, even to open shopping centers or supermarkets—if, for example, they are creating new jobs and bringing prosperity to a depressed area. Ostensibly, the young royals work for free, but it is an open secret that they expect a donation to go to a favorite cause before they commit themselves.

Of course, sometimes charity work can be a delightful mix of business and pleasure for Sarah and Diana, and everyone benefits. Diana was able to get in a game of tennis at her club last October and raise £3,000 for Birthright just by lifting her racquet. She partnered the Marchioness of Douro in a charity tournament, and though the pair lost in the second round to a team that included Marilyn Oppenheimer, a former junior Wimbledon champion, the real victor at the end of the day was the charity.

At another sporting event in summer 1987, $500,000 (toward an ambitious target of £40 million) was collected for one of Sarah's charities, the Tate Gallery Foundation, which raises cash to buy new works of modern art for the Thames-side museum. The money came from the sale of tickets to an exclusive polo match and black-tie ball in Greenwich, Connecticut. The polo club enlisted Sarah's quickie visit—her first to America in the company of her husband—via a good word from Major Ferguson. As far as Sarah was concerned, the idea couldn't have been more appealing; her stepfather, Hector Barrantes, would be playing in the match, which meant the chance of a rare heart-to-heart with her mom. Her dad would be there, too, standing in for Prince Charles, who decided to stay home at Windsor. And not only would it be great publicity for the Greenwich Polo Club but also an unmissable opportunity for Sarah to raise megabucks for her charity. The British will rarely part with more than £100 a head for even the most lavish charity affair (perhaps because charity donations aren't tax deductible over there), but the price tag for anyone wanting to dine and disco alongside the Duchess was a cool $1,000, and a sellout at that.

Sarah's participation in one particular fund-raising event—alongside her husband and Princess Anne—did raise many eyebrows. That summer, Prince Edward—who had recently quit the tough British Marines—organized an "It's a Knockout" tournament based on a successful British TV show. The idea was to assemble four celebrity teams, led by royals, who would take part in rowdy televised events. Dressed in medieval costumes, the royals indulged in such inelegant games as lobbing plastic fruit at one another. The well-intentioned Prince's idea was to raise hundreds of thousands of pounds for charity—he succeeded—while enabling the world to "see the royals as normal people."

It was all rather down-to-earth and, in the eyes of most royal watchers, rather undignified. (Diana and Charles, aware that it wouldn't really do a lot for the monarchy's image if a future king and queen were seen being splattered with custard pies, wisely stayed away and watched it on television.) Sarah got carried away by the whole event and perhaps overdid the cheerleading, shouting deafeningly into the presenter's microphone that her team were "the best Blue Bandits there are!" Even her father, Major Ferguson, was prompted to declare, "Personally, I don't think that any of the royals should have participated. I don't think that kind of thing is terribly funny. But I don't want to get too critical of it," he added, "because it is something that Prince Edward organized. It raised a great deal for charity, and we all do things for charity that perhaps we shouldn't do. . . ." The Queen is thought to have taken a dim view of the end result, and it's doubtful that there will be a repeat performance.

Much more elegant was Sarah's trip to New York early last year—*The Phantom of the Opera*'s much-heralded Broadway premiere was too good to miss. Again, her mother was part of the bait—Mrs. Barrantes joined her daughter in New York for the gala—and it gave Sarah another chance to raise money, with high-society New Yorkers fighting tooth and manicured nail for tickets to the play and to an Edwardian-style gala dinner at the Waldorf-Astoria afterward. (Sarah may also have secured a generous donation from Donald Trump, who hosted a prepremiere cocktail party in her honor, delightedly declaring afterward, "She's very pretty, very bubbly, with lots of personality.") Sarah was also flying the British flag on Broadway, another royal coup for Andrew Lloyd Webber (who created the record-breaking musical for his wife Sarah Brightman); Webber has just signed up Prince Andrew's star-struck younger brother Edward (who coordinated the "It's a Knockout" debacle) as a glorified gofer—though his official title is production assistant. Unlike most of the New York audience, Sarah wasn't seeing the hit show for the first time. She told Michael Crawford afterward, "You made me cry. Yet again, for the fourth time, you made me cry."

With her husband away in the navy, Sarah sees no reason to twiddle her thumbs back home when she could be combining pleasure with good deeds, earning valuable dollars for charities close to her heart. She's been criticized for her increasingly frequent overseas jaunts—but few of her detractors have bothered to discover how much of this globe-trotting's in a good cause.

Of course, for the early part of her marriage, Sarah had to

schedule in her charity commitments alongside a real-life, paying career. Her resume reveals that she's had several office jobs, including working for an apartment rental company and a small commercial art gallery. Her first job, in fact, was with a Knightsbridge public relations company, and former boss Peter Cunard reminisces: "She used to spend a lot of time on the telephone arranging her social diary. I had to remind her there was work to be done as well and that we were paying the bills." But somewhere along the way, Sarah developed a more serious, careerist approach to her work, and she's made history by keeping her job after joining the royal ranks. With a new baby, she's announced that she will no longer be working full time, but she hopes to keep her manicured hand in as a freelance editor.

Nobody could believe it, to begin with; a working princess didn't fit the fairy tale somehow. The photographers who turned up on the doorstep of BCK Graphic Arts in Mayfair, to take snaps of Prince Andrew's girlfriend as she entered and left her place of work, imagined that she must spend her day at the typewriter, filing her nails, and biding her time while the Prince made up his mind to whisk her away from her humdrum office existence and into a life of luxury behind closed palace doors.

But the Duchess proved she was made of sterner stuff and continued to work for the Swiss-based publishing company headed by Richard Burton (*not* the late actor), who squashed any rumors that Sarah was just "dabbling" when he declared to journalist Christopher Wilson: "There's been a great deal of speculation as to whether she does any work. Let me tell you that as an acquisitions editor you don't just sit around behind a desk. I think she enjoys the job because it keeps her feet on the ground and keeps her in contact with reality. She'd be very unhappy if she was locked into a royal role with no outlet. If she wasn't allowed to work, she'd feel caged."

What did Fergie's job entail? She is fascinated by the art

world and has acquired quite a knowledge of the fine arts; it's a passion reflected in her charity patronages, too. Basically, until she gave up work last year, she edited and coordinated sumptuous coffee-table art books, acting as liaison with authors, photographers, designers, and proofreaders to produce glossy tomes like *The New Painting*, a heavyweight work on the Impressionists, which sold an amazing 155,000 copies around the globe. Another book was *The Palace of Westminster*, and Sarah had hoped to get her teeth into a pet project of her own, a hefty volume based on an incredible collection of over two thousand architectural plans and drawings amassed by King George III, one of her husband's ancestors.

Sarah and her boss, who lived in Geneva, spoke constantly on the phone and got together for "totally informal" monthly editorial meetings at Buckingham Palace. For security reasons—with her mother-in-law's blessing—she shifted base camp there after her engagement was announced. Sarah was also responsible for expanding the company's staff. As Burton explained in his interview with Christopher Wilson, "She lassoed one member of my staff as she was walking around the Dulwich Picture Gallery with Princess Margaret. She just said, 'Are you any good with a word processor?' When the girl said yes, Sarah said, 'You're hired,' and she was on her way to Geneva." (The Duchess just happens to be the gallery's patron, incidentally.)

Until her pregnancy, Fergie's commitment was anything *but* part time. "The real thing about it is that I can do it because I think the busier you are the more you get done," she declared. "For me, it is a tonic. It keeps me in touch with the world around me. It takes about twenty-five hours a day, but I just make sure there is time. The girls in the office insist I am a workaholic. It drives them mad, but I just do it and I want to do it." One of her authors revealed that Sarah was even in touch with him during her honeymoon at Balmoral to ensure that the book was progressing smoothly!

Only now that Sarah has a daughter has she given up work for BCK. But nevertheless, she is hard at work in her precious spare time on a book of her own, entitled *Budgie*, about a helicopter-flying bird. The proceeds of this are likely to go to charity. But this project—like the job at BCK—are, to Sarah, symbols of her own fragile independence. As she pointed out in a television interview with David Frost, "At the end of the day, when Andrew comes home, I have actually done something too. I'm not just sitting there wondering what to put on next day."

The punishing schedule occasionally takes its toll on Diana and Sarah. At the launch of a scanner appeal at a South London hospital, Sarah confided to one patient's wife, "Behind every good man there is a good woman—sorry, an exhausted woman!"

As princes' wives, neither Diana nor Sarah receives an *official* royal salary, but they probably deserve to. (The Queen is alleged to give Sarah a generous "dress allowance"; but Diana, like most executives' wives, must rely on handouts from hubby. She does, however, have a small income of her own from Spencer family trusts, a fact with which she can parry Prince Charles's occasional thrusts if he feels she's splashed out on too many new frocks.) Diana, without the benefit of her sister-in-law's secretarial training (or her handful of "O" levels), has had to learn to do reams of daily paperwork, dictate letters, and write speeches of her own. They both carry off their duties with the utmost professionalism and plenty of warmth.

Most of the time, at least when they're not throwing plastic bananas around or twanging a president's suspenders (as the Princess did to Portugal's President Suarez), the Princess and the Duchess are the best team of public relations executives that the royal family's ever had. Just when there was a danger that the British public would get bored with the stuffy royals who seemed so far removed from real life and begin to entertain anarchic thoughts that the monarchy had outstayed its welcome on the throne—as many European countries, like France and Greece, have done—along came Diana, then Sarah, giving the royal family's image an injection of life, vibrance, and style. Every megawatt smile flashed at a camera is beamed around the world. Every hand they shake earns the royal family another fan for life. But most important of all, every charity they commit themselves to gets an undreamed-of boost, which will enhance the lives of the people they help—or perhaps even save them.

8

Homes, Sweet Homes...

It's a bizarre notion that, in London, the royals live in apartments. But these are no mere shoeboxes; instead, they are triplex-style living quarters worthy of Park Avenue and palatial enough to turn Donald Trump emerald green with envy. These domiciles are allocated to the royals by the Queen, enabling her family to live in cozy sections of either Kensington or Buckingham Palace (the two royal homes, just over a mile apart). On a practical level, it saves on maintenance costs, and the Queen is always thrifty. But, more importantly, dividing up the warrenlike, rambling royal palaces enables the royals to turn their rooms into homes.

The higher up the royal tree you are, the more rooms you'll be given. These homes, of course, may be filled with antiques, swagged with silk, and sumptuously carpeted, but the more priceless treasures are out of harm's way, out of bounds to scampering royal children who might carelessly knock over a million-pound vase while chasing one another around the couch. Behind the closed doors of their apartments, the royals can relax, watch TV, and keep warm and cozy. (The cost of heating Buckingham Palace means that the larger rooms, except for ceremonial occasions, can be positively as cold as the Arctic in winter.)

The London base for Diana and Charles is Kensington Palace. Sarah and Andrew are closer to the Queen in Buckingham Palace, where Sarah maintained a small office so she could continue her freelance work for her Swiss-based publishing company, overseeing the production of glossy coffee-table books and hosting meetings with her authors.

Before her marriage, Sarah always loved popping around to see her friend Diana at Kensington Palace, the sprawling red-brick mansion in the midst of one of London's loveliest parks. This palace is home not just for the Waleses but also for their aunt Princess Margaret and several cousins—Prince and Princess Michael and the Duke and Duchess of Gloucester. Before she took on royal duties of her own and wed her prince, Sarah would regularly descend to visit Diana on Thursday afternoons, sitting on squashy couches in the drawing room that Di and Dudley Poplak, her accomplished decorator, worked on together. There the two women would drink endless cups of tea out of mugs. But there's less time for idle chatter now that Sarah, at last, has her own rather controversial home to plan and look forward to.

Sarah and Andrew have never felt at home in the houses they've so far rented, in spite of the dozens of beautiful historic houses within striking distance of central London on the real estate agents' books and despite the couple's unlimited means to restore anything less than perfect to its full glory. Therefore, instead of settling for an existing property, Sarah and Andrew have roped in the services of Law, Dunbar and Nasmith, an architectural firm, and chosen to build their own multimillion-pound mock-Tudor mansion not far from the Queen's castle just outside London at Windsor (where she likes to weekend). It's a downright weird choice—totally suburban-looking by royal standards and a design that would be far more at home in nouveau riche Beverly Hills than stuck in the middle of a beautiful, walled garden in Sunninghill Park. There's little to distinguish it from the architecturally mediocre minimansions that this "stockbroker belt" (so called because its closeness to the city has prompted many wealthy leaders of big business to make their homes there). Plenty of British TV stars live nearby and, from the look of the drawings, the York home would be far more appropriate to a TV game show host than a royal couple. It's *Dallas*-style, not palace-style. There is more than a touch of Southfork about the Duke and Duchess's first proper home.

Still, Fergie must be relieved that they will have their dream home at last and she can get out from under the Queen's feet. (The two may be firm friends, but it is hardly ideal to kick off married life with your mother-in-law breathing down your neck—especially when, technically, she must be curtsied to.) With Andrew assigned to the naval base in Portland, Dorset, for the next two years, Sarah wanted to be in striking distance of her new husband. She has resigned herself to frequent partings in what may, for years, be of necessity a long-distance love affair, since Andrew has signed up in the navy for the long haul. She grew tired of being driven from Buckingham Palace to Dorset and to neighboring Somerset, Wiltshire, to look over houses that failed to live up to the real estate agents' colorful descriptions. The interior was never as she'd imagined it, or the place would be too drafty.

Then the couple heard that Charles Weld had decided to move out of Chideock Manor, a five-bedroom yellow-stone historic home he'd been given by his father in 1971, located conveniently just fifteen miles from Andrew. This turned out to be their first home. It was a book-lined library with inviting salmon-pink easy chairs and a grand dining room for entertaining. The massive stone chimneypiece (rescued from Chideock Castle, which was destroyed by the Roundheads) just cried out for a crackling log fire. The asymmetrical house actually has a Catholic Church attached, a stone chapel dedicated to Our Lady, Queen of Martyrs (which means that parish churchgoers had access virtually to the Yorks' backyard—a security aspect that worried their bodyguards).

The garden itself was a bit of a letdown, just some topiary, handsome trees, and a sweeping gravel drive. Sarah just loves flowers—the Queen invited her to tag along to the preview of the world-famous Chelsea Flower Show soon after her engagement was announced—but getting down on her knees to attend to the herbaceous borders will have to wait. At just £200 a week, the place was a bargain the Yorks couldn't afford to pass up. And, a real bonus, it also had a swimming pool for sporty Sarah to splash around in on languid summer days. The thousand-acre estate should have kept Andrew happy too, with pheasant shooting and trout fishing. The local hunt meets there, and the Chideock estate runs almost down to the sea—perfect for bracing walks along the beach.

But Chideock Manor *wasn't* the answer to the Yorks' housing problem, as it turned out. The lack of security was a worry, and the cost of installing a full alarm system, complete with cameras and electronic beams, was high—quite apart from the potential damage and disruption to the decor. A more important reason, though, is that perhaps Sarah was lonely so far from their friends in London. With Andrew away, she'd be left to rattle around on her own, listening to the creaks and drafts that suddenly seem so loud when you're alone. (Although, of course, with her security man, her maid, and sometimes a lady-in-waiting, Sarah—like any princess—is never *really* alone.)

In the end, the Yorks never spent more than a few weekends at Chideock and never really moved in most of their possessions. The year had been packed with overseas visits—Canada, Mauritius—so they were away from home a great deal anyway. And it seemed just as easy for Andrew to drive at breakneck speed (of which the royals are so fond) to London if he had a weekend or an evening off rather than to isolate Sarah from her friends and new family. As a princess, her mantelpiece positively groans with invitations. In London, she could never be lonely. But at Chideock, she would simply be waiting for Andrew to come home, and no new marriage thrives on that.

But having packed up their few possessions from Chideock (and honoring the terms of their lease), where to? The Queen took pity on her second son and his new wife, of whom she'd grown so fond. As it happened, she could spare them a plot of land used mostly as a humble vegetable patch, at Sunning-hill Park, five miles from Windsor and near to Ascot race-course—where, poignantly, Sarah and Andrew first started to fall in love. There had been a house there once, a mansion given in 1947 to the Queen by her father, King George VI, but before she and her new husband Philip could move in, Sun-ninghill burned to the ground in a terrible fire. If Sarah couldn't find her ideal home among the real estate agents' effusive particulars, then let her build it. There was no need for the Yorks to mortgage themselves up to the hilt to build a home, either; the Queen had given Andrew and his bride a most generous capital sum as a wedding present. The figure whispered in royal circles is a cool £5 million.

Sarah is reported to have confided in her friends, "We never dreamed we would have such a gift. We had been looking for ages but nothing was right or safe. We just didn't know what we were going to do. Then the Queen surprised us by coming up with this super idea. It's fantastic." Having agreed on the style of home they both yearned for, Andrew left the rest to Sarah. Certain features were essentials: a helipad (to escape traffic jams, the royals have found helicopters the swiftest and most comfortable form of travel—and now that Sarah can pilot her own, it will be even handier) plus stables and a tack room, a large swimming pool, and tennis courts to keep the sporty, horse-mad Duchess amused while her husband's at sea.

The master suite comprises a large bedroom with a luxurious bathroom and separate dressing rooms to house Sarah's ever-expanding wardrobe and Andrew's numerous official uniforms. And there is, of course, to be a nursery suite. The house will offer guests every comfort: each bedroom with an en suite bathroom and many with their own sitting rooms. The mansion, out of sight behind electronic gates, will be protected by the latest in high-tech security. It will, in fact, be a veritable fortress and has been cruelly dubbed "Trust House Fort" for its hotel-like architecture. But to ensure the newlyweds plenty of privacy, security staff will sleep and take their meals in a separate building. At last, there will be room to unpack nearly a million pounds' worth of wedding presents, which created such havoc at Buckingham Palace that for a while, tables, chairs, rugs, sofas, and a thousand tinier gifts were stacked in the palace's private cinema, where nobody could trip over them.

With the announcement of their plans, however, the Yorks sparked off a major controversy. The remaining area of countryside bordering London's suburbs is a conservation area or greenbelt; local residents and government officials fight tooth and nail to protect it and other remaining areas of greenery around England's capital from development. Otherwise, the leafy lanes and beautiful woods would be razed to the ground in no time by unscrupulous developers just itching to erect fifty houses on every field. Like everyone who wants to build on the greenbelt, the Yorks' architects had to submit plans for permission.

To the royals' shock and horror, a planning subcommittee initially refused them the right to build, and Sarah must have begun, tearfully, to wonder whether she would ever again have a place to call home, where she could raise the family she was so keen to start. But realizing that the area would get a boost from the resident royals, that earlier refusal was over-turned at a later meeting. The controversy over the house's design, however, still rages. And one wonders what Prince Charles, whose particular bugbear is, as he sees it, the appalling state of modern architecture, has said to the couple behind closed palace doors. Since he's so fond of his younger brother and obviously has a soft spot for Sarah, he may well have bitten the royal tongue.

The two royal princesses may well, for quite different reasons, envy each other's homes. Sarah must still wait while the construction workers steam ahead to build her home, and then she must delay still further while the team of interior decorators she's enlisted set about their work with tape measures and endless yards of chintz. More eyebrows have been raised here, in fact, by her initial choice of the design team Parish Hadley. America's well-known Sister Parish boasts a celebrated list of happy clients, including Jacqueline Onassis, Ann Getty, Brooke Astor, Happy Rockefeller, and a generous sprinkling of the "ladies who lunch." The original selection of white-haired, ladylike Sister Parish (a nickname given her by her four brothers) put the noses of London's interior design elite—including royals David Hicks (the Queen's cousin) and Princess Michael—firmly out of joint, but it offers a clue to Sarah's tastes: chintzy, romantic, with flowers everywhere—the personification, in fact, of English style, executed with the emphasis on comfort and warmth so essential to Americans. Her trademarks are needlepoint cushions, crocheted throws, and homely touches that take the edge off the grandeur. (Since Sarah's not famous for her love of handcrafts, perhaps Diana—who's passionate about needlepoint—can be inveigled into stitching a few pillow covers.) It's a look that is pure "old money." Ironic, when money doesn't come much older than the royal family fortunes, that the royals have to employ the services of an outsider to re-create the look for them. But Sarah's plans to use Parish Hadley have now been quashed.

According to one rumor, the Queen declared that the budget for the job was too high. More likely, however, is that Sarah has realized that it would give the English interior design industry an enormous boost if she selected a homegrown decorator—and has opted for Nina Campbell, whose utterly English style shows distinct similarities with Parish Hadley's. Nina Campbell is unquestionably qualified and talented enough to be able to give the Duke and Duchess's new house the homely, intimate ambience they crave.

Still, Sarah can't finalize her plans and color schemes for a while yet. It may be a year still before she and Andrew get to sleep somewhere they can truly call home. For the moment, she and Andrew (and the new baby) are "camping" at Castlewood House, in Egham, on the edge of Windsor Great Park (near enough to the site of her new home for her to nip across for almost daily supervision), rented from King Hussein of Jordan and, as such, already amply fortified for the British royal couple. So while she waits patiently for her builders to finish—it's unlikely to be this year—Sarah is allowed to be a little jealous of Di's comfortable setup, as she sees her well-organized sister-in-law dividing her time between Kensington Palace and Highgrove House, in the county of England called Gloucestershire (which, with Princess Anne and Prince and Princess Michael near neighbors, may soon be known officially as Royal Gloucestershire).

But Di, for her part, may well feel a frisson of jealousy that Sarah got to *choose* her future home. Diana was presented with a fait accompli, and although she's been heavily involved with the decor, she had to accept her husband's choice of home.

The historic, £500 million Kensington Palace—referred to by the family as "KP"—is where Charles and Diana have their twenty-five-room London base. This suite was created by combining the palace's apartments eight and nine. On a site that has been in the royal family for five hundred years, the house is set in one of the capital's loveliest parks, Kensington

Gardens (which even features a charming statue of Peter Pan, the enchanting children's storybook character. Di often points it out to her boys, who are taken for walks in the gardens each afternoon). Until the Queen allocated them to her son and heir—back in pre-Di days, with a scheme to move out Charles totally away from Buckingham Palace—the rooms had been empty for years, run down almost to the point of dereliction with damp and rot. The Countess of Granville, mother-in-law to the Queen Mother's lovely sister Rose, had been the last occupant, but an incendiary device that fell on the palace in 1940 had so damaged her quarters that the Countess never returned to live there. Prince Charles wasn't exactly thrilled by the first tour of his future home, solemnly declaring, "It's just like a pigeon loft."

Charles must have felt very unsettled at this point in his life. His country seat, at Chevening in Kent, had proved to be less than ideal, since it was badly served by roads. Those leading to London snaked through narrow suburban thoroughfares often jammed with rush-hour traffic. Plus, he wasn't wild about the decor and, to cap it all, as he was quietly enjoying the newspapers on weekends, the rural peace Charles craved would be shattered by the bugle of the hunt, in pursuit of foxes nearby. The idea of being near to his sister, Anne, and to many friends who'd moved to the West Country, appealed enormously, so he began a search there, sometimes using the alias of Mr. Brown. The surprise of opening the door to the heir to the throne—when only "a regular guy" had been expected—may have led some ladies of the manor to wish they'd been a bit more diligent with the dusting.

Highgrove came onto the market and seemed the perfect solution—£800,000 worth of sandstone mansion set back from the road among 350 almost flat acres of farm and woods in Gloucestershire. It was the family home of Maurice Macmillan, a member of Parliament and publisher, and Charles liked it very much, paying the full asking price without haggling.

(This included carpets, drapes, and several large pieces of furniture that the departing owners no longer wanted.) But the Prince then found himself with two homes to work on. Architects and decorators became practically a feature of his daily life, and by now Charles had another distraction—his romance with Lady Diana Spencer, which was getting warmer all the time. Charles had a feeling that at last he'd found his bride, and he no doubt cherished visions of a happy home life at Highgrove. His lonely bachelor days would soon be ending.

Diana had for some time shared an immaculate three-bedroom apartment in Coleherne Court, in London's Earl's Court, with two girlfriends. It was a generous gift from her father, Lord Spencer. (Residents of Coleherne Court have the Princess to thank for boosting the value of their properties enormously. And while they were sorry to see the pretty, polite young woman leave, nobody missed the swarming hordes of reporters who'd lurked on the doorstep from the first intimation of the royal romance.)

Filled with little knickknacks and silver-framed snaps of blissful holiday scenes and portraits of her family, Di's apartment was comfortable rather than grand but nevertheless stylish. Now she would have to leave the happy little bachelor-girl setup and sell her home, leaving her girlfriends to go their separate ways. She wasn't exactly bowled over by the guided tour of her future country home, full of the Macmillans' unwanted objects. Her mother was even less thrilled; a woman of great taste, she promptly declared, "My daughter cannot live here," which must have enabled the still timid Diana to breathe a huge sigh of relief.

So a decorator was summoned to revamp Highgrove and Kensington in a way that would make them suitable for the royal couple. The royal family has two "in-house" interior designers, David Hicks (who is revered around the world) and Princess Michael of Kent. Instead, however, the task went to South African-born Dudley Poplak. Poplak proved a popular choice all around; he'd worked for the Queen herself on several rooms at Buckingham Palace and for Diana's mother and stepfather. The latter, as a wallpaper magnate, knows the interior design business inside out. Very importantly, royalty and the prestige of his twin commissions wouldn't faze him, and he could be relied upon to be discreet and refrain from leaking details of the work to the outside world. (Understandably, the public were desperate to find out what color the royal bedroom would be, and whether Charles and Di had the luxury of separate bathrooms.)

Recently, though, Poplak is rumored to have been replaced by Nicholas (or Nicky) Haslam, a decorator who's worked on homes for rock stars like Bryan Ferry and Mick Jagger as well as countless society figures around the world. The Princess, with her love of pop music, may well have found the combination of Haslam's more contemporary style and his link to the world of music irresistible. He favors the use of illusion-creating mirrors and soft furnishings upholstered in watered silk-taffeta; he also likes to hang pictures from the wall with decoratively tied bows. Now that she has become very much a woman of the world, Diana no longer needs to rely on her mother's tips, however sound.

Others' initial verdict on Poplak's transformation of the Waleses' two homes, though, was that they had turned out just slightly dull, with the mediocre decor of a comfortable upscale hotel: trellised wallpaper and patterned carpets commissioned especially for the palace, but no strikingly flamboyant touches. Diana has steered clear of rich, dark colors and stayed with the pastel favorites of her single days: peach, lemon, pale blue, and plenty of green. Both Charles and Diana were accustomed to grandeur—Diana having grown up amid Althorp House's legendary treasures—but they were determined their *home* should be just theirs. No doubt chocolatey fingerprints on the upholstery and scuffs on the wallpaper have lent the place a lived-in feeling by now.

The royal family has a huge collection of antiques, enough to fill several palaces, and the couple were able to select favorite pieces for their new home, adding to the bounty from their wedding list. (Unwanted gifts have been forever banished to a former chapel, where the palace's residents store unwanted junk.) Like many of the world's wealthiest people, Charles watches every penny, and it must have gladdened his heart to get useful items like a French polished dining-room table (which seats sixteen in comfort). Rich silk carpets, oriental lamps, and porcelain figurines were all generous gifts from friends and foreign heads of state. Diana likes dried flower arrangements for the fireplace and, like all the royal family, she will call in the services of "horticultural inventor" Kenneth Turner, one of the world's top florists (who loves to use unusual items like fruit and vegetables, or beautiful chunks of driftwood in his arrangements), to decorate her home with fresh blooms for special occasions. (Turner is so popular with American clients that he has a department at New York City's Bergdorf Goodman.)

At Kensington Palace, apartments eight and nine are grouped around the pretty quadrangle court on the palace's west side. A huge Georgian staircase dominates the house, which is, in fact, not a duplex but a triplex. Diana, craving more light in her new home, had its dark wood painted ivory. In the entrance hall is a visitors' book that guests are asked to sign; the first entry in this reads simply, "Earl Spencer (Daddy)." Just as soon as the high-gloss paint was dry, Diana summoned her beloved father to show her finished home off to him.

Rooms off this magnificent three-floor central stairwell include a sitting room for the Princess, her favorite room (aside from the nursery). Its unique, especially commissioned wallpaper features a delicate blue-and-white diagonal check with pale-pink Prince of Wales feathers, and the draped curtains echo the motif. Visitors are reminded not to light up by a "No

Smoking" sign—and the Princess means it; she hates the habit. A reminder of her happy days at West Heath sits on the windowsill: her "tuck box" (for supplies of cakes, biscuits, and other treats to snack on between school meals, a valued tradition among boarding-school students), humbly labeled "D. Spencer." Surrounded by her best-loved treasures, she loves to retreat here to watch her favorite soap operas—*Dallas, Dynasty,* and *East Enders* (set in the Cockney stronghold of London's East End)—or the BBC's *Top of the Pops* music rundown on a Thursday evening, since her sitting room has the apartment's only TV set. Since her trip to Australia, where she met some of its stars, she's become glued, too, to the hit Aussie soap *Neighbours.*

There's also a study for the Prince—a book-lined room that overlooks the Prince of Wales quadrangle—where Charles can find some peace and quiet amid the frenzied hustle and bustle of palace life. Charles loves to read; he's a great philosopher who meditates every day, and his eclectic taste is evident from the bookshelves. (Publishers will often send along advance copies of new books on their lists which they think the Prince and Princess might enjoy.) He has studied works on Eastern religions, and one of his closest friends is the explorer/author Sir Laurens van der Post, whom he chose as godfather for William. The pair have visited the Kalahari desert together on one of Charles's increasingly frequent retreats from the pressures of royal life, and Sir Laurens's books feature heavily in the Prince's collection. A sentimental soul, he likes to surround himself with family snapshots and mementos from his seafaring days.

As future king, Charles has assembled a coterie of advisers on industry, politics, and conservation; he is kept constantly abreast of world events. When Bob Geldof began Band-Aid, which raised millions for famine relief in Ethiopia, he received a summons to the palace so that Charles, who gave the project his wholehearted support, could hear about his plans. (It led to an amusing exchange between the scruffy, long-haired Irishman and Prince Charles's son William, who's known burst into the study unheralded to check what his dad's up t Geldof recalls it with amusement in his autobiography, en tled *Is That It?*: "William came in and wanted his father to g and play with him," writes Geldof. "He said he couldn't, ▌ had to talk to this man, indicating me."

"Why do you have to talk to that man?" said the young prince.

"Because we have work to do," said his father.

"He's all dirty," said the boy.

"Shut up, you horrible boy," I said. I was wearing my jeans and sneakers, as usual, and I had my normal five o'clock shadow.

"He's got scruffy hair and wet shoes," said the boy, indicating my beloved and comfortable, but admittedly scuffed, suede yellow sneakers. "Don't be rude, run along and play," said the now mortified father.

"Your hair's scruffy too," I retorted, to the boy who would be king.

"No, it's not, my mummy brushed it," answered my tormentor before leaving the room.

Charles's mortification at this exchange, however, was not ing compared to his wife's horror when she discovered ho cheeky her young son had been to the Band-Aid hero. Sl redoubled her efforts to keep the little ones out of Daddy way, to avoid a repeat performance when Charles has guest is going over a speech, or is planning his daily schedule wi his private secretary. But secretly she knows that it's importa to let William have his fun now; one day, the heavy respons bilities that Prince Charles shoulders will be his.

The main double drawing room is for welcoming guests o more formal occasions. It is lined, at Poplak's suggestion, wi mustard-colored, velvety flocked wallpaper with a rich yellow border and dominated at one end by a giant antique tapestry. There's a fabulous grand piano on which Diana loves to play for Charles, who's particularly proud of his wife's talent.

The Waleses' sense of humor can be guessed at from the downstairs bathrooms. They're hung with cartoons, usually featuring themselves, from British newspapers, that amuse the royal couple. A call is made to papers publishing any cartoon that raises a particular giggle over the royal breakfast table, and the artist in question is usually only too pleased to dispatch the original sketch to Kensington Palace, where it will join the Waleses' collection on the wall of the smallest room. The toilet stalls themselves, fitted with genuine antiques, are referred to wittily as "the throne rooms"! The Duchess of York calls the archaic toilets "amazing. They don't have cisterns and chains. You have to pull a chain up from the ground, water comes rushing down, and the whole thing opens up. They're great." (But there is little doubt that at Sunninghill, Sarah will be opting for something more contemporary.)

Upstairs is the great master bedroom, which truly befits a prince and princess. It is dominated by a huge four-poster bed, a staggering 7½ feet wide, which Charles had transported from his earlier apartment at Buckingham Palace; the couple's respective soft toys are cutely piled up on it. (Diana goes for furry frogs; Charles has a weatherbeaten bear who goes by the name of Teddy and has circled the globe with him many times.) Occasionally, the royal couple sleep apart—but that's no evidence of a rift between them. Either Charles or Di may have have to be up at the crack of dawn to dash halfway across the country for an official visit. For one to wake the other with a jangling alarm clock would be downright selfish, since the Prince and Princess need every wink of sleep they can steal. Sometimes, then—if he has a cold or an early call— Charles will sleep on the bed in his dressing room, allowing his wife her well-earned rest.

The master suite incorporates separate bathrooms and dressing rooms. Diana's wardrobes, in fact, occupy a significant chunk of the apartment, possibly to Charles's chagrin. He had planned to move out of Buckingham Palace totally and to bring his office to Kensington Palace too, but his romance with the Princess of Wales put an end to that idea. There wasn't room for her clothes *and* his office, so some days, Charles makes the short drive to another royal palace, St. James's, and gets on with his work there.

Lined with full-length mirrors so that she can admire her svelte figure in her new designer frocks from every angle, Diana's dressing room leads off the master bedroom. There's another, smaller room where her dressers can make emergency repairs to Diana's clothes, air them, press them, or steam the creases out. They can check for any tiny stains that will have to be dry-cleaned out. Since the Princess's clothes are made only of the richest, most sumptuous fabrics, her dry-cleaning bill must be extortionate. Like many rich women who can enjoy the luxury of silk, satin, wool, and the purest cotton every day, it's doubtful she even knows what polyester feels like. Drawers in the dressing room are filled with colored and patterned pantyhose that Diana teams and tones with her outfits to such effect. She has great legs and she knows it. If she can't wear her skirts quite as short as she'd no doubt like—royal duties mean plenty of bending down to receive bouquets and plant trees—then she's damned well going to flaunt a well-turned ankle instead.

The dressing room has run out of hanger space—after all, Diana probably has the world's most extensive wardrobe—and clothes from earlier seasons that can't be shortened or have simply been seen in public once too often are wrapped in cellophane and tissue and stored in a special room downstairs, meticulously recorded by her wardrobe assistants. Diana's friends and sisters have often gratefully received royal cast-offs, and the dressers are more than glad to have a fraction more breathing space.

Charles has his own "brushing room," where his personal valet oversees the royal wardrobe, including a huge collection of service uniforms. (The Prince is colonel-in-chief of dozens of regiments.) One man, Stephen Barry, a former footman who'd acted as Prince Charles's manservant for twelve years, sometimes accompanying his employer on official duties but working mostly behind the scenes, was responsible for the immaculate royal wardrobe, keeping Charles's petty cash, doing his shopping, and bringing breakfast to the Prince each morning. He learned the hard way that discretion is the better part of valeting.

He grew swellheaded, and his name began cropping up too often in the newspapers' gossip columns for either of the Wales's liking, including one famous occasion when Barry, a homosexual, was involved in a fight in a gay club. The Prince had relied on Barry over the years, but a parting of the ways was now inevitable; Diana had never taken to him, and when the royal couple returned from their honeymoon, Barry resigned. He later capitalized on his insight into the royals' life and made a fortune with a book about the royal family (which was banned from publication in England due to its sensitive revelations). Nevertheless, Charles evidently forgave this indiscretion, because he was deeply upset when his former aide contracted AIDS and died. He wrote with deep sympathy to Barry's sister and has shown an interest ever since in the work of the Terence Higgins Trust, the British AIDS charity, which counsels victims of the fatal disease.

The present valet is spared the task of polishing the royal hand-stitched Lobb shoes, a duty usually delegated to an orderly from the Gurkhas, but he does prepare the following day's clothes from top to toe—although Diana frequently intervenes to pick out a snazzier tie or shirt, since she's revamped Charles's ultraconservative style and insisted on a more modern haircut. All Charles has to do in the morning is stumble out of bed, shave, and dress, and he's ready to hit the road. Or, as is more usual, the skies, since a helicopter whisks him away most mornings.

The sight of a bright-red whirlybird hovering over Kensington Gardens is well known to passersby. Only from a helicopter can Charles and Di's private roof garden be seen. Diana likes to soak up an even suntan there (rumors are that, blissfully out of sight, she even goes topless at times), and Charles shows off his skills at barbecuing for friends and close family. They're both mad about gardening; Charles has his organically grown vegetables and Diana likes flowers. She'll pick her own blooms for little vases to give the palace a really homey touch. There's another walled garden downstairs with its own fountain, but it lacks privacy, since it is overlooked by other apartments belonging to royal relatives. Just snatching a few quiet moments outdoors might prompt an unexpected—and not always welcome—visit from Princess Michael, Princess Margaret, or the Gloucesters. But the little princes love to play there, screaming with laughter as they whoosh down the slide or fly through the air on swings, enthusiastically pushed by their parents.

The Waleses don't often have overnight guests at their London home, but, when rumors were flying about her prospective engagement to Prince Andrew, the Duchess of York retreated to one of the two guest bedrooms to escape the journalists who were besieging the Lavender Hill apartment she shared with a girlfriend.

Right at the top of the palace, beneath the eaves, in a suite with sloping attic ceilings and dormer windows (securely barred so that the boys can't climb or tumble out), is William and Harry's territory, the nursery. The walls are beige with an apple design, but the overall effect is highly colorful, with bright toys everywhere, including beautifully painted rocking-horses, one of which was a gift from Nancy Reagan. The nursery has a playroom where the boys may sit at a small table to draw pictures and complete tasks assigned for homework. The lads share another room to sleep in. Both Mum and Nanny encourage them to pick up their own toys and not rely on the servants. The boys, of course, also have their own bathroom.

Nanny—former nurse Ruth Wallace—sleeps just along the corridor in case one of the boys has to get up in the night. Forty-one years old, Miss Wallace is a disciplinarian with a deep love of children. She had dedicated her life to caring for sick children, most recently at St. Bartholomew's Hospital in London, in the emergency and radiotherapy units. She proved that she was well equipped to handle royal youngsters when she served a part-time stint for the family of ex-King Constantine of Greece, a friend and relative of the Waleses. The boys call their nanny "Roof," and she has proven herself well able to control two rowdy boys. Miss Wallace was engaged initially to replace Barbara Barnes, who resigned in January 1987 after having cared for William from his birth. Miss Barnes was totally devoted to the boys, but perhaps a little too soft, since young men need a firm hand.

For Sarah and Diana, who live in unimaginable luxury surrounded by millions of pounds worth of antiques, there is no single spot that allows them to feel more at home than the nursery rooms. There, they do not have to worry about sitting on spindly chairs or accidentally knocking over a Sevres vase worth hundreds of thousands. They may have elegant drawing rooms, silk-draped bedrooms, and hundreds of yards of closets to make them feel regal. But for the Princess and the Duchess, the nursery—with its unbreakable plastic toys, miniature furniture, and most of all, the children they treasure—is truly that corner of home where the heart is.

9

Clock the Rocks!

Baubles, bangles, and bijoux are a priceless perk of a princess's job. Between them, Diana and Fergie have a collection of sensational sparklers that must make Elizabeth Taylor emerald green with envy.

Diamond Di and the Dazzling Duchess have made flaunting fabulous jewels both fun and fashionable. Their tiaras, necklaces, bracelets, and engagement rings are worth a king's ransom, and at the drop of a hat (or perhaps it should be the drop of a crown—Diana and Sarah do *so* love to don their diamonds). Before Di and Fergie came along, jewels had a middle-aged image. (As master faker Kenneth Jay Lane, purveyor of diamanté to the rich and famous—even the Queen has some—declares, "Jewels used to be something you acquired when older. If you saw a younger woman in real rocks, it implied that she'd done something frightfully naughty to get them. . . .")

Of course, what the Princess and the Duchess had done to earn the jewels and treasures that have been showered on them was utterly respectable, a fantasy: to win the heart of a prince. Indeed, Diana and Sarah began to build up their magnificent collections on the memorable day each accepted her prince's proposal. Before their weddings, they wore the gold status symbols popular with their Sloane set: fine gold chains (Diana's had a gold "D," Sarah's a gold "S" and another pendant, "GB," referring to her father's nickname for her. "To me she'll always be GB," he says. "Nobody else in the world calls her that, and nobody in the world will ever find out what it stands for." However, there are some who suggest it may be "Ginger Bush"!). Sarah also loved to wear a pretty blue enameled butterfly brooch and her chunky gold Rolex watch.

Sarah's particularly sentimental about her three-colored-gold linked Russian "wedding" ring, since it was her first gift from Prince Andrew; he slipped into the Regent Street shop of Crown Jewellers Garrard to pick it out himself late on the eve of the first Christmas of their romance, and Sarah still loves to wear it, even though it has been eclipsed by later jewels. (Diana has one, too, which she's worn since school-days; in fact, the Russian wedding ring, slipped onto the little finger, is a trademark of the Diana-Sarah set, and no self-respecting young lady's outfit is complete without one.)

The engagement rings—swiftly copied on a less expensive scale by jewelers around the globe—are themselves breathtaking. Diana's choice was a dazzling sapphire, just a shade darker than her clear blue eyes, surrounded by diamonds and set in gold. It was commissioned by Prince Charles from Garrard's, who have long held a royal warrant. Its value was estimated, at the time of their betrothal, at £28,500; indeed, anyone with that amount of cash to splash out on the ring of a lifetime could have later ordered its twin through Garrard's catalogue.

Sarah's choice for an engagement ring was an unusual one and proves she's not a superstitious soul. She decided upon rubies and diamonds—a combination of red and white viewed by some as unlucky—and Andrew designed the ring himself, discovering a new passion and artistic talent. The main stone is an oval Burmese ruby picked out from the huge royal collection and surrounded by ten football-shaped perfect blue-white diamonds. All these are set in an eighteen-carat yellow-and white-gold band. Down the ages (particularly during Empire days), the royals have been showered with unset gems and treasures by visiting dignitaries or as welcoming gifts on overseas tours. Thus they built up unquestionably the most valuable collection anywhere in the world. (The royal vaults known as the "Jewel Pool" are laden with all kinds of baubles—studded with diamonds, sapphires, emeralds, and rubies—from bygone days.)

The rich red ruby was probably chosen to symbolize Sarah's flame-colored tresses, which Andrew loves. "We came to the mutual conclusion that red was probably the best color for Sarah, and that is how we came to the choice of a ruby," Andrew explained. Having slightly refined Andrew's blueprint, a team at Garrard's worked for four nights and days to finish the ring in time. Thus an overjoyed Sarah was able to flaunt it at the official announcement of their engagement, in front of the assembled press in the gardens of Buckingham Palace, on Wednesday, March 19, 1986. Sarah positively beamed and pronounced her ring "stunning." She wore another special item of jewelry in her ears that day: delicate diamond-and-enamel heart-shaped earrings. These seemed so appropriate for the happy event that the Princess of Wales was only too glad to lend them to Sarah, a gesture of fondness from the Princess showing that she was desperately excited at the prospect of having a new sister-in-law and justly proud of having done her bit to help Cupid along.

For Sarah, even more than Diana, the jewels she's received are an unexpected joy. Diana's family have several priceless treasures of their own, including the Spencer tiara, made world famous when the Princess wore it to keep her veil in place at her wedding. Another Spencer treasure is the three-strand pearl choker with a teardrop-shaped pearl pendant, which Diana wore with her going-away outfit. (Her sister Sarah had worn it earlier in the day to the royal wedding and had to wave the ancestral jewel good-bye as Diana and Charles rode away from their reception in a horse-drawn carriage.) Exuberant Fergie still can't disguise her awe and wonderment. At her prewedding party, Sarah toured the room, letting all and sundry take a close look at diamond-studded gifts from her future family, demanding that one and all "clock the rocks"!

Tiaras are an essential item in the royal wardrobe for state occasions like the official opening of Parliament, big banquets, and some charity events, and Diana and Sarah wear theirs with particular pizzazz and flair (although they've yet to acquire the Queen's knack; Princess Margaret, who jokingly mispronounces it "terrara," insists that the Queen is the only family member who has mastered the art of keeping a tiara in place while descending the stairs). It can be a heavy burden, seeming by the end of the evening to weigh a ton and occasionally sparking off splitting royal headaches; ladies-in-waiting make sure to carry a couple of aspirin in their evening purses. The tiara Diana wears now is the Queen's magnificent gift to her daughter-in-law. Once the property of Queen Mary, the Queen's own grandmother, it is a crescent of pretty diamond-studded lovers' knots from which hang nineteen perfect pearl teardrops.

Sarah's tiara, with its curlicues, flowers, and leaves in its elaborate design, is something of a mystery. When it was revealed to the world on her wedding day, nobody was quite sure of its history, though it may be a family heirloom. Now the treasure has been matched by flower-shaped earrings and a grand diamond necklace (again, commissioned from the

Crown Jewellers Garrard), which Fergie shows off to perfection on her generously proportioned décolletage.

For her wedding, Sarah wore a lovely modern piece believed to be another royal gift: a single strand of pearls with a diamond-shaped, diamond-studded pendant and matching earrings, which first glittered in public at the 1986 Ascot Races. It may even have been a generous love token from Andrew to commemorate the beginning of their love—which was kindled over a plate of profiteroles during lunch in the royal box during Ascot week one year before. Like all royal males, he loves to shower gifts of jewels on the woman he loves; another anniversary gift is a pin of diamonds and gold with a teardrop-shaped ruby and the outline of a bee, the insect featured in the Duchess's coat of arms. Every Christmas, the sight of small, square boxes tied with satin bows under the tree must cause the princesses' hearts to skip a beat at the prospect of glittering joys in store!

As queen consort, however, it is Diana who'll have the thrill of dripping with the present Queen's jewelry when Charles accedes to the throne; these include huge stones—some of them expertly cut from the world's most famous and largest diamonds—which will make Fergie's current collection of sparklers look like mere fragments by comparison. But, while Diana will shine in crown jewels such as the Diamond Diadem, Queen Victoria's Emerald Bracelet, and the famous Victorian bow brooches, Fergie may not have cause to envy this thousand-carat booty. It is generally believed that Andrew's grandmother, the Queen Mother, is reserving some of her finest bijoux for Sarah. She was herself the last Duchess of York, until Edward VIII's abdication catapulted her husband, the new King George VI, to the throne.

Upon Diana's marriage to the Prince of Wales, one of Earl Spencer's wedding gifts to his daughter was supposedly an empty jewel box. He knew that it was one wedding gift which she'd most definitely use daily! It was rapidly filled with glorious wedding gifts: a diamond-faced watch from the United Arab Emirates, a pearl watch, and, from the Emir of Qatar, earrings and (for Charles) cufflinks. By now, Diana's once empty box must be bursting at the seams with precious items. One of Diana's favorite gifts from Charles is a fabulous oversized crucifix set with diamonds and amethysts; it was displayed to breathtaking effect dangling at her trim waist from a string of sensational pearls, over a dark velvet dress with a ruffled collar. Diana wore this outfit as a guest of Crown Jewellers Garrard—who had executed this latest royal commission. It had fellow guests swooning with envy (and costume jewelers reaching for their sketchbooks).

Diana also prizes a highly sentimental gift from the Prince: her gold-link charm bracelet, which was one of his early love tokens. At birthdays or special occasions, such as the birth of their sons, he adds a tiny new treasure to it. It is too private a gift to be worn in public, and only friends and family have the pleasure of admiring each new charm. It is far less grand than Charles's official wedding present to Diana—an important antique diamond-and-emerald bracelet—but infinitely more romantic. As a legacy from her past life, she still prefers pearls over diamonds; in the early days of her courtship, she was never photographed without a string of pearls peeking out from beneath her demure cotton blouses, a style still favored by Sloane Rangers today.

In his self-appointed role as the royal design connoisseur—a bent evidenced by his passionate interest in architecture—Charles has also begun to patronize younger jewelers. He commissioned a baroque pearl necklace from Leo de Vroomen, and a pretty little pin featuring five feathers—his Prince of Wales trademark—from Wendy Ramshaw, one of Britain's best-known designers, who likes to work with humble stones like garnets, milky moonstones, and amethysts. Other lovers' keepsakes include the gold medallion in which is engraved the name "William" in Charles's own handwriting, to commemorate the birth of their first baby.

Most famous of all Diana's jewels, though, must be her cabochon emerald-and-diamond Art Deco–style necklace, another wedding present from the Queen that had once belonged to her granny, Queen Mary, though the Queen never wore it. On one overseas tour, Diana was planning to show off the choker at a dinner. The burning noonday sun ruled *that* scheme out, however, since Diana acquired a touch of sunburn on the back of her neck. A heavy necklace would have been too painful, but not to wear jewels was out of the question; her public expect a glittering show! With her innate sense of style, Diana and her lady-in-waiting fashioned the emerald choker into a stunning Hiawatha-style headband. It took everyone's breath away.

She likes to play around with jewels. Since the early days of her courtship, when her image was refined with the expert assistance of senior editors at *Vogue,* Diana's confidence in her own unique style has swelled. She is fond of wearing chokers made of velvet ribbon with a necklace clasped above the fabric. The velvet shows off the jewels to perfection. This is a display trick of the world's top jewelers, who will show customers bijoux nestling in velvet-lined trays or on plush cushions.

On official visits overseas, particularly on recent trips to the Arab nations, Diana has also been showered with millions of dollars worth of diamonds by sheikhs. (At Diana's wedding, the Saudis bestowed on her a huge sapphire pendant and a diamond necklace, part of a suite that is made up of matching earrings, bracelet, and watch.) Many of the Arab gifts are refreshingly modern designs. (The royals seem to err on the side of tradition and caution when they commission new baubles to add to the royal jewels, aware that classic designs can be worn for years to come.) The Arabian royals, however, are more interested in creating a stir with their generosity; their motto seems to be the flashier, the better.

A stunner clasped around the Princess's swanlike neck recently (believed to be just one of those generous gifts) is a cascade of diamonds and rubies with matching earrings. Another gift, from King Fahd, alleged to be worth a million pounds, is a diamond-encrusted gold choker and earrings in an avant-garde design. (Any gifts from heads of state that aren't to the princesses' tastes are carefully catalogued and stored away, to be retrieved and worn if the dignitary in question pays a visit to the United Kingdom or they are to meet the donor once more abroad. No doubt the royals would much rather have the unwanted items reset, but they must be careful not to offend.)

But not every day brings a banquet or a royal film premiere. Diamonds are hardly appropriate for a visit to a coal mine or a submarine, for attending to paperwork, or for thrashing around on the tennis court. When the sun goes down, the glittering diamonds come out. But for day wear, both Diana and Sarah sport a nice line in less flamboyant gold jewelry. For horseback riding, Sarah has a pair of small, perfectly plain pearl studs, probably a gift from her family dating back to the days when she was footloose and fancy-free. Diana's favorite low-key earrings comprise twists of tricolored gold (like a Russian wedding ring) which she wears through her pierced ears. A peek inside any Sloane Ranger's jewelry box would turn up an identical pair; they're virtually standard issue! Sarah—who's turned bows into her own personal trademark, wearing them in her hair, on her shoes, and as bustles on her clothes—has a small pair of bow-shaped gold earrings, too. Cleverly, the bows have detachable drop-jewels—pearls and hematite heart shapes—for a variety of looks. Sarah also boasts a matching necklace incorporating three more bows on a simple gold neckband, all modern designs from the workshop of jeweler Kiki McDonough.

Several items from Ms. McDonough have, in fact, made their way into the York trinket box. Another favorite is a three-strand black-and-white necklace set with a chunky, heart-shaped hematite jewel.

But the Duchess and the Princess share another passion, and nobody fakes it with more style than Fergie and Di. A glance at them will often reveal that diamanté can be a girl's best friend—and it's comparatively easy on the royal pocket. Both of them love to visit Butler & Wilson, the Aladdin's Cave costume jewelers in the Fulham Road, and pick out guilt-free gilt and bargain baubles from the semicircular showcases. Diana has a stunning necklace of starfish-shaped paste and fake onyx beads which match petal earrings. On one memorable night out with Charles (for a rock concert), Diana stole the show by wearing her husband's tuxedo with a diamanté serpent snaking down the lapels. Sarah has some reptilian dazzlers, too: a couple of linked diamanté lizards that she wears as a pin.

The riotous redhead has single-handedly revived the fashion for wearing hair jewels, which glitter and gleam against her flowing auburn tresses. She will often ask that pins and brooches be converted into hair clips, like the witty ones shaped like biplanes that she wore for her first moment of flying achievement the day she earned her wings. Another beautiful hair ornament is crescent-moon-shaped diamanté studded with paste.

The chic royal starlets borrow jewels, too. The Queen will reach into her velvet-lined jewelry boxes for a brooch or a bracelet to set off a new outfit, but the princesses are lent major trinkets for special occasions by leading London jewelers (many of whom have their high-security showrooms in Bond Street). Sarah, as the royal newcomer with the fewest treasures of her own, often takes advantage of short-term loans. There is no finer or more refined showcase for jewels in the land than the persons of the Princess and the Duchess, who, together, have the cashiers singing a hallelujah chorus—and Britain's jewelers are eternally grateful. They've even rejuvenated the image of the "full set"—an overpowering combination of tiara, bracelet, necklace, and earrings piled on at once—which used to smack of crusty old dowagers.

It's no coincidence that, since the glittering new royal brides appeared on the sparkling scene, diamond sales have soared. Even the famous jeweler Tiffany's feels there are now enough well-heeled jewel connoisseurs in London to warrant the opening of a Bond Street branch, so that Britons need no longer make a pilgrimage to Fifth Avenue for one of those famous, dear little turquoise shopping bags. Or could it be that they were just hoping their traffic-stopping window displays might attract the beady eye of a gem-loving royal princess or two?

10

Shopping
the Tiara Triangle

Imagine that you had virtually limitless funds; a social calendar packed with dances, lunches, and overseas travel; plus literally billions of people to impress. Fantasize a while about shopping for that life-style, about making private visits to the world's top department stores (all the while being followed by security a few paces behind, someone to carry your shopping bags and make sure that you and they reach home safely). Dream about having a personal assistant to unpack and hang your chosen treasures up—unless, that is, you fancied diving into the endless rustling layers of tissue paper yourself for a change. Just visualize the bliss of inviting the world's top dressmakers to visit *you* at home—to help you choose and ultimately to fit clothes in sumptuous fabrics tailored to your every curve.

Real life is like that for the Princess and the Duchess. And boy, do they love to shop! Actually, their ability to spend, spend, spend is perhaps the most enviable aspect of the young royals' life-style. When Andrew first took a shine to Fergie (who already had favorite shops, like Ralph Lauren, and—along with all of her set—a dressmaker to run up taffeta ball gowns and silk dresses for Ascot), Diana was able to take her potential sister-in-law under the royal wing and steer her toward other London treasure troves on her regular shopping beat.

The women delighted in joint expeditions, with a pit stop for lunch, often fitting in a rendezvous with friends. Fergie, perhaps, lacks the true dedication of a champion shopper like Di, who loves buying presents and hardly ever returns to Kensington Palace without some little treat for her boisterous boys. But they have enjoyed countless hours together browsing through London's finest stores, forging a firm friendship, and handing out honest appraisals of each other's choices.

So let's take a closer look at this pair of power shoppers and discover more about the area of London aptly known to top people as "The Tiara Triangle" (probably because so many millions of pounds have disappeared there!) Here, on any day of the week, innocent customers might find themselves standing right next to one of the world's most famous women as she pops in for a gift or to pick an outfit off the rack.

Very often, Di and Fergie will simply drop into a shop, unheralded, perhaps on their way to another appointment or simply on a day off. I myself was inspecting the strands of fake pearls in Butler & Wilson, the Fulham Road's celebrated costume jewelry shop, when out of the corner of my eye I noticed two striking young women poring over a glass counter, looking at the diamanté and paste gems so fashionable that season. While the Princess and the Duchess selected a few pins to take home, their personal bodyguard (inconspicuous-looking but nevertheless with lightning reactions and crack training to protect the royal shopaholics from danger) stood casually by, near the door, keeping an eye open more for the traffic police than for would-be assassins. As usual, the unmarked royal car—as is the princesses' custom—was illegally parked outside. Apart from gently nudging one another to point out the blonde and the redhead excitedly selecting baubles, nobody batted an eyelid. A royal shopping spree is not an uncommon sight in The Tiara Triangle, since, having leafed through the glossy magazines each month, Diana and Sarah like to see the latest styles for themselves, to compare prices, and to try on clothes—just like in the old days.

Except for state occasions and official appointments, the Princess and the Duchess are able to travel without a huge entourage—just their personal officers, assigned by Scotland Yard's Royal Protection Squad. No limousines with tinted windows for protection, no motorcycle escort outriders, just dull-colored sedans. The girls are able to drive themselves if the mood takes them. (Diana, who now travels in a family car big enough for William and Harry, used to have a gleaming silver compact, complete with a silver mascot of Kermit the Frog.)

Carefree alone or as a formidable duo, the two women are able to visit favorite haunts from their single days; only now, there's no longer any need to watch the pennies. But contrary to popular belief, the royals don't get "free gifts" of clothes or jewels. A little discreet "product placement" can *make* a designer's career—which is precisely why the royals pay for everything, although occasionally (if they are buying direct from a designer's showroom) at wholesale prices. Very often, Di and Fergie's purchases are delivered to their homes with a bill, which is promptly paid—so there's no need for credit cards or wallets full of crisp new notes.

Probably as a holdover from their single days, they both still like to carry some cash or at least a checkbook—from the royal bank, Coutt's and Co.—unlike the Queen or Prince Charles, who never carry money. (Diana still smiles at the memory of a Benetton shop assistant who, failing to recognize her royal customer, insisted she produce some identification.) If all else fails, the royal detectives can always step forward with a Duchy of Cornwall American Express card.

As for favorite shops, Butler & Wilson (109 Fulham Road) is a must to visit, as is Cobra & Bellamy, another purveyor of fakes to the rich and famous. The chic lacquer-red interior of Monty Don's shop in Beauchamp Place, which sells cute diamanté Scottie dogs and zodiac brooches (Di's is a crab, for Cancer, Sarah's a Libra, symbolized by the scales), has tempted the princesses on several occasions. Despite an impressive collection of real-life rocks, under lock and key back home, and the famous tiaras and crowns behind glass in the Tower of London (which Diana will one day wear when she becomes queen), it seems that the other man's glass is always greener.

For Diana and Sarah, underwear is a passion and one of the greatest luxuries their new life affords them. Well-off women may dress expensively, but (apart from the occasional underwear fanatic) only the truly rich can afford equally costly undies, which will be seen only in the privacy of their boudoirs. Almost undoubtedly, before their marriages, the princesses' frillies would have been from Marks and Spencer (where the vast majority of British women buy their underwear). Now, they have both learned to love the luscious feel of pure silk nightwear and frothy lace undies—and of having their underclothes made to measure to flatter and fit. A visible panty line is a royal no-no.

Thanks to telephoto lenses wielded by photographers from the royal Rat Pack, pictures of Sarah and Diana in their bikinis have been splashed across the front pages of newspapers in every country of the world. But there are a few, discreet souls—besides their husbands—who have seen the pair in even less as they take the princesses' measurements for hand-embroidered, lace-trimmed luxury lingerie. Diana and Sarah are spared the indignity of slipping into the shops' changing rooms. Their choice will be delivered to Kensington or Buckingham Palace for the women to try on in private, where their husbands are able to give a royal thumbs-up or thumbs-down to the fabulous fripperies.

Beneath the Ralph Lauren, Jasper Conran, or Saint Laurent clothes lurk beautiful, handmade undergarments from, perhaps, Janet Reger (2 Beauchamp Place), Night Owls (78 Fulham Road), and Rigby & Peller (next door to Harrods), all of whom have boxed up exquisite unmentionables for the Princess and the Duchess. They've both fallen for—and given a boost to—the vogue for miniskirts. But when she was first undertaking royal duties, Diana—whose skirts *used* to reach almost to her ankles—confessed publicly that "if I didn't wear longer dresses, you might see my Janet Reger underwear."

Diana has also nipped in and snapped up silk satin underpinnings from the Emanuel ready-to-wear boutique at 10 Beauchamp Place, London SW3; it is owned by Elizabeth and David Emanuel, who became famous overnight for creating the Princess of Wales's love-it-or-hate-it ivory-silk wedding dress. This narrow street, pronounced "Beecham," is an important landmark on the royals' map. The princesses also frequent Courtney of Sloane Street, where the sugar-almond colored bras, panties, and slips are irresistible. Amazingly, according to one royal insider, Di's preferred color for her lace-trimmed negligees is *gray*. Amazing, since that's the color most underwear, over time and frequent washes, gradually becomes.

These sensual slivers of silk, however, aren't enough to keep out the biting wind when you're planting a tree or going for country walks in the Scottish glens. Diana once let slip in public that her secret for keeping warm was "my thermals" from Courtney or thermal underwear specialists Damart (whose ultrawarm long johns and vests are equally suitable for the palace—or the poles!). Since the company has a mail-order division, Damart's showroom in Regent Street is one address that needn't feature on the royal agenda.

Foreigners flock to Fortnum & Mason (Piccadilly, W1—where, in the food hall, even the humblest customer is waited on by a tail-coated shop assistant), Harrods, and Harvey Nichols (both in Knightsbridge) for the best in fashion or food, but they have occasionally been delighted by an unexpected sighting of the princes' wives. (A friend of mine, shopping for pantyhose in Harvey Nichols, was struck dumb to see a stunning blonde, obviously pressed for time, zoom up to the same counter, grab half a dozen pairs each of black and ivory-colored hose, pay, and disappear before anyone had time to recognize the Princess of Wales.) In a single, efficient burst in 1987, Sarah is reported to have done all her Christmas shopping at Harvey Nichols.

Both Diana and Sarah have donned head scarves (to hide those highly recognizable coiffures) and wheeled a trolley around Sainsbury's in the Cromwell Road, the Sloane set's favorite supermarket—presumably on cook's night off. Mingling with regular shoppers—rather than being trailed by overawed assistants at a time when the stores are closed to the public—is one way in which Diana and Sarah can reassure themselves that there *is* real life outside the palace walls. It reminds them comfortingly of the life-style they left behind, even if rubbing shoulders with the hoi polloi does give their security men palpitations.

There aren't too many household necessities when you're a princess. Wedding gifts from foreign dignitaries and fans all over the world have taken care of glassware, china, and crisp white linen for the table and the bedroom; the Waleses had their wedding list at Peter Jones department store, in the heart of the Sloane zone, facing Sloane Square; the Yorks placed theirs at the General Trading Company, which took care of just about everything from dinner services to dishcloths. But although the women's own linen closets and kitchen cabinets may now be fully stocked, Peter Jones and the General Trading Company, just around the corner at 144 Sloane Street, are still on the princesses' beat. The pair are surrounded by young friends setting up home for the first time, and it is a rare Sloane whose wedding list can't be found at PJ's (as it's known) or GTC. And, of course, the priceless Waterford crystal and the finest bone china selected by the royal brides aren't exactly practical for everyday use. They like to keep an eye open for something more modern and less expensive for day-to-day tableware, no doubt to the eternal relief of both palaces' washer-uppers.

In the early days of her courtship, Diana wore distinctive, brightly striped knitwear with a cute llama motif from Inca, a Pimlico shop specializing in Peruvian imports. (A measure of the Princess's fashion influence is that within days of Di's first public sortie in the sweater, Inca was swamped with 400 orders.) But these days, both she and Sarah prefer to riffle through the shelves of rainbow colors at Benetton for their pullovers. Casual clothes by chic Italian and French designers like Mondi, Kenzo, Erreuno, and Gianni Versace suit them both (although the Princess of Wales, in her appointed role as savior of the British fashion industry, is careful to be seen on duty almost exclusively in British designers), and they may well decide to buy off the rack. (Fittings can be tedious; all that standing around while nervous fingers try not to treat the royal personages like pincushions.)

One essential to royal life is comfortable shoes. Both girls are tall, and Diana, in particular, tries not to tower over her husband in public—he's barely an inch taller than her five feet ten. So she saves her high heels for solo sorties. French Charles Jourdan shoes (conveniently available from the Knightsbridge shop, equidistant between Harvey Nichols and Harrods) have long been the royals' choice of footwear and are bought, Jackie Onassis–style. When the footsore royal feet find a perfect fit, the order will include a pair in every color. Or, a true luxury, several pairs will be purchased in one color, so that, if endless walkabouts wear the shoes out, there will still be a standby pair in the closet. Bruno Magli shoes are snapped up in the same way. For less formal dates, Pied a Terre and Bertie (both chains of shoe stores) make sure that the princesses are always stylishly shod, and both girls frequent Manolo Blahnik, in Old Church Street, where Diana found her over-the-knee black suede "Puss-in-Boots" boots.

Charles Jourdan also supplies the clutch bags Sarah and Diana favor (although, for casual summer days, Diana still loves the Provençal-print quilted purses she bought at Souleido, in the Fulham Road, before her wedding). Unlike most women, the merry wives of Windsor don't need to cram their bags full. A lady-in-waiting trails behind on official outings with spare tights, a needle and thread, the day's itinerary, and emergency funds. Paperback books for boring journeys and bulging diaries can be left in the chauffeur-driven car. All Diana and Sarah need to slip into their purses is a lipstick and compact. If not from Charles Jourdan, these may have been picked out at Fendi or, once again, at Harvey Nichols, which carries a huge range.

For their delicate English skins, Body Shop cosmetics (which promise not to be tested on animals and are made only of natural ingredients) are ideal, and with branches all over London, it's a rare car journey from either palace that doesn't pass a Body Shop that the princesses can dash into. They experiment, though, with all the major names—Fergie loves Chanel, and Di, with her sensitive skin, Clinique. The Princess has also been glimpsed trying out the latest lotions and potions in Fenwick's, the Bond Street department store.

Sarah loves to drift around the Ralph Lauren shop, a little further up Bond Street, looking at tailored navy blazers with heraldic buttons, virginal white-lawn blouses, or flowing silk skirts; she's often worn Lauren, on and off duty, and it's perfect for hanging out at the polo field. It's no wonder that the Princess and the Duchess feel so at home in Ralph Lauren's shop, decorated with burnished leather Chesterfield sofas, shiny antique riding boots, and tartan throws. For Sarah and Diana, this perfect imitation of upper-crust English life (stylishly polished up on the other side of the Atlantic) ensures that Ralph's shops are just like home!

When they've finished indulging themselves, Diana and Sarah both have plenty of presents to buy for youngsters. Not surprisingly, anyone who can snare a royal to serve as godparent has made a real catch. Such a request is difficult to resist, especially for these two women, who adore little ones. Therefore, Di and Fergie have an ever-longer list of friends' children to buy birthday and Christmas presents for. Sarah is now in a position to indulge the children of her father's second marriage, Andrew, Alice, and little Eliza, the last of whom is barely out of diapers but already horse-mad.

When the enchanting store Dragons opened, selling personalized, pastel-painted furniture often stenciled with fairytale favorites like Winnie the Pooh and Peter Rabbit, it was a godsend to the godparent set—and the Highgrove nursery of the Windsor lads is itself dressed in Dragons' rocking horses, chests of drawers, and toy boxes painted with their royal Christian names. (No doubt now that Andrew and Sarah have started a family, Dragons will be called upon to personalize their newborn's nursery, too.) By coincidence (or the shrewd design of Dragons' owner Rosie Fisher), you'll find lots of items bearing the names William and Harry in the store.

Of course, Diana has a special shopping interest—her sons. Though she's worked wonders on her husband Prince Charles's wardrobe, updating a sartorial style that had barely changed in decades with brighter ties and colored shirts, he's still deeply conservative and difficult to buy gifts for. In fact, ever since she announced in public that he likes silk boxer shorts, she's been able to strike that item from her shopping list. (With a swish and a flourish, well-wishers have presented both Diana and Charles with these roomy undergarments in public—to the royals' considerable embarrassment!)

At first sight, William and Harry's formal English clothes can look ridiculously impractical: pale-blue, velvet-collared overcoats worn over shorts, so that the wind whips around their little blue knees! (In time-honored tradition, William and Harry won't graduate into long trousers for several years yet.) Their sensible shoes—often black patent with a single strap—are a design that most kids would simply refuse to wear, perhaps with a stamp of their little feet. But the Queen takes particular pride in seeing her grandsons dressed smartly, because it reminds her of the time when her own sons were small. (However, William and Harry's rough-and-tumble antics in pale wool coats or Chelsea Design Company white sailor suits must lead to awesome dry-cleaning bills. A few weeks after her sons, in their little blue coats, had a ball climbing over a shiny fire engine for a New Year's royal photo session, Diana remarked, "Sketchley's really had fun with that," referring to a dry-cleaning chain.)

A short stroll from Kensington Palace is a favorite shopping nook of the Princess's, tucked away off the main drag in Victoria Road, W8. On a day off, Diana often arranges to meet a girlfriend, books a table at Launceston Place (a popular English-style eatery run by two handsome young restaurateurs, Nick Smallwood and Simon Slater, whom she greets warmly). Pretty as a picture amid the pink tablecloths, she enjoys a leisurely but light lunch (and a good portion of girlish gossip) before stepping across the road to the Frog Hollow toy shop.

If William and Harry have been good, a Paddington bear or a Lego set might be in the cards. If they've been up to their usual tricks, they may have to make do with a gruesome plastic tarantula. Diana buys some of the boys' clothes from the expensive, old-fashioned children's store owned by Anthea Moore Ede, next door at number 16. She may pick out sailor suits, classic coats, or little white shirts and ties. And no doubt she becomes a touch broody over the beautifully smocked dresses that look so heavenly on little girls.

At some point in the future, Diana will be given permission by her mother-in-law to grant royal "warrants," the ultimate seal of shopping approval. At present, only the Queen, the Queen Mother, and Princes Philip and Charles share the right to bestow the royal seal of approval on their favorite emporiums. Royal warrants are the ultimate stamp of monarchic approval, issued to merchants who've regularly been patronized for at least three years by the royal granting this honor. The companies in question apply, to the lord chamberlain's office, for royal warrants in writing. An approval gives them the privilege of using the phrase "By appointment to . . ." and displaying the royal coat of arms for a decade (although the right to a warrant is reviewed every five years and must not be unduly capitalized on by, say, advertising what the royals have selected from the store's stock. If this strict royal rule is greedily broken, the warrant can be revoked). Shops all over London are poised for Diana's go-ahead.

Who, in Sarah and Diana's privileged position, wouldn't grasp the chance to "shop till they dropped"? To some people, it is a flagrant waste of money. But Di and Fergie's shopping sprees have transformed the Tiara Triangle into boomtown, inspiring millions of consumers to follow in their stylish footsteps. Every pound the princesses part with brings in hundreds more in tourist dollars, deutsche marks, or drachmas. Top London public relations dynamo Lynne Franks declares, "Diana—and now Sarah—have done incredible things for British fashion and its exports."

In truth, there's little danger of getting carried away. After all, wouldn't *you* keep your spending in check if every bill you handed over carried your mother-in-law's solemn, watchful portrait?

11

Food, Glorious Food

$\mathcal{E}$ ating out in the Sloane zone is like a game of royal roulette; visit the same restaurants often enough and, eventually, you'll encounter the Princess or the Duchess lunching or dining with their set. Unlike the Queen—who never eats out except when she's arranged a royal celebration, perhaps a pre-wedding dinner or a sumptuous supper to mark a wedding anniversary or a landmark birthday at a five-star hotel like the Ritz—Diana and Fergie love the combination of fine food and people watching.

Diana and Sarah both belong to the exclusive clique of "ladies who lunch." They may only toy with the odd salad leaf and sip mineral water, but then, to these ladies, eating and drinking take a back seat to gossiping. There are secrets to share and romances to discuss (who's seeing whom—and what on *earth* does she see in him?). The Duchess and the Princess like to keep up with their old friends' news, views, and love lives. So—well away from the palace, their chatter drowned out by everyone else's small talk—where better than their favorite London eateries?

Maître d's usually get plenty of warning about when to give the crystal an extra polish or put a pretty bouquet on the table for the princesses. Very occasionally, royals will drop in unannounced, but since most restaurants "hold back" a couple of tables for unexpected diners, they're rarely turned away. More normally, a phone call from "Buck House" or "KP" a couple of days in advance will reserve two discreet tables for lunch or dinner. (The extra table is for the ever-vigilant detectives, known to revel in this delicious perk of their job.) Not *too* out-of-the-way, however: where's the fun if you can't see who's lunching whom?

Beauchamp Place proves to be not only a favorite shopping haunt but the place to eat out as well. Ménage à Trois has been a firm favorite with Diana for years; since she befriended Lady Tryon—an Australian whom Prince Charles playfully nicknamed "Kanga"—the pair have often lunched in this whitewashed cellar restaurant hung with modern lithographs. It offers nothing but appetizer-sized portions, perfect for a figure-watching princess. As it's slap next door to Lady Tryon's dress shop (Diana and Sarah have publicly given her brightly colored frocks the royal seal of approval), Ménage à Trois makes a convenient pit stop. Every now and then, rumors surface about the nature of Dale Tryon's relationship with Diana's husband—before his marriage to Diana, this mother of four, married to Charles's friend Lord Tryon, was probably his closest woman friend—but it's always been purely platonic. Diana knows full well that to lunch with Kanga will instantly quash any press speculation.

Just down the street is San Lorenzo, one of London's best-known restaurants, where Diana and Sarah are assured of the warmest welcome. Mara and Lorenzo Berni are the jeans-clad owners, who for twenty years have served pasta and the unique, mouthwatering crepe San Lorenzo (an irresistible pancake filled with whipped cream, laced with Tia Maria liqueur, and sprinkled with crushed amaretto biscuits) to the famous. For Joan Collins, Elizabeth Taylor, Robert Redford, Dustin Hoffman, and a galaxy of international celebrities, a trip to London would not be complete without a languid lunch or lingering dinner at San Lorenzo, with its potted palms, rattan furniture, white ceramic-tiled floor, and giant mural of nuns marooned on a desert island! Mara greets regulars with an Italian-style peck on the cheek and, with the Latin love of little ones, never fails to ask a mother about her children's progress. And to star-struck Diana—tucking into her mozzarella, tomato, and avocado salad and sipping on San Pellegrino—it must be as thrilling as it would be to anyone to find Meryl Streep or Clint Eastwood seated at the next table.

Italian food has become incredibly popular with the figure-conscious "lunch bunch," since nutritionists have declared that pasta needn't be fattening provided you stear clear of creamy sauces. Only thirty calories an ounce, in fact, with plain tomato pomodoro sauce (and easy on the parmigiana). The Princess of Wales has indulged her love of Latin food as a guest at Cecconi's (a riotously expensive restaurant just off Bond Street, where lunch for two can easily top $180) and at Ziani's, in Chelsea's Radnor Walk.

But both the Duchess and the Princess like to hang out at La Nassa, on the fashionable Kings Road, a canteen-style restaurant filled with Sloanes and snobbish "Hooray Henries" who love rubbing shoulders with royalty and celebrities. Its walls are lined with autographed pictures of Frank Sinatra, Michael Caine, Michael York, and other well-known visitors. Diana's often been seen lunching at Luigi's in the Covent Garden area of London with ballet dancer Wayne Sleep, discussing their mutual passion for the dance. There are six small paneled drawing rooms that give the place an intimate atmosphere, and it's handy for the Royal Opera House, where the diminutive Sleep once persuaded Diana to dance onstage—to the enormous surprise of the audience (and her frowning husband)—as the star turn in a charity gala.

Wayne Sleep has also invited Diana to accompany him to the members-only Groucho Club, which is always packed with media folk from television, radio, and the press. It must have taken guts for the Princess to stroll nonchalantly into this lion's den, no doubt causing several journalists to topple off their bar stools and wonder whether they'd had one kir royale too many. It didn't take long for word of this particular sighting to reverberate around Fleet Street. Di prefers to eat upstairs in one of London's prettiest dining rooms, a stuccoed white room with a navy-blue carpet flooded with daylight from a huge, glass conservatory roof. (The club's management, unlike its membership, is notoriously discreet; Bob Geldof had his stag night there, while Madonna and Michael Jackson have held parties in the club's private dining rooms—and not a detail of those revelries leaked out.)

One of Fergie's favorites is Green's Champagne Bar in Mayfair. Bubbly is known to be her favorite (though only occasional) tipple, and the place positively echoes with the sound of vintage corks popping. It's a wood-paneled restaurant near the auction houses of Sotheby's and Christie's, and it therefore attracts the well heeled and wealthy craving a break from the bidding. Its patrons also include many local art dealers and fashion-conscious businessmen buying suits, ties, and striped shirts in Jermyn Street, the most gentlemanly of shopping zones. If there's an "R" in the month, oysters feature heavily on the menu. (The royal family, however, steer clear of the aphrodisiacal molluscs, since a single dodgy oyster can wreak havoc with a royal digestive system—and a royal, action-packed itinerary—for several uncomfortable days.) The Duchess's favorite is dressed crab, another house speciality.

Almost as soon as it opened, Diana fell in love with the light and airy Launceston Place restaurant, which is a short hop from Kensington Palace in a residential street of white-fronted

Regency houses. It's reported to be her favorite spot, hung with watercolors and vast ancestral oil paintings in gilt frames—a place where she can lunch on dishes like spinach roulade and fresh Scotch salmon while seated at a pink, damask-covered table in the main dining room and still be in time to fetch William and Harry from their nearby schools with a tiny gift (perhaps a bag of marbles to roll along the royal corridors) picked out from the Frog Hollow toy shop opposite.

Gourmets flock to Launceston Place for the nouvelle Anglais food; gossip lovers go there to take a peek at the rich, famous, and frequently royal diners; and there are plenty of upwardly mobile younger guests of Diana's own age, who have faithfully followed owners Nick Smallwood and Simon Slater from the Zanzibar (which, before the Groucho Club, was the preferred hangout of London's media and advertising crowds) and L'Escargot, a West End restaurant beloved of authors and literary agents. Now Smallwood and Slater have also opened a California-style high-ceilinged restaurant a mile or so away in Kensington Church Street. Its location—conveniently close to KP—will probably ensure continuing royal patronage. Fergie's already been sighted there.

If it's lunch with Daddy, though, both the Princess and the Duchess adore the discreet dining room at Claridge's—Sarah lunched there with her papa the day after her engagement was announced—where aristocrats often take teenage children to initiate them into the "grown-up," sophisticated world of restaurants. It is a small and pricey top-notch sanctuary where delicate melba toast is offered in place of rolls, and excellent English cuisine, such as grilled meats or giant lobster salads, dominate the menu. Meals are served on exquisite bone china with crystal goblets for the wine and heavy silver flatware. (I saw the Duchess's sister Jane lunching there with friends, too, just before the wedding.) Walking through the marble Art Deco foyer of Claridge's hotel (the *only* hotel many rich

Americans will even consider during a London stay), guests are greeted by the sight and melodious sound of a string quartet, and ushered by a tail-coated maître d' to their table—complete with heavily starched tablecloth. A lunchtime spot check any day of the week will reveal a good smattering of lords, ladies, and other nobles.

Another popular choice for a date, especially with the older set, is the Grill Room of the famous Savoy Hotel in the Strand, presided over by Italian maître d' Signor Maresca, who will escort father and royal daughter to a plush red banquette seat at the edge of the room, guiding them through a traditional English menu that always offers a sizzling roast, kept warm on a trolley under a giant silver dome. Depending on the day of the week, the dish of the day might be liver and bacon or sausage and mash, a pleasant change from banquet fare!

The day before Sarah's wedding, savoring her last moments of freedom, she lunched at Mimmo d'Ischia, in Pimlico's Elizabeth Street, with Lady Leonora Lichfield, sister of the Duke of Westminster, whose massive property interests—he actually owns a large chunk of central London real estate—make him the richest man in Britain. Leonora was then married to the Queen's cousin, photographer Patrick Lichfield, who took Di's wedding pictures (though Sarah herself gave that privilege to top fashion snapper Albert Watson). Sarah and Andrew had dined in Mimmo's, as it's known, during their courtship. (Andrew also held a dinner there for his navy squadron of twenty-five, tucking into spareribs and chocolate mousse.) Obviously, wedding nerves had done nothing to rattle Fergie's hearty appetite—she thoroughly enjoyed her mozzarella salad and grilled sea bass—though she said a firm no to the sweets trolley. She paid by check—the last she ever signed with her maiden name of plain Sarah Ferguson—and Mimmo himself never cashed it, keeping it as a cherished souvenir.

Chinese food? It isn't a big favorite with the figure-conscious princesses, but if a craving for sweet 'n' sour or chop suey sweeps over them, there's Poons, just off London's bustling Leicester Square in the heart of Chinatown, where Diana's been sighted deftly wielding a pair of chopsticks.

Popular with all the young royals (just a very short drive from Kensington Palace) is Julie's Restaurant in Portland Road, Holland Park, which has been going strong since the sixties. The decor hasn't altered much since then—gothic furniture and Victorian antiques give one a certain sense of eating in a church. Julie's Restaurant (there's a less expensive wine bar next door) is a subterranean warren of small dining rooms where the royals can eat in peace and privacy—making it perfect for stag-night celebrations before royal nuptials! Prince Charles had his bachelor event there, and so did his brother-in-law, Princess Anne's husband Captain Mark Phillips, several days before the wedding itself, leaving plenty of time for the hangover to clear.

On the subject of pre-wedding parties, one of the most famous of all is the Duchess of York's hen night, an occasion that still brings Fleet Street's journalists out in a cold sweat at the memory. At the suggestion of Sarah's friend, the outrageous Australian comedienne Pamela Stephenson, she, Sarah, and Diana borrowed wigs and police uniforms and spent a night on the town in their fancy dress! They wound up the evening inside Annabel's in Berkeley Square, one of the world's ritziest and most exclusive nightclubs, a mecca for the rich, famous, and aristocratic. There, the trio propped up the bar, to the bewilderment of fellow guests who couldn't figure out what several uniformed policewomen were doing in the club.

Ironically, a posse of top Fleet Street journalists was also enjoying a night on the town at Annabel's. It could have spelled disaster for the princesses' prank. However, the group of newsmen—who had been drinking all evening—were too well oiled to see through the disguises. Amazed by the vision of the lasses in blue, they even went up to Diana and Sarah and chatted with them. One "news hound," noticing that the spectacles Diana wore had no glass in them, playfully poked a finger through the frames. *Still* they didn't catch on, and by now Diana and Sarah were stifling tumultuous giggles. But for the off-duty journalists—one of whom, incredibly, even had an auto-focus camera in his pocket to record the men's antics on their evening out—another freshly chilled bottle of Möet beckoned, and they returned to their table to enjoy it. It wasn't until news of the royal joke leaked out a couple of days later that some of Britain's top journalists realized they had missed the scoop and the photo opportunity of the century.

Annabel's is out of bounds to the paparazzi, so royals and stars alike know that they can boogie on the dance floor away from prying lenses. Supremely discreet, it is lined with booths and has a string of circular tables in the center for dinner. The menu includes scrambled eggs and corned beef for late-night feasting and what many concur is quite the richest, most sinful chocolate ice cream in the world. Champagne is a standard tipple. For any royal itching to get down and get funky—Di loves to dance till dawn—there's really no choice. Annabel's ought to be awarded a plaque, "By Royal Appointment." Although, for one group of journalists on that never-to-be-forgotten night, it was a royal *disappointment*.

12

Glittering Globetrotters

The job description promises "plenty of foreign travel," and today's princess had better have plenty of extra pages glued in the back of her passport. Diana has already circled the globe several times—and Sarah is hot on her Charles Jourdan heels. The royal family has traditionally spent much of the year paying overseas visits, building goodwill around the world while promoting Britain and its exports. The Queen is head of the Commonwealth—a group of countries including Australia, New Zealand, Canada, and some of the more obscure corners of Africa—who all want to get a peek at the Sovereign, her offspring, and their glamorous wives. Britain is part of the European Economic Community, too, which means plenty of short hops to major European capitals, perhaps staying with some of the remaining crowned heads—a case of "You show me your palace, I'll show you mine."

And they really do travel in style. Forget the "two-piece baggage restriction." Royal luggage may weigh in at several tons. It's a case of "If in doubt, throw it in," even though these royal sojourns may be planned down to the last detail up to a year in advance. Fitness fanatic Diana, for instance, likes to be ready for any eventuality; carefully catalogued, wrapped, and stored in her baggage will be a tennis racquet, bikini, and jodhpurs. Several tons of baggage are loaded onto the aircraft of the Queen's flight: waterproof trunks and suitcases color-coded for easy recognition. Diana has her aluminum custom-made luggage; the Queen's is yellow; Prince Philip's is mauve. Even the staff are allocated red or yellow—depending on their rank in the royal household—or basic white.

When the Queen travels, a retinue of as many as a dozen tag along (and for Di and Charles, it's almost as many): body-guards, dressers, ladies-in-waiting, valets, private secretaries. Only her precious corgis get left at home; British laws require that even royal mutts who've spent time overseas be caged in quarantine for six months on their return. Two doctors go along, with a complete medical kit including blood plasma and sterilized equipment. This is particularly crucial, for instance, should the worst happen in Africa, where AIDS is reaching epidemic proportions and is transmitted, in many cases, through unsterilized hypodermic needles. The doctors take turns staying close to the royals at all times.

The Queen's list of "must haves" in her baggage makes her sound distinctly picky. Into the trunks go her favorite blend of China tea—with a monogrammed teapot to serve it—straw-berry jelly, and fruitcake. Well, you never know when you're going to get a decent meal abroad! The doting grandmother travels with her collection of sterling-silver-framed family snaps (so does Diana), and the monarch's baggage also con-tains a white, kid leather toilet seat! Better still, on many overseas journeys, the Queen has her own royal yacht, the *Britannia*, sail out ahead giving her the unimaginable luxury of a real "home away from home," which she occasionally lends to her children. But still, no royal traveler is quite so endearingly eccentric in her requirements as the Queen Mother, who insists, wherever she goes in the world, that a kilted bagpiper travel along, to play beneath her window every morning and wake her up. An alarm clock, it seems, just won't do.

When Charles was small and travel took so much longer, he would be left at home for long, lonely chunks of the year while his parents went off visiting abroad. When Diana gave birth to Prince William, she hated being parted from her little prince so much that she insisted on a change of plans to include him on an upcoming visit to Australia. In fact, the Princess put her foot down and issued the ultimatum: either he comes along or I stay home. The Australians were delighted when they got three royals for the price of one, including a particularly cute boy taking his shaky first steps.

A couple of years later, they paid a return visit with another new prince—and among the ninety suitcases and trunks were fifty-five pounds of disposable diapers! But nowadays, though she misses her sons terribly (and looks forward all day to the ritual 7 o'clock [Greenwich Mean Time] phone calls), Diana must secretly be delighted that her sons are now independent enough to be left back at home; since this makes room for at least an extra couple of gowns in the baggage. Whenever there's a royal tour, that means dozens of new outfits. After being accused of flagrant extravagance, Diana in 1985 toured Italy with barely a new designer gown in her wardrobe; they'd all been seen in public before. The Italians—consummate style watchers—were extremely offended. From then on, for Diana and Sarah, the prelude to any overseas visit is a round of dressmakers' appointments.

Traveling by private jet around the globe helps combat jet lag. As another royal confided in me, "It makes all the difference. You don't have to sit in transit lounges while the plane refuels; you can just remain in comfort in your seat and have a cup of coffee. And there aren't any stewardesses poking you to wake you up for the next meal! When you get to the other end, you just waltz past all those people queueing at immigration. I feel hugely lucky to be able to travel this way even occasionally. It really does take away all the hassle."

But unfortunately, the aircraft from the Queen's fleet can't always be spared. When the Yorks visited Los Angeles last year, Andrew and Sarah traveled by a scheduled British Airways flight. Restlessly pacing the plane rather like the expectant father that he was and finding the thirteen-hour flight unbearably long, Andrew—who has mellowed so much since his wedding that friends comment happily, "It's as if he's had a personality transplant"—rolled up his sleeves and pitched in with the washing up in the 747's cramped first-class galley. "He was wonderful," enthused a smitten stewardess afterward. "He said he was grateful for something to do because he was bored." Indeed, the only time he sat still was for the movie, entitled appropriately, *Baby Boom*.

Di and Fergie don't always take travel and the crossing of time zones so easily in their stride. Arriving in Washington on one occasion, Diana confessed: "I didn't get any sleep at all on the plane. I don't know if I can keep my eyes open," and in Australia, she confessed that the legacy of jet lag from her twenty-three-hour flight had left her unable to remember a thing about the events she'd witnessed a few days earlier to celebrate Australia's bicentennial, when the royal couple had been whisked by launch to view the historic tall ships sailing into Sydney Harbor and had joined in a rousing chorus of "Waltzing Matilda."

Though she'd rather curl up on a plane with a Barbara Cartland novel, instead Diana's far more likely to spend the journey under a warm tartan blanket leafing through her "homework," absorbing the biographical details of dignitaries she'll have to sit next to at dinner or learning facts like population figures (although she's also been known to heed the advice of John Travolta, who danced with her at a White House gala and whose anti-jet lag theory is to exercise as soon as you get off the plane and sleep as long as you can on board). In fact, royal tours have been described by some attendants as 1 percent glamour and 99 percent misery, yet the princesses must keep a smile permanently on their lips lest they offend or disappoint the host nations. To the outsider, however, waltzing around the dance floor with Travolta (as Diana did in Washington) or arriving to sip Pimm's at a polo match (as Sarah recently did in Los Angeles) seems like the epitome of the good life.

For the pretty princesses, it is a taste of true superstardom, second only, perhaps, to standing on the balcony at Buckingham Palace and waving at hundreds of thousands of royal fans. But the red-carpet treatment they've come to expect back home doesn't hold a candle to the luxury laid on abroad, complete with rapturous flag waving and screams reminiscent of Beatlemania in its frenzied heyday. In America, particularly, they're treated like the film stars who seem to line up to meet them, and they upstage every one. In this classless society, there is never any problem rounding up glittering personalities for a party; indeed, Sarah and Diana find these celebs infinitely more fun than the stuffy aristocrats they're more likely to meet in Europe or back home in England. It's a TV addict's dream come true; both Diana and Sarah have rubbed shoulders with most of their screen heroes at soirees that can make the "Night of a Thousand Stars" look like a room full of nobodies.

At the 1985 White House gala in Charles and Diana's honor, dance-crazy Di—whose husband is described as "all feet and no rhythm" on the parquet—had the time of her life. First off, she was whisked onto the empty floor to open the dancing by *Saturday Night Fever* star John Travolta (who'd been primed by Nancy Reagan—as if he needed to be—to invite her to get down and get funky). Afterward, cherishing memories of the moment he slipped his arm around the slender waist of the future Queen of England, he declared, "She got wind that it was a special moment, and she really seemed to take off. She has great rhythm. We did a kind of modern fox trot and she followed me very well. She seemed freed up for the first time in months," he added. Nearing the last few bars of their second dance, he whispered, "Maybe someday we'll get to do this in a less watched situation." "That would be great," whispered the future Queen, in her usual flirtatious style. Following in Travolta's quick steps was a somewhat humbled Tom Selleck, who claimed that "I spent most of the time apologizing." Lining up for *their* turns were Neil Diamond and Clint Eastwood, who were treated to royal charm that had been turned up to full power for the star-studded occasion. "She made *my* day," pronounced Dirty Harry himself, who'd joked with the coquettish Princess that she was too old for him. "But I'm only twenty-four!" laughed Diana.

For Sarah and Andrew's Los Angeles debut, half of Hollywood clamored for an invitation to the charity dinner to promote the British Arts Festival UK/LA '88—where the Yorks got to talk to, among others, Joan Collins, Dudley Moore, Julie Andrews, and master of ceremonies Roger Moore. (Later in the week, at a charity film lunch, Travolta got to charm his second princess, too. She confided to him that after the birth of her baby she planned to tackle flying fighter jets. He'd been especially invited—along with Jack Nicholson—as one of the Duchess's Hollywood pinups, and Fergie was able to relate that Diana still cherishes memories of that White House dance.)

Even princesses get star-struck; back home, they like to thrill friends with inside gossip on what the stars are *really* like—not grandly gloating, but simply as eager as any normal young woman to share star-studded gossip with their green-with-envy girlfriends.

But for every twirl around the dance floor, Diana and Sarah must endure a dozen guided tours around power stations, army barracks, hospitals, and factories, always remaining charming and trying to ask intelligent questions despite sometimes being bored rigid. As Harold Brooks-Baker, editor of *Burke's Peerage,* a directory of who's who among the top people, explains: "I know the dinners and lunches with celebrities sound wonderful. But to the royals they are just a day's work. I have seen Charles and Diana at dinners where they have only been able to sit down for about thirty minutes in an entire evening. And they are plagued the whole time by people who don't know how to approach royalty, especially when they are abroad on tours." And there is little time to put the royal feet up. As Diana explained after her first official visit to Australia in 1983, "The first week was a shock. It was like a baptism by fire, but having got into the feeling of it, it got better. By the time I left Australia, I felt I'd actually been able to achieve something. But people tend to think that if you're going to Australia or New Zealand it's a holiday, but actually, it's our busiest time, much busier than over here."

They must contend with living their lives even more under the microscope than usual. Every step of the way, they are surrounded by the royal Rat Pack, there to photograph every gesture and capture every bon mot for posterity, or at least, for the following morning's edition. "Crocodile Dun-Di!" screamed the front page when Diana visited a croc farm in Australia's Northern Territory; a couple of days later, it was "Bondi Di!" and "Di-Centennial!" By now, they're used to hogging the headlines (and both princesses claim that they "never read" what's written about them—though it must be hard to avoid if a princess wants to keep abreast of world news). Arriving in Germany muffled against the freezing cold in a giant yellow-and-black coat with flat black-suede boots, Diana switched on a 1,000-volt smile and said to the press, "Open fire."

There can be truly unfortunate moments, too—lived out in the public eye. Host nations are informed in minute detail of the royals' preferences—the sorts of food each prefers, how many pillows they prefer on their beds, and so on. But there are some unavoidable faux pas, like the time Sarah was confronted with a twelve-foot python just before a lunch for the World Wildlife Federation, in Canada, and the world discovered she has a phobia about snakes. She reached for a handkerchief proffered by her concerned father, Major Ferguson, but, wiping the tears from her eyes, could not conceal her distress. The British Embassy was forced to admit later, "Snakes make the Duchess physically sick." At least she can rest assured that it is one well-publicized episode that will not be repeated.

Just why *do* the royal family seem compelled to travel so compulsively? Ask any royal, and they'll tell you, for sure, that it isn't for the hell of it—or the fun of it. There's a sound reason behind all this jet setting: to promote British goods and good relations. Not only is the Queen head of the Commonwealth, but Britain is also part of the twelve-country European Common Market, and there have been plenty of semiformal visits by the young royals to Europe—where, there are many sumptuous royal palaces to stay in, as guests of Europe's crowned heads, and where the princesses can sleep easy, safe in the knowledge that the palaces enjoy the strictest of security.

That's one reason, quite apart from the close friendship that has grown up between Diana and King Juan Carlos and Queen Sofia of Spain, that she accepts their annual invitation for a sunbathing sojourn at one of the Spanish royals' summer homes. With their armed guards, electric fences, and the very latest in high-tech antiterrorist protection, Diana can truly relax while her sons frolic in the sand and she soaks up a deep and even suntan. King Juan Carlos also owns a gleaming white yacht—more a floating palace, really—where Diana can sip cooling glasses of Perrier in absolute luxury, occasionally diving off the side into warm Mediterranean waters when the sun becomes unbearably hot.

Another favorite destination is Princess Margaret's sumptuous Caribbean hideaway on the secluded paradise island of Mustique, beloved of rock legends like Mick Jagger and film stars such as Raquel Welch and Robert De Niro. Les Jolies Eaux—the beautiful seas, named after the sparkling azure waters a pebble's throw from the house—is a white stone, palm-clad home set in luxuriant gardens. Princess Margaret gladly lends it to young royals. It can also be rented to an elite clientele in the royals' absence—if you have the $4,000 per week wherewithal. The 1,400-acre island (whose 160 residents are known as the Mustiqueers) has the strictest of visitor-control policies; no one can stay on the island after dark without the consent of the Hon. Brian Alexander, official of the Mustique Company, which runs the island's affairs. This scheme successfully keeps interlopers at bay and enables the royals to swim, sunbathe, and enjoy beach barbecues utterly undisturbed.

Elsewhere, special arrangements have to be made to protect the jet-setting royals and their entourage. At Le Tousserok, in Mauritius—a favorite jet-set spot frequented by topless bathers where Sarah and Andrew spent a blissful week—no less than thirty rooms are rumored to have been cordoned off to offer the royal lovebirds complete seclusion and to accommodate a sixty-strong security staff. There was no danger of the well-endowed Duchess following the example of her fellow sun worshippers; ever careful not to fry her fair English complexion under the sun, she spent most of her holiday in a T-shirt, swathed in a sarong from a local market. (Andrew, meanwhile, sported a natty pair of flower-print bermudas.) Rarely rising before lunchtime, Sarah and Andrew for once turned their backs on the water sports available to Le Tousserok's chic clientele, preferring to lounge by the pool with paperback books the size of telephone directories and indulging in nothing more energetic than beating a path to and from the barbecue, where delicious seafood from the Indian Ocean was sizzling temptingly.

To shield them further from lone madmen or organized terrorists, the planes used by royals nowadays are equipped with the very latest antiterrorist devices. When Sarah, courtesy of the Royal Air Force, visited the Alps for a skiing holiday, she traveled on a plane whose security devices were like something out of *Star Wars:* instruments to counter heat-seeking missiles, electronic sensors, and other warning devices. Similar systems have been fitted to the VC10s and Tri-Stars that allow the royal family to sleep easy as they speed through the skies to their destinations.

Abroad, security on the ground tends to be far greater than in the United Kingdom, where gun ownership is very limited; most of Britain's police force is unarmed save for an archaic truncheon. Jittery host nations, who would be mortified if the royals came to any harm while visiting their turf, lay on motorcades, armed guards, and countless secret servicemen to protect the visitors from attack. Both Diana and Sarah have had their brushes with danger; Sarah was ushered to safety in New York when a banner-waving IRA supporter lunged at her, trying to penetrate the phalanx of security men around her. And in Los Angeles, a man with an automatic rifle was spotted lurking in an alleyway. The princesses' attitude, however, is that "you can't live your life in fear, or you'd go crazy."

And they can't just leaf through the glossy holiday brochures and decide to spend the summer in a secluded Provençal farmhouse, or on a Florida beach. Diana's known to love America and would like to see more of it at close range, but she can hardly pack Harry and William into a Winnebago and zoom off along the Appalachian Trail. And she's often left behind to attend to her own engagements while Charles jets off. When Prince Charles attended Texas's glittering 150th birthday celebrations, Diana was left back at the Kensington ranch. "I'd love to go to Texas, but that trip was boys only," she lamented. "It's not up to me where I go."

Sarah shares Diana's wanderlust; her passion for travel was kindled when, as a teenager, she hitchhiked around South America with her friend Charlotte Eden. It was fueled still more when she commuted between the magnificent Swiss Alps and London to visit her ski-mad lovers. For Sarah, the golden opportunity to see the world probably outweighs the magnificent jewels and fabulous fashions.

Indeed, Sarah's been accused of treating royal life like one long "freebie"—barely a month seems to go by, in fact, when she doesn't go jetting off to some foreign part for work or for play. An example is her Concorde trip—in the company of stars like Elton and Renata John (close friends of the Yorks); George Harrison; and Ringo Starr and his wife, ex-James Bond girl Barbara Bach—to see the curtain rise on Andrew Lloyd Webber's *The Phantom of the Opera* on Broadway. She spent just forty-eight hours in the United States before returning home. In 1987, for example, Sarah spent a staggering ninety-nine days outside the United Kingdom—though in 1988, the impending birth of Beatrice clipped her wings somewhat. Nevertheless, when Princess Beatrice was six weeks old, Sarah spent several weeks in Australia, having left her baby behind, initially on an official visit, but later, following her sailor husband everywhere his ship dropped anchor. In 1987, though—a blueprint, perhaps, for Sarah's jet-setting life—her schedule began with three weeks at Sandringham (where the Queen likes to spend New Year's); this was swiftly followed by a short skiing trip in Switzerland with some friends. She came back to London just long enough to get her ski suit dry-cleaned; then it was off to the slopes again, joining Diana and Charles on their annual skiing holiday in the top Alpine resort of Klosters. Some of the princesses' horseplay on the piste had Prince Charles—how shall I put it—just a fraction piste off?

There were several short hops to Paris (where she has friends) and back to London for couture fittings before Sarah sped off to spend time in Barbados with Andrew. In June, she was a guest at chateaux in France for wine-tasting, and in July came the famous hiking and canoeing trip tagged onto the end of Sarah and Andrew's first official overseas tour, of Canada. August was spent winding down at Balmoral, joining the rest of the royals for their summer break; the Queen, not fond of the heat, prefers the rolling Scottish hills to a warm, sandy beach anytime. In October, Sarah could be found fund raising in Palm Beach, before accompanying Andrew to the Indian Ocean paradise isle of Mauritius—tagging several days' vacation at one of the world's top hotels, Le Tousserok, onto the end of the official itinerary. This was not so much a second honeymoon, in the Yorks' case, as a fifth or sixth. The bill for the Mauritius trip, as for many of Sarah's overseas jaunts, was footed by a willing host only too pleased to be graced with royal company.

Diana and Sarah's idea of the perfect holiday couldn't be more different. Diana readily admits, "I like going to sunny places so I can work up a tan"; she likes nothing better than to play on the beach with her boys, building sand castles, like any normal mother—except that they're replicas of the ones William and Harry will themselves live in one day.

To Andrew's great delight, his wife is game for anything—a fact proved once and for all when, wearing a Davy Crockett hat and carrying a bowie knife tucked into her waistband and designer army fatigues, she donned a heavy fifty-pound knapsack with a somewhat less than Duchess-like "cor, blimey" and joked that she wasn't at all certain she'd survive ten days of the vicious blackflies that plague the tundra at that time of year. In the company of five hearty old friends from Andrew's time at Ontario's Lakefield College, Sarah proved that she was most definitely "one of the boys."

The trip came just after the Yorks had completed their first official tour of the country, visiting such attractions as rodeos and Niagara Falls, and where the Duchess was presented with a giant stuffed buffalo's head. Laughing gaily, she instantly declared, "I'll call it Andrew and hang it on the door." The Yorks loved their stay, and it's just as well; Canada is a nation they may well come to know still more intimately, since it's rumored that after his twelve-year stint in the navy draws to a close, Andrew might be appointed governor of this Commonwealth nation. In a speech thanking her hosts for their hospitality, the Duchess rose to her feet at the end of a meal—to the delight of the assembled crowd—to declare, "I could not go through a whole tour letting my darling husband of a year and a day," (they'd celebrated their anniversary the preceding day) "do all the public speaking. So we agreed for once that I should have the last word tonight. You are very lucky to be living here and I now count myself along with Andrew equally fortunate to be an honorary Canadian."

Official duties over, Sarah next day gamely paddled off in a canoe in hot pursuit of her husband up the Caribou Narrows. Her vessel was inscribed, appropriately, with the motto "Never underestimate the power of this woman." "Don't blame me," laughed Sarah, "I didn't put it there, ask my partner," she laughed, pointing at her husband, who was wearing a T-shirt with "Almost Famous" emblazoned across the front; you didn't need clairvoyant powers to deduce who'd given it to him. Sarah's an all-action holiday girl. In the future, we may well see her trekking through the Himalayas or whitewater rafting—that is, if motherhood doesn't make her lose her nerve.

It isn't hard to imagine Sarah keeping her brother-in-law Charles company on the kind of "Boy's Own" adventure holiday *he* enjoys the best, like a Kalahari safari in the company of his old friend Sir Laurens van der Post, with a 5:30 A.M. alarm call and dozens of miles to trek each day, fending off scorpions and lions. He likes to disappear to remote Scottish islands and live the simple, humble life for a few days, too, like the three days he spent in the company of a crofter's family in the Hebrides last year, planting potatoes, building walls, and fishing. Sarah would feel quite at home in such seclusion, where Charles's own wife would be bored and isolated—and would miss her creature comforts. As for risky exploits—well, they aren't Diana's cup of tea at all.

Sarah and Diana both look forward to the annual royal skiing junket in Klosters, although the disaster in which a royal pal was killed on the slopes, cast a shadow and a question mark over future trips, until Sarah and Andrew paid a return visit in January last year. The royal skiing event has made February the most fashionable month among the Sloane set for skiing, since they can then hope to bump into ski-borne royals on the piste. It is one holiday when Diana, Charles, Andrew, and Sarah seem to be able to mingle, unharassed, with the hoi polloi. Barely anybody bats an eyelid, though, when the royal quartet, clad in anonymous-looking ski suits, take their seats at the mountainside chalet restaurants for omelette, apple strudel, and salads. A bearded Swiss detective will case the joint first (followed by one of the royals' own bodyguards), and then the royal party troop in, slip off their hefty ski boots, and wiggle their white-socked toes, just like any other skiers, while waiting for the mountainous plates of food that will satisfy skiers' notoriously hearty appetites.

Diana's skiing has improved vastly since her marriage, but she's still careful. Sarah and Andrew are very accomplished. And Charles, according to one ski expert, is now "verging on the reckless," as the accident seems to back up. But the meal over, they would usually push off down the piste at their own pace before taking the twenty-minute train ride (second-class seats, nonsmoking) back to the luxury chalet rented each year for the young royals.

One of Diana's greatest frustrations is that she visits some of the world's greatest shopping cities yet has to make do with window shopping from behind the bulletproof glass of a chauffeur-driven limousine. She could barely conceal her delight in Thailand recently (where she and Charles stayed as guests of King Bhumikol) when she got to souvenir-shop like any normal tourist, snapping up two lengths of multicolored Thai silk to transform into dresses, a pink silk shirt for her husband, and a couple of yards of white silk to have made into another. Though the bill only totaled around $80, Diana is one tourist who never carries money—her detective, Graham Smith, had to reach for his Mastercard to settle the account! Elsewhere, she apparently snapped up a crab-shaped pillow (her star sign is Cancer), a kimono, and a cotton jumpsuit. In a city renowned as one of the world's great shopping meccas, it was a rare opportunity for Diana to see how the other half holidays.

13

Royal Baby Boom

$\mathcal{P}$ublic pressure on a princess to get pregnant is enormous. No sooner had Diana, then Sarah, hitched themselves to the royal wagon than everyone wanted to know when there would be a happy event to have them billing and cooing and knitting bootees.

As if to order, Diana, fulfilling her most crucial royal obligation, duly provided Charles with a son and heir, little William, not quite eleven months after the magnificent St. Paul's Cathedral nuptials, just before her twenty-first birthday. If she did nothing more, she had earned her keep forever by giving birth to William. So important, indeed, was it for the Prince's consort to fulfill this demand that (in line with tradition) she had undergone the ritual medical examination—an experience shy Di is known to have hated and resented—to ensure that she was gynecologically healthy enough to give Charles an heir to his throne.

But that fleeting moment of discomfort and embarrassment was forgotten when, on June 21, 1982, at 9:03 P.M., little

William Arthur Philip Louis—to be known as Prince William of Wales—made his bawling way into the world, greeted by overjoyed parents. And at least Diana didn't have to suffer the indignity of earlier royal moms, who gave birth in the presence of the home secretary, the government official who has been required by custom to witness royal births ever since James II's wife is alleged to have switched a stillborn baby for a healthy infant (smuggled, so it is said, into the royal chamber in a warming pan). Diana should be grateful to Charles's grandfather, George VI, for the abolition of *that* one. Prince Charles, however, held his wife's hand throughout the uncomplicated birth, describing it as "a very adult thing to do." He'd never looked happier than the moment he emerged onto the doorstep of the famous Lindo Maternity Wing of St. Mary's Hospital. When asked if the boy resembled his dad, the proud new father quipped, "Fortunately, no."

Diana's made no secret of the fact she didn't much enjoy the experience of being pregnant, plagued by morning sickness (sometimes morning, noon, and night sickness) while still trying to carry out her royal commitments. No sooner had she lost her puppy fat and acquired a figure she could be proud of than nature conspired to give her a bump that even the most skillful British designer could do little to disguise. All those slim-line, prepregnancy designer frocks had to be consigned to the back of the closet unworn—though to everyone but the burgeoning Princess, she looked 100 percent swelegant. (She's supposed to have confided in a friend, "I feel just like an elephant.") But nothing could compare with her obvious joy at being a mother—something she'd longed for almost all her life. Diana's always had a soft spot for little ones, and, as it rapidly became clear, so had doting Prince Charles.

The new mom, who breast-fed both her sons, was determined to do things "her way," but she didn't always win. Royal freshwomen are often confronted by a brick wall to bang their pretty heads against. When trying to initiate changes, they're often thwarted by courtiers or fellow royals who simply declare, "But historically, it's always been done like *this.*" For instance, the name William itself was a compromise; she rather fancied the sorts of Christian names favored by her Sloane set friends: Tom, Rupert, Oliver, Sam. But they don't sound quite right, somehow, with "King" tagged on the front. By contrast, Sarah and Andrew are free (as Princess Anne was, when she picked the name Zara for her daughter) to call their child by any of the more unusual names currently popular. It was undoubtedly Diana's influence, however, that led the Waleses' second-born to be known to the world as Harry right from day one, even though, officially, he was christened Henry Charles Albert David—every name rousingly, patriotically, historically royal.

Doting Diana has successfully broken another royal rule when it comes to traveling with her sons. The Queen and Prince Charles never fly together for fear that a tragic accident might rob the British nation of its sovereign and her heir. Although William had traveled on the same plane as his parents when he was tiny, while they made the laborious, exhausting journey to Australia, the Queen hadn't been at all smitten with the idea. And when little Harry arrived, the Queen put her foot down; Diana, Charles, William, and Harry weren't to fly together again, thus safeguarding the royal line of succession against attack or accident.

For a while, Diana stuck to the dictate issued by her mother-in-law, sadly waving good-bye to two-year-old William, his favorite soft toys, and his nanny as they boarded a separate aircraft whenever they made trips to Scotland or Europe. (Not that William is likely to have complained; he's enraptured by anything with wings, and his first word was reputedly "plane.") But not surprisingly, deep down Di felt that her mother-in-law's worries were outdated and unrealistic. Statistically, for instance, the Waleses are in far greater danger when they simply get into an automobile together, and no planes in the world are flown with as much care and attention to safety regulations as is the fleet that transports the royal family.

So when the King of Spain issued his annual invitation to the Waleses to join him for a summer holiday, Diana persuaded her husband to let the family jet off to the sun together. An insider told journalist Judy Wade, author of *Inside The Royal Marriage*, "Finally, the Princess won her husband over to her side. Prince Charles has decided that the advantages of flying as a family group outweigh the risks of an appalling accident—at least, while his children are small and not flying very often. The cost of separate flights for William, the nanny, and a detective helped to tip the balance. The Prince always loves a chance to save money, so he persuaded the Queen to agree." Even one of the world's richest women—whose wealth was recently estimated to be £3,340 million—has her thrifty side, it seems.

These days, though, now that her sons are more independent and less clingy, it is often simpler to leave the wee Waleses at home. When Diana and Charles first traveled to Australia with William, their entourage occupied thirty-three rooms of an Albury hotel and four bedrooms at the royal couple's chosen residence, Woomargama; Diana and Charles flew back from the four corners of Australia a total of seven times in order to play with their nine-month-old darling. Now, though, Mom is keen that her sons' education shouldn't be interrupted and that their lives have a sense of continuity, even though leaving them behind tugs on the heartstrings. When Diana and Charles travel without their princes, there are daily telephone calls at an appointed hour, awaited expectantly in the royal nursery. But there's no disguising the fact that for Diana, long-distance laughter and love are no substitute for the real thing. On the official royal tour of Australia last year, she paid a visit to a group of children from broken homes and got a "fix" of surrogate motherhood, cuddling a cute little five-year-old blond girl and beaming that it was "just heaven to be back among children again." As the overexcited children dragged her by the hand to join them, Diana declared herself to be "very, very happy—so happy that I'll do whatever they want me to," and stayed contentedly with her miniature playmates for nearly half an hour before anxious, clock-watching royal aides pried her away. The Queen would be hard-pressed to find fault with her daughter-in-law's devotion to her sons. But ironically, it could be this very dedication that she finds jarring. The Queen certainly adores her own children, and *their* children, but Prince Philip has always been closest to her heart, followed by her three sons and her daughter. For a while recently, Diana's affection for her husband seemed to everyone to be visibly fading—they spent long periods going their separate ways—yet she has never disguised her love for the little princes. Di persists in doing the school run at every opportunity, even though it could equally well be handed over to any one of forty servants. But she has not always seemed so keen to rush to her husband's side at the drop of a hat.

In Sarah, however, the Queen can see a woman whose husband is unequivocally *numero uno*. The Duchess is only too aware that she's married a man with a notoriously keen eye for the ladies; she's witnessed what the glamorous competition for his affection and attention was like, and she'll do whatever she can to ensure that his royal blue eyes rove no further. If that means putting Andrew first, even leaving the little Yorks at home while they travel overseas, then Sarah will unquestioningly do so, just as naturally as she learned to pilot a plane, then a helicopter, to delight her darling prince. For their first trip to Australia (September), Beatrice didn't go along for the ride, though Sarah's schedule was rearranged to enable her to spend plenty of time on the phone with her baby.

She made it clear, like Diana, that being pregnant wasn't going to stand in the way of official duty. Lying on a chaise longue for nine months with her dainty feet up, leafing through glossy magazines and picking at healthful snacks prepared in the royal kitchen isn't Sarah's idea of the perfect pregnancy. Sarah once hinted that—in line with many other career women of her generation—she wasn't planning on starting a family until she was thirty. But fifteen months into her marriage, the press and public's patience were running out. Like many new brides, she found herself bombarded by questions about when the announcement of a happy event could be expected.

The tabloid press ran stories that she was having trouble conceiving (after years on "the pill") and was paying secret visits to a Harley Street gynecologist for doses of the fertility drug Clomid, which can sometimes result in multiple births. But all this was hotly denied by her angry father, who was deeply irritated by having to endure a barrage of inquiries about whether he was to become a granddad again. Her friends, however, were let into the secret with a usual flash of wit. When Sarah accompanied her husband on a pheasant shoot at Sandringham before Christmas, she wore a jaunty hat shaped like a Christmas plum pudding, complete with a sprig of holly sticking out of the top—a clue to alert her pals that she was "in the pudding club."

Speculation about the impending royal event rose to baby-fever pitch while she was in Switzerland enjoying a skiing holiday, guest of brewing heir Peter Greenall and his wife Clare. (As much as any royal *can* enjoy a holiday while they are being pursued by ski-borne, sensation-seeking paparazzi.) Throughout her stay, however, Sarah remained mum about the whole matter; back home, the besieged press offices at Buckingham Palace were being equally guarded.

When a devious radio reporter rang the chalet where she was hiding, a somewhat flustered Sarah—or someone sounding exactly like her—picked up the phone, insisting that the Duchess was "um, er . . . out." When pressed about the rumors of a pregnancy that were circulating, the plummy voice insisted, "I'm fed up with so many calls here. I don't know anything about it. We are here on a skiing holiday and I don't know quite what you are talking about. So I suggest that you ring Buckingham Palace." In their attempts to get a royal pregnancy confirmed, the press pursued her through the Alps—but black-run skier Sarah outdistanced them all, tackling the most advanced slopes. Even her detective was hard-pressed to keep pace. "I'm game, I'll try anything," she laughed at a fellow expert. When the press finally caught up with her, she would smile sweetly for the cameras and zoom off again. The closest anyone got to a scoop was an interview with a local Swiss restauranteur, who claimed that Sarah had tucked into a hearty meal of french fries and appeared to be "eating for two."

The reason for the secrecy surrounding Sarah's pregnancy became clear a week later, when she dashed off to New York for the premiere of *The Phantom of the Opera*. She had been waiting to make an announcement because she first wanted to tell her mom in person. After Mrs. Hector Barrantes had been let in on the glad tidings, Buckingham Palace was finally able to let the kitten out of the bag: that the Duchess of York was expecting a baby in August, who would be fifth in line to the throne. A week after that, the Duke and Duchess made their first public appearance since the announcement, attending the gala premiere of the movie *White Mischief*, in aid of the Nordoff Robbins Music Therapy Centre for handicapped children. Sarah's radiant glow brought a rousing cheer from those of us present, including stars like Geraldine Chaplin and Sarah Miles, even if we did wonder whether the four-letter words, on-screen nudity, and graphic murder scenes were quite the thing for the eyes and ears of a newly pregnant royal. But the Duchess, clad in Saint Laurent and swathed in a padded pink shawl of parachute silk, seemed to be loving every moment.

Indeed, Sarah showed no signs of letting her action-princess image fade now that she was expecting the Queen's fifth grandchild. The only activity scratched from her itinerary—at her gynecologist's recommendation—was horseback riding. The very day after her pregnancy was announced, she took to the skies again at the controls of a helicopter for an eighty-minute flight and swooped low enough over her father's Hampshire home to read the cheery message that her thrilled father and stepmother had scrawled in red—"Congrats Ma'am!" "She will be a wonderful mother," beamed Susan Ferguson. "Absolutely radiant. She's 100 percent healthy and I am delighted for them both." But within a fortnight, Sarah had hit the ski slopes again, arousing fears that in the thin air, at high altitude, with the ever-present risk of a tumble on the hard ice, she could be placing the health of the royal baby at risk. There's a history of problems in her family; her sister Jane suffered two late miscarriages before giving birth to a healthy daughter, Ayesha. In fact, there's a strong rumor that Sarah herself lost a baby just a few weeks into a pregnancy the summer before last.

But Fergie is no fool, and neither is her gynecologist, Mr. Anthony Kenney (who was never far away during the pregnancy, accompanying the royal mum-to-be on her overseas visits). If the flying Duchess took to the skies and the slopes with gusto early on in her pregnancy and kept her diary chock-full of commitments, it can only be because the eminent obstetrician gave her the green light. With her husband away working, Sarah had to endure the early months of her pregnancy without her husband's beefy shoulder to lean on, occasionally to cry on. Keeping active would stave off any loneliness she might feel, even though Andrew dashed home whenever he could to be by her side. Other gynecologists applauded her energetic approach, declaring, "The more normal a life a woman leads during her pregnancy, the better. Physically, doing so helps the muscles keep in trim."

Her choice of doctor, Mr. Kenney, showed yet again that the

spirited Duchess was determined to do things her way. For years, royal mums-to-be have opted for the services of Mr. George Pinker, Surgeon Gynecologist to the Queen (all surgical consultants are called Mr., not Dr., incidentally). Father of four, sixty-one-year-old Pinker has safely delivered Princess Anne's two children and the Princess of Wales's two little princes; he attended Princess Michael of Kent and the Duchess of Gloucester during the births of their babies, too. He's been known to leave his favorite opera in mid-aria or to make a speedy exit from a dinner party if a baby's on the way. He hands out his home phone number to expectant mothers, encouraging them to call if they have even the tiniest nagging doubts. And above all, Pinker shows a healthy sense of humor. Apparently, George Pinker is likely to write—in front of a patient who's just been asked how her sex life is—"satisfied customer"! When and if Diana has another child, George Pinker will be the first to know—and to remain in on the act until he's delivered the newest prince or princess.

Both Charles and Diana would love a little sister for their boys. Obviously finding his noisy heirs a little too much to handle, Charles once wistfully said to the father of two teenage girls, "Girls are so much nicer than boys, don't you think?" And Diana, visiting a play group in North London, remarked to one mother, "I don't think I would like three boys. But deep down, I would love a little girl." They're believed to have reserved the name Elizabeth, a tribute to both the Queen and Queen Mother (known respectively as "Lilibet" and "Grandmama").

As a woman of experience, Sarah, however, already had a gynecologist when she joined the royals, and she's sticking with him. Kenney, who is forty-four years old, is favored by her set and is well known for his risque jokes and wacky impersonations of Mickey Mouse!

Only time will show us Sarah's style of motherhood, though she's had plenty of vicarious experience, with her younger half-brother and sisters and Paddy McNally's two sons. She's no stranger to diaper-changing. And even though princesses can delegate the messier aspects of motherhood to their staff, they tend to find that mundane, daily chores like changing and bathing their children help them retain a sense of reality. Sarah's love of children is as obvious as Diana's ever was. They're naturals, who never miss an opportunity to bend down and chat eyeball-to-eyeball to the little children appointed to hand over bouquets during royal visits; while touring Wales, Sarah noticed a couple of small children crying their eyes out and promptly produced a slab of chocolate for each from her pocket.

Tongue-tied, nervous little ones soon loosen up, transformed into chatterboxes in an instant once they've been treated to the princesses' naturally warm smiles. At the Children of Courage Awards staged annually by Britain's *Woman's Own* magazine, where prizes for acts of youthful bravery were given out, protocol was thrown to the wind when Fergie arrived. She picked up the winners for a hug, stroked their hair, and made endless jokes. When one of the children, feeling a touch neglected, poked her in the rear, she roared with laughter, wheeled around and gave him her undivided attention.

Both the Princess and the Duchess are resigned to being working mothers with brutal itineraries, unable to devote as much time to their own children as they yearn to. Often, they spend their time fund raising for those far less fortunate than their own families. Diana, who has to prepare for the day's engagements, rarely sees her sons until after breakfast; they're roused by nannies from their slumbers in the royal nursery at the top of Kensington Palace (where the stairway has been roped off with netting, to prevent the little princes from climbing through the banisters). Fed, hair brushed, and in their smart school clothes (the previous day's muddy stains miraculously removed by a valet), they may get to kiss Mummy and Daddy good-bye before leaving home—that is, if their parents haven't already sped off in chauffeur-driven limousines or the bright-red helicopter that so enchants William and Harry to fulfill the day's commitments.

At the end of the day, though, Diana always strives to be home to collect her sons from school in the family Ford Granada. She often whisks them straight off for swimming lessons at Buckingham Palace. If they're well behaved, they may be allowed to join her in her private sitting room for four o'clock tea, a royal ritual, with cucumber sandwiches and cream cakes. (Diana insists, however, that the boys' diet is as healthy as possible. When she once caught William in a Highgrove outhouse, having given his security men the slip for the umpteenth time, he was swigging down an entire bottle of cherry cola. Diana took one horrified look at the additives on the label and banished processed foods from her sons' diet immediately.) If they're really good, Diana lets them stay up to watch their favorite TV shows: *Postman Pat* cartoons and *Blue Peter*, a long-running magazine program for children with a smattering of news, games, live animals, and things to make and do.

Before their sons' bedtime and preparations for their own evening engagements, Charles and Diana may play with their boys on the swings in the garden or help them with a jigsaw puzzle. And there is always bath time, followed by bedtime stories—old faithfuls like *Winnie the Pooh* and the Beatrix Potter books, by which Diana and Charles were themselves enchanted as children. On weekends, which the Waleses try to spend at Highgrove, the nannies get to put their feet up. Diana and Charles spend as much time as possible in the great outdoors, leading the princes around on their ponies, teaching them the names of plants and flowers (Diana and Charles are both fanatical gardeners), taking long walks across the meadows, and generally attempting to tire the boys out before it's 7:30 and time for bed. William used to have a gleaming miniature replica of his father's Jaguar, but he was so fond of ramming all the other vehicles like a demented driver that it's been exchanged for a small bicycle, which he soon learned to ride without stabilizers.

Sarah's life as a mother will be different from Diana's. She's said that "all that matters is that a child is healthy and happy." *Her* children—further down the pecking list of succession to the throne—will have a fraction more freedom than Wills and Harry. The Queen will never worry about the Yorks traveling together—probably with their parents at the controls! But Sarah will have to be content raising Beatrice, and any future children, as a single parent for much of the year, while her seafaring husband continues his career. Sarah, raised by her army officer father, is a believer in discipline—more so than softie Di. "You mustn't be too soft or easy with children," she's said. "They need to know where boundaries lie and what they can and cannot do." She'll also pass on the most valuable lesson Major Ferguson ever taught his flame-haired daughter: "Always be natural, be yourself." This is something Sarah seems never, for one moment, to have forgotten.

Luckily, the Duchess is likely to have fewer commitments than is her sister-in-law, the most in-demand royal, leaving her free to perform, at times, the work of two parents. Andrew's committed to the navy for the foreseeable future—possibly for life—and Sarah's lot will be that of any serviceman's wife, doling out treats and punishments and unable to wield the ultimate deterrent, that of saying "You just wait till your dad gets home!" Because in Andrew's case, that could be weeks. However, when Sarah says no, her children will realize she means it.

Actually, royal tots today are raised far more leniently than their parents were—in the case of rambunctious little William and his brother Harry, some suggest *too* leniently. They aren't bowed and scraped to, and their titles are never used within the royal household, so that the children can grow up with a feeling of normality for as long as their parents can string it out. Though they're showered with toys and playthings on tours and visits, many of these never reach the royal nursery for fear the princes will become spoiled. Instead, they're given to hospitals and charities like Dr. Barnardo's, of which Diana is a devoted patron. Like any other small children, the boys go to kindergarten, because, in the words of Prince Charles, "It teaches you how to look after yourself." But though Diana once worked in one, she's admitted that the choice of where to send the little princes is still tough. "We're open-minded about William and his education," she explained in a TV interview with Alastair Burnet, "because the bad luck about being number one is trial and error. Number two skates in quite nicely. So we're still learning the tricks of the trade."

At school, the sole concession to the boys' specialness is the bodyguard who shadows each of them from the corner of the classroom. William now attends the Wetherby School, where he'll stay until he's eight, and little Harry's followed in his elder brother's footsteps to Mrs. Mynors's nursery school, less than a mile away from Kensington Palace in Notting Hill Gate, where, to the amusement of his parents, an excited William dragged his little brother indoors on the first day to show him around, like an old pro. The school itself had already been especially modified to cater to the princes' arrival, fitted with bulletproof windows and other security devices believed to have been paid for by the royal couple; the kindergarten enjoys the added security of being housed in the basement of Jane Mynors's own home, where she lives with her city wheeler-dealer husband and their two children. The Wetherby School, too, has been equipped to guard against kidnapping or terrorist attack.

There's the occasional barrage of press attention: first day at school, the annual Christmas pageant (for which, one year, Harry was dressed as a pixie, in bright-red tights, a green tunic, and a Wee Willie Winkie hat—photos that he'll cringe to look back at later on). But so far, their destiny does not seem to have dawned on the boys, and Diana deploys the occasional little white lie to keep her sons in the dark for a little while longer, explaining that the assembled press cortege is there only to photograph her new frock. "I know it sounds arrogant, but so far it's worked," Di is on record as saying. She is less happy, however, at invasions of her own palace territory. Driving up to the gates of Kensington Palace one day with William, she saw red, treating waiting photographers to a rare flash of Spencer spirit. Winding down the window of her car, she shouted, "Leave him alone. *Alone*, do you hear. How would you like your children to be treated like that?"

But the boys are clearly at home in front of the cameras that have been poised since the day they were born. Practically before they could walk, the little lads were practicing the "Windsor wave" in preparation for a life that will turn out, as their parents know only too well, to be one long photo opportunity.

Before long, no matter what pains his adoring parents take to protect their eldest son from the realization that he's different—so *very* different—from other boys, Prince William may start to understand the enormity of the role that lies ahead for him as a boy who will one day be king. Prince Charles touchingly explained it once as "something that dawns on you with the most ghastly, inexorable sense. I didn't suddenly wake up in my pram one day and say 'yippee!' Slowly you get the idea that you have a certain duty and responsibility, and I think it's better that way, rather than somebody suddenly telling you."

Prince Charles takes fatherhood mighty seriously. He got involved well before his children were born, listening to a lecture with other fathers-to-be on their vital role during the big event, and he studied up by reading countless baby-care books. He learned to enjoy small children when he was almost a teenager and his mother presented him somewhat belatedly with new younger brothers. He wrote and illustrated (with wonderful watercolor drawings) a story for Andrew and Edward called *The Old Man of Lochnagar*, which has even been turned into a stage play. And there can be no doubt that on the shelves of William and Harry's royal nursery lurk a few more priceless fairy tales created especially by the Prince. He's also a favorite among his countless godchildren, nephews, and nieces for the box of tricks—like squeaky toys, false noses, and grotesque teeth—that he keeps on hand to delight tots.

When second son Harry was born, Charles flung himself even more wholeheartedly into paternity; the future king's diary was unusually empty for the first year of his son's life as he devoted himself to his baby's development, bathing and playing with the little redheaded child at every opportunity (and it's alleged to have sparked fireworks between Charles and his father, Prince Philip, who accused him of dereliction of his princely duty). But perhaps this diligent fatherly attention can explain the fact that Harry, unlike his elder brother, has grown into a quiet, thoughtful, and gentle little boy, described as "very advanced for his age."

Charles knows that nobody is better equipped to school William in the rules of royalty and the special lessons a prince must learn, and he has become the boy's doting coach, referring to him fondly as "Willie the Wombat," in public and private, after a particularly cute native rodent of Down Under. Charles had a lonely childhood; he was often left at home for weeks on end while his parents were on royal tour and was taught at home until the age of eight, almost as if he were in solitary confinement. By the time he was signed up for Hill House Preparatory School, he was shy and somewhat insular. He agreed with Diana that their sons should be sent out into the big wide world as early as possible, but it's believed that there *were* clashes over other aspects of child rearing. "Liberal upbringing" seemed to have a different meaning to each of William's parents.

For a while, it appeared that willful William was growing up into a right royal tearaway—and Charles may have felt that it was a result of Diana's determination that her children should be reared in the modern, relaxed style most child experts today favor. In the charge of royal nanny Barbara Barnes, who'd reigned over the royal nursery from the day of his birth and is thought to have pampered her favorite little prince, William was becoming increasingly rambunctious and prone to chronic misbehavior. Despite his parents' well-meaning desire to allow their son to grow up as normally as possible, one insider described the prank-loving prince as "too full of himself by half." Diana acknowledged publicly that her toddler son was a "mini-tornado" who ran riot at home. He once set off the intricate alarm system at Balmoral and flushed his father's handmade Lobb shoes down the toilet. During the Queen's annual Christmas Day broadcast, the monarch was seen grabbing her wayward heir by the arm and trying to distract him with her cuddly new corgi puppy. William wasn't having any of it; he exited, stage left, to torment Zara Phillips, Princess Anne's daughter.

Any hope that he would have calmed down by the time he started school were dashed. Rough-and-tumble tactics earned him the nickname "Billy the Basher," for supposedly barging to the front of the lunch queue, picking fights in the school yard, and bullying classmates by boasting, "My daddy can beat up your daddy—my daddy's the Prince of Wales." When Diana, leaving the nanny behind, took Prince William off to see his father play a few chukkas of polo, he could be seen dangling dangerously over the edge of the royal box (with Diana holding onto the seat of his pants for safety) and was overheard bombarding his exasperated mom with whining questions like, "Where are the horses? Can I have an ice cream? I want a drink!" Finally, she simply scooped him up in her arms and drove him back to Windsor Castle.

Diana confessed to being exceedingly nervous about William's official debut—as pageboy at his Uncle Andrew's wedding to Sarah Ferguson, the first formal duty in a lifetime destined to be crammed with ceremonial occasions. But in the end, except for poking out his tongue at the TV cameras and tickling a bridesmaid, William was remarkably well behaved. He has inherited every ounce of his mother's charm—and he knew how to use it to wriggle out of trouble, which appears to explain how he was allowed to get away with blue murder. "William is just like me," Diana once said, "always in trouble." But soon after the royal wedding, it was decided that doting Nanny Barnes should be replaced with a woman who would rule the nursery with a firmer hand. In Ruth Wallace, a former children's nurse, Diana and Charles stumbled upon the perfect person. "William and Harry are changed children," reports a relieved insider.

The drawing room at Kensington Palace—filled with priceless ornaments and silk upholstery that doesn't take well to chocolatey fingerprints—is still out of bounds. But to the relief of both his parents, William has calmed down enormously. The boy who will be king, Diana's adored firstborn, is beginning to grow up. But the Queen now has a new grandchild to delight in.

Of course, what Sarah discovered—like Diana before her—is that in the public's imagination, there is nothing that rounds off a royal romance more neatly than the patter of tiny royal feet. And when little Beatrice Elizabeth Mary arrived in this world, the love story had a perfect happy ending. For she made her debut on the day that—so Chinese legend goes—is the luckiest of the century, 8/8/88 (eight being, in oriental numerology, the sign of good fortune). And as if all those eights weren't already enough, Beatrice made her debut at the extremely lucky hour of 8:18 P.M.

The British public were becoming decidedly restive by the time Beatrice arrived, but probably nobody was quite so relieved about the royal birth as Fergie herself. During the early days of her pregnancy, Sarah had lived life in the fast lane at her usual pace, skiing, flying, and taking on an itinerary of royal appointments that would exhaust even someone who *wasn't* expecting the Queen's grandchild, fifth in line to the throne. Andrew had been at her side, there had been plenty of foreign travel to exotic places, gifts for the new child were thrust at them wherever they ventured, and the excitement that the royal couple felt at the prospect of parenthood shone out from their joyful faces.

But after the idyllic days of her early pregnancy, Sarah found that impending motherhood had a definite downside. After a couple of months, the moment finally arrived for Andrew to pursue his career where it beckoned, taking up a posting thousands of miles away aboard the guided-missile destroyer HMS *Edinburgh*. Suddenly, Sarah was all alone, at a time when she craved her hand to be held, her back to be rubbed, and to be told that she was still beautiful. She admitted to friends that she was, in fact, worried that "Andrew may not be around to see the baby born." By the time her due date came around in mid-August, he was due to be on the other side of the world, in the waters of the Orient, although, eventually, it was announced that the Duke of York would be allowed compassionate leave to be at his wife's side during the birth—to the chagrin of many fellow officers denied such a privilege when *their* wives went into labor.

It seems as if Sarah turned to food for the comfort she craved from Andrew, because, by the time Beatrice appeared, her weight had ballooned by sixty pounds. The slenderness she'd striven so hard to achieve in the early days of her romance—when butterflies and excitement ruined her appetite anyhow—was a thing of the past. Size 10 dresses hung accusingly in her wardrobe, and there must have been times when she despaired that her homely body would ever look svelte again. "I'm trying not to put on too much weight," she laughed with friends, a champagne glass in her hand. (Her gynecologist, Anthony Kenney, believes women should try to be at their most relaxed during a pregnancy, and if that means an *occasional* glass of wine, then perhaps the benefits of a laid-back mom outweigh the disadvantages.) Fergie did her best to follow the antenatal exercises prescribed to her, although she confesses that "I can't stand being stretched out on the floor in a leotard trying to do something I know I won't achieve." She regularly went for Alexander Technique classes, the body-alignment therapy and gentle exercise that is designed to improve posture; but still the pounds piled on.

Rather too late in the day, Sarah realized that she had done nothing to organize a maternity wardrobe; her regular designers couldn't run up something stylish in time. (Apparently she pleaded with the couture house Saint Laurent, whose clothes had transformed her from frumpiness to chic, but no luck.) She moaned anyhow that maternity clothes made her look like "a sack of potatoes," and on all but the most formal occasions made do with billowing long shirts and sweaters in an attempt to conceal her rapidly blossoming figure. At Ascot, she wore a far-too-girlish sailor suit with a hat jauntily perched on her titian curls when she should unquestionably have picked a more sophisticated, sleeker outfit.

Sarah certainly listened to the advice of old hands in the maternity game, such as her friend comedienne Pamela Stephenson (whose own baby had been due at the same time as Sarah's—Scarlett, in fact, arrived just a couple of days earlier) and her sister-in-law the Princess of Wales, who had perfected the art of retrieving her prepregnancy slenderness in a flash. But still the cookie jar beckoned, and Sarah's will power had all but disappeared; she frequently seemed to be eating for rather more than two.

By the end of her confinement, Sarah looked unhappy and bloated whenever she was seen in public; she was obviously feeling the ill effects of having put on so much weight. She seemed almost to have abandoned wearing makeup (though early on in her pregnancy, Sarah—who'd always had perfect skin—had been troubled by an outcropping of pimples, which had to be concealed). Much as Sarah yearned for a child, the seal of her love for Andrew, the pregnancy itself was something to be endured rather than enjoyed. Skiing early in 1988, she had revealed to a friend, "I want it all over and done with before I go skiing again this time next year." And there is no doubt that, last year's tragic avalanche notwithstanding, we'll see Sarah on the slopes for years to come.

Sarah's pregnancy was particularly trying by any standards. Not only was her husband on the other side of the globe and her weight skyrocketing (while, irritatingly, her sister-in-law looked ever more glamorous), but there were problems in her family, too. The British yellow press revealed that Major Ferguson, her father, had frequented the Wigmore Club, a "health club" where sexual favors were found to be on the menu. "Relief massage" was featured alongside the more regular, Swedish variety, and a prostitute who worked at the club claimed that Major Ferguson would regularly visit the establishment for the sake of "a sexual act." He apparently made no secret of his identity—even boasting of his royal connections—and he was not the only celebrity, the newspaper revealed, to have partaken of the club's proffered entertainments.

The word of any prostitute must certainly be held in doubt, particularly when it is common knowledge that certain British newspapers offer quite substantial financial incentives to people who can dish the dirt. But Major Ferguson refused to issue a denial, maintaining, instead, a discreet silence on the matter. This, in turn, prompted several leading lights in polo circles to call for Major Ferguson's resignation from his post as Prince Charles's polo manager. He refused to stand down and, twice, a committee met to decide whether he should indeed be sacked. By one vote on each occasion, he retained his job by the skin of his teeth. Nevertheless, for the first couple of weeks after the *News of the World*'s startling revelations about Fergie's seemingly so-proper pa, the royal family seemed to treat him like a pariah, avoiding contact with the Major whenever possible—a difficult task when the polo season was in full swing. The Duchess, in the fragile emotional state common to pregnant women, was extremely upset and is said to have shed many tears over the affair.

Later on, she suffered further shocks when a hit-and-run driver rammed the Jaguar in which she was being chauffeured at high speed. The Duchess was shaken but unhurt; her car, however, suffered some damage and was taken off the road. Sarah was transferred to a police car escorting her own favorite Jaguar and apparently laughed the incident off with her customary sense of humor. Nevertheless, it was a trying time, and it must have seemed like yet another blow. The cards were stacked against her.

But every cloud, so they say, has a silver lining—in Sarah's case, it was gold-plated. Though her husband was away, Sarah sought comfort and solace in the company of her own mother (Mrs. Hector Barrantes), getting to know her better than ever before. Through a stroke of fortune, the latter months of Sarah's pregnancy coincided with the English polo season, when Mrs. Barrantes and her professional polo player husband are traditionally to be found in the United Kingdom. Together, mother and daughter shopped, lunched, shared front-row seats at Wimbledon, and forged a steely bond. It was her mother's calming presence that enabled Sarah to endure the stressful months of her pregnancy. Insiders say, in fact, that Mrs. Barrantes was prepared to be present when her daughter was giving birth if Andrew couldn't make it back from Singapore in time. If Beatrice had indeed arrived early, the uncomplicated birth might well have been over before Andrew could dash halfway around the world to be at his wife's bedside.

Luckily, Andrew made it with just a couple of days to spare, and the evening before Beatrice was born they took a spin in a brand-new powder-blue Jaguar XJS which had been delivered to the Duchess after her accident. They appeared happy and relaxed, driving through the leafy lanes surrounding their rented home at Windsor. And next morning, the patience of the public, photographers, and reporters, who had for three weeks been occupying the sidewalks opposite London's private Portland Hospital, finally paid off. Looking somewhat tense, the royal couple arrived at 9:55 A.M., though, to the disappointment of the assembled crowds, they sneakily came in through the back door. A couple of hours later, Sarah's mother arrived—destined to spend the day with her daughter and her son-in-law, who obviously has more affection for his mother-in-law than do many men.

London was starved of important news, since August is notoriously the "silly season," when Parliament is in recess and the newspapers have trouble filling their columns. Curiosity was at fever pitch all day. Eventually, shortly after 9 P.M. that evening, the birth was announced in the traditional manner at the Portland Hospital (the first entirely private hospital chosen for a royal birth) and Buckingham Palace, where a notice was posted at the cast-iron gates announcing that "at 8:18 P.M. the Duchess of York was safely delivered of a daughter." Jubilation engulfed the land on that balmy evening, and when, a couple of hours later, the new father appeared on the doorstep of the hospital, he was clearly elated.

By the time Andrew left, the flowers, bouquets, gifts, and telegrams of congratulations had already started to flood into the Portland Hospital. But none must have seemed quite so touching to the new mother as the bunch of full-blown roses Andrew arrived with next morning; he had clearly picked them himself from the gardens at Buckingham Palace. They were even fastened, rather inelegantly but touchingly, with an elastic band! Andrew later "went walkabout" outside the hospital, accepting flowers and compliments from well-wishers with charm and grace—a Prince Andrew quite unrecognizable from his early, surly days when he was the press corp's least favorite royal. In answer to questions, he replied that "fatherhood is wonderful," and that the new baby resembled "both her parents."

The birth itself had been quite straightforward and had taken no longer than most first-timers. Rumors that the baby was in breech position and would have to be delivered by caesarean section or that it was overdue and would have to be induced were quite unfounded. The new Princess of York (at this stage, her name was still a secret) weighed in at six pounds, twelve ounces. And in celebration, Andrew is believed to have bestowed on his wife a substantial item of jewelry; for weeks beforehand, London's elite jewelers had been on standby.

The Queen was reportedly overjoyed at the birth of a granddaughter—her second, although the first to bear a title. (Princess Anne married a commoner, Mark Phillips, so her daughter is plainly and simply Miss Zara Phillips.) She's extremely fond of Sarah and, though touring Scotland at the time of the big event, was most impatient to see the new baby. Over the next few days, very important people in the new princess's life arrived for their first glimpse: her great-grandmother (Mrs. Barrantes's mother), her grandfather Ferguson, stepgrandmother Susan Ferguson, and the Princess of Wales and her two little boys, who were greeted with a kiss from Uncle Andrew (in his shirtsleeves) on the doorstep of the hospital and who arrived bearing a huge card and a gift.

The rest of the world had to wait until Friday for *their* first look at the Princess of York. Sarah and Andrew and a little, crumple-faced bundle appeared on the doorstep, to a resounding cheer, for the baby's first photo session. Sarah (who'd obviously had a visit from her hairdresser) was still wearing a dressing-gown-style maternity frock, which prompted some cruel comments that it looked as if she hadn't yet had the baby; but she did wear a funny pin that proclaimed what a delighted world already knew: "I'm a Mum!" Her figure looked likely to be a problem for some time to come, and though obviously happy, Sarah seemed tired and wan for fleeting moments when her face wasn't lit up by that famous grin.

The Princess of York slept like the babe she is throughout the cheers and clapping. In response to photographers' requests to "show us the baby's face, Fergie," Sarah duly obliged, tipping her precious bundle (in the most exquisite, white-crocheted shawl) so that the world could see her button nose and a telltale wisp of hair. *Red* hair, inherited from her mother, to the joy of Andrew—who was attracted to his wife's russet curls from the word go. At one point, Andrew proved that he's been perfecting the role of father, expertly taking the fragile bundle from his wife. A wisecracking onlooker demanded to know if he was looking forward to the sleepless nights that lay ahead. "There won't be too many, I hope," he grinned—knowing, naturally, that he'll be away from his home, his wife, and his daughter for many of them. There will no doubt be lonely nights aboard the HMS *Edinburgh* when the Duke of York *dreams* of being awakened by the squalling of his first child.

At that moment, however, disaster nearly struck. Fergie's independent streak forever to the fore, she could not resist making a bee-line, to collect a bunch of flowers, toward the crowds who'd waited so patiently outside the hospital. To the horror of Andrew and their private detectives, she made an unscheduled dash across the wet road, slipped, and almost fell. She recovered just in time, with the help of a detective who'd sprung into action, before she slipped right over. Undoubtedly highly embarrassed—she will forever be haunted by the photographic record of her near miss, which was emblazoned over every newspaper the next day—she regained her composure and collected the bunch of flowers being proffered by an American tourist before entering the chauffeur-driven limousine with her child, who was by now tucked beneath a coverlet in a Moses basket lined with blue-sprigged fabric (which surely put an end to suggestions that Fergie knew the sex of her unborn child, or it would certainly have been pink-sprigged). Her luggage and Prince Andrew's camera bag—for he's said to have captured Beatrice's earliest moments on film—had already been loaded into a police backup car.

The royal duo—now, of course, a trio—waved good-bye to the entire Portland staff, who had assembled on the steps of the hospital, and sped off to an unknown destination. It was expected that they would return to their own home, but instead the Yorks jetted direct to the Scottish highlands to join the other royals who'd assembled for their annual holiday at Balmoral. It was there that Prince Andrew took the first official photographs of his wife—her face rather extraordinarily scrubbed clean of makeup—and their baby. Sarah was casually dressed in a crisp white shirt and a paisley-printed Ralph Lauren house robe. The charming portraits were released to coincide with the announcement of the baby's name, Beatrice Elizabeth Mary. She will probably be known to all as Bea. This has an added symbolism for the Duchess, since the bee is incorporated in her family crest and was embroidered on the train of her wedding gown. Beatrice is also a name with historic royal associations; it was chosen by Queen Victoria for her youngest daughter. Interestingly, the fact that Andrew and Sarah *didn't* choose Elizabeth as the first name for their baby—in tribute to her regal grandmother and great-grandmother—implies that Diana and Charles may well have earmarked it for a child of their own and that they don't plan to stop at two boys.

The carefully screened, handpicked nanny for Princess Bea—twenty-year-old Alison Wardley, from Cheshire, a graduate of the Princess Christian College for nannies, in Manchester—was not summoned to join the royal couple until several days after their arrival. Presumably, in the meantime, Sarah assumed all the diaper-changing duties herself, and as a modern dad, Andrew may also have taken a turn at this least favorite of paternal duties.

In an ideal world, Sarah would no doubt like to apply her customary businesslike approach to the role of motherhood, too—but as any mother can tell you, hormones don't always go along with your plans. There had been much debate about whether or not the baby would accompany her parents, six weeks after she was born, on their official visit to Australia, coinciding with that country's bicentennial. In any event, it was decided that little Princess Beatrice would stay behind with her nanny, prompting fury among the ranks of child-care experts who insisted that the Duchess was missing out on crucial bonding with her baby. But just three weeks after the birth, it looked as if that plan was still on the cards when Sarah left Baby Bea (as she's quite likely to be nicknamed) behind at Balmoral, flying to London to spend the night and attend the wedding of her lady-in-waiting—in a tight-fitting suit that showed she'd shed few pounds but was still decidedly matronly in shape. (She's apparently been in almost constant contact with her homeopathist, who is prescribing herbs and mineral treatments that will help curb the Duchess's appetite and boost her energy.) She could not have been nursing her child at that point, or such a lengthy separation would be impossible. It's likely that for the first couple of weeks, Princess Beatrice of York was breast-fed and after that took to the bottle, on which she would have to rely when her mother left her behind and joined Dad on the other side of the world.

In reality, there's no doubt that even for a daredevil duchess with such an independent streak as Sarah, leaving a baby behind is a huge wrench, tugging on her heartstrings every moment she is separated from her darling daughter. As a close friend says, "As the months go by, she will want to hold the baby in her arms rather than give her nanny the pleasure. She has said that she wants to bring up the children rather than leave the task to others." The Duchess of York, separated from her seafaring husband for so much of the year, is going to want to channel the love and affection she cannot show to Andrew on her children. Which, over the months and years to come, as duty calls for this active, tree-planting, statue-unveiling, foundation-stone-laying member of the royal "corporation," will mean that Sarah will find it harder and ever more of a trial to be parted from Beatrice (and in due course, one supposes, from her little brothers and sisters).

And Baby Bea? With father enjoying a life on the ocean waves, her godparents are likely to assume a more important role than most in the little girl's life—perhaps taking her to tea at royal grocer Fortnum & Mason and certainly lavishing gifts and toys on the pampered princess. There were suggestions that Andrew and Sarah would include in their selection some of their famous friends, like comedienne Pamela Stephenson and outrageous funny man Billy Connolly, her beau, or perhaps Elton John. In any event, it was a sedate quintet: architect Peter Palumbo (which must have irritated Prince Charles, since the Prince has publicly criticized Palumbo's designs, denouncing one as "a giant glass stump"), royal carpenter Viscount Linley, Gabrielle Greenall (whose Swiss chalet Fergie stayed in during the early speculation about a baby), the Duchess's old friend Carolyn Cotterell (with whom Sarah shared an apartment), and, romantically, the Duchess of Roxburghe, chatelaine of the castle where Andrew proposed to his bride.

The christening proved a happy family occasion. Diana and Sarah looked radiant, but nobody outshone the little princess, growing up not only surrounded by love, but by all the privilege in the world.

It is, of course, Diana and Sarah's good fortune that they're free from money worries about who'll foot the bill for the countless disposable diapers, from having to get up at 4 A.M. to escort a sleepy-eyed tot to the toilet, and from the hassle of finding a babysitter so they can enjoy a night out on the town with their husbands. Even though Sarah may be a self-confessed softie with her friends' kids—"I just love giving presents; it gives me so much pleasure to see their faces," she's said—the Yorks and the Waleses try to see that their children aren't ruined by having too much too soon. And despite the fact that they could buy all the toys in F.A.O. Schwarz without denting their bank balances, Diana and Sarah, children of broken homes themselves, are going to make damned sure that the commodities *their* children never go short of are those that all the money in the world can't buy: security, love, and affection.

14

Star Wars?

Firm friends, or royal rivals? Sarah and Diana are impeccably qualified to help each other through the rough patches and enjoy together the magic moments in a princess's life. But if they aren't careful, the essential differences in their life-styles could be a breeding ground for discontent and jealousy.

Sarah and Diana knew each other socially for several years before Prince Andrew made the flame-haired Miss Ferguson his wife. Sarah had even been mooted as a possible lady-in-waiting for the Princess—but Buckingham Palace vetoed that suggestion because it was felt, for all her administrative skills and social graces, that Sarah was too inexperienced for the role of official companion.

Unofficially, though, the friendship flourished anyway. The problem with being a princess, as Diana discovered, is that too few people in this world can be trusted. Her close circle is restricted to the few young women she knew before she was married. They staunchly stood by, never breathing a word about the flourishing romance to the press and thus proving their absolute discretion once and for all.

When a young woman marries into the royal family, everyone's attitude except that of her family and the closest of friends changes. No longer can a princess be sure that the new friends she makes are interested in her personality or humor. There must always be a question mark hanging over the friendship. Do they like me for myself, or because I'm rich, famous, and royal? Are people genuinely laughing at my jokes or putting on an act, hoping that some of my glamour will rub off onto them? Few people are able to act completely normally in the presence of royalty. They become awestruck, embarrassed, flushed. Their hands go unattractively clammy. They sometimes blabber unintelligibly. Hardly the most auspicious start to a friendship.

In Sarah Ferguson, however, Diana found a young woman who *was* at ease in royal company. She, too, proved over time to be discreet, and since they are the same age and from similar privileged backgrounds, she was the perfect choice for promotion to the status Diana refers to as B.F. (or best friend), although Major Ferguson declares, "I think 'best friends' is corny. They are great friends. Incredibly close." Diana's former Highgrove housekeeper added, "Fergie is a frequent visitor. It's nice for Diana to have someone to talk to at last who really understands what it's like to be watched whenever she sneezes, yawns, or coughs. I don't think she's jealous that a new face on the scene will steal the limelight from her. In fact, she's probably just glad to have someone to share it."

But that was back in the early days of Sarah's marriage, when it really did look as if the introduction of a new royal sister-in-law, an outsider who hadn't been born to the role but had to be coached and educated as Diana herself had been, would be the answer to Diana's gnawing loneliness.

However, their relationship is a minefield of potential conflict for the royal pair. Diana has been able to observe that

Sarah enjoys far greater freedom than she ever had or can ever expect to. Diana had to be a virgin, where as Sarah brought to her own marriage a worldliness denied her sister-in-law. The Princess of Wales is one of the relatively few women today who entered into marriage with no history of sexual experimentation or knowledge of the important lessons learned by men and women who've already had close emotional relationships. Diana was a real first-timer, and she had to get it right the first time.

Though the Princess has now, one hopes, ironed out many of the problems in her own marriage, reaching a comfortable status quo, her obvious marital malaise coincided neatly with Sarah's appearance on the scene. One wonders if, for the first time in her life, Diana began to see, through Sarah's eyes, precisely what she had missed out on. And, of course, the idea that you can *never* have something is very likely to make you desire it all the more. Diana must always be thought of as untouchable, her reputation beyond reproach. She is forbidden even the most harmless of flirtations, beyond merely batting her mascarade eyelashes in the direction of her official dinner companion. Sarah is permitted to be just a little risque. Most British concur that Diana is beautiful, but that Sarah is, well, dead sexy.

Diana's role is that of dutiful, beautiful wife, a woman who must symbolize and personify loyalty—to her husband, to her Queen (who happens to be her mother-in-law, rarely the easiest of relationships), her country, and her children. Sarah can virtually carve out any role for herself that she chooses. She must certainly play the devoted wife—but that seems to come effortlessly to her; plus, there is no age gap or interest gulf to cast a shadow over her marriage, and her husband, unlike Prince Charles, is free of the awesome knowledge that he will one day be King of England. Just as Princess Margaret has always been free to have a whale of a time (because as soon as Prince Charles was born, she knew she'd never be queen), so Andrew is able to enjoy an unburdened existence. Sarah can join him in that and enjoy it to the full, whereas Diana's responsibility is to be the shoulder on which her husband leans and occasionally (as he did after last spring's Alpine skiing disaster) cries.

Diana knew that Sarah could never compete with her in the looks department. The Princess of Wales was as surprised as anyone to discover that lurking under her own puppy fat was an incredibly photogenic beauty. The camera absolutely loves Diana, and, though not unbearably vain, she does for the most part relish the attention. But she yearns to be able to switch that spotlight on and off at will, to pass unnoticed when she's feeling low, having an off day or a zit, or is unhappy. Instead, she has to contend with the reality of being pursued and photographed even when she's nipping into Harvey Nichols for pantyhose.

Sarah, so far, has never been subjected to quite the media pressure placed on her sister-in-law, and anyhow, Diana was only too glad to be able to give insider trade information about just what horrors to expect. Thus, Sarah entered royal life with a head start over her friend. Diana learned about the pressures the hard way. As royal biographer Ralph Martin declared, "Even when Diana was living in Buckingham Palace before the wedding, never once did the Queen invite her for a private lunch or dinner and say, 'This is how it's going to be, kid.' " Yet when Sarah accepted her Prince's proposal, she knew *exactly* what she was taking on in a way Diana never could, because until Diana appeared on the scene, interest in the royal family had dwindled almost to nothing. Diana gave it a shot in the arm—of pure, 22-carat glamour—and unwittingly ensured that she would almost never have another moment's peace.

Diana must have felt fairly secure in her position as number-one royal princess. But Sarah, perhaps aware that only a handful of women in the world could compete with Diana in the beauty stakes, chose to win the nation's hearts in quite a different style. She certainly laps up the glamorous aspects of royal life, but she decided it was more her style to become a walking, talking, daredevil "action princess," as game for canoe trips as couture fittings. Better to understand her husband's passion for flying, she even enrolled in a challenging flying course, earning her pilot's license in just four weeks with forty hours of air time. "Flying is his life and I want to be part of his life," she declared, touchingly, expressing just the sort of love we hope for for our princes.

The course itself was a wedding gift from the Oxford Air Training School, and a leading British industrialist later put a helicopter and pilot at her disposal, so that "Chatterbox One"—the nickname given to her by air-traffic controllers—could master the complicated controls of a whirlybird, too. Sarah described it as a "great challenge," and the admiration of her husband (who piloted a Royal Navy Lynx helicopter during the Falklands war) was clear when, presenting his wife with her second set of wings, he beamed: "She's amazing, learning to fly a helicopter in just forty hours. It took me eighty-five hours to get my wings, but then it was a slightly different course." In the unlikely event that Diana might have chosen to learn to fly, she would probably have been talked out of it by members of her circle, anxious for the future consort's safety. And, it's almost certainly true that she would have been unable to be seen accepting such a generous gift as the flying lessons. Sarah's place further down the royal pecking order enables her to live her life with many fewer constraints.

With her obvious affection for her husband—Andrew doesn't mind one bit if she expresses it in public—and her go-for-it attitude (unchanged even during her pregnancy), Sarah was able to earn the public's affection in a way Diana never did. She winked, joked, and nudged her way into our hearts, where Diana just smiled and looked drop-dead gorgeous.

Sarah's rambunctious romp through the royal corridors infected the rest of the family with a sense of fun. She blew a breath of fresh air into their stuffy world, instantly endearing herself to the family, who, notoriously, love a laugh. She learned to drive carriage horses to please her father-in-law and rode out with the Queen, whereas Diana's popularity in the royal family was somewhat shadowed by her reluctance to saddle up.

Perhaps, seeing how Sarah, with her relaxed style, had infiltrated the royal ranks—to the point, when her seafaring swain was away, of cozy tête-à-têtes with the monarch herself—Diana felt keen for the first time to kick up her heels and let her immaculate hair down.

Diana is endowed with a chameleon nature; she tends to assume the mannerisms and characteristics of whomever she's with. Among foreign royals, she is the most regal of women. With hospital patients, she becomes genuinely concerned and caring, aware that she can do enormous good, like the time she shook hands with dying patients in an AIDS ward, at a time when the British public was first reeling with the horror of the disease and extremely concerned that it could be passed on by simple social contact. Diana's simple gesture single-handedly knocked that notion on the head. But when she's around younger folk, particularly Sarah, then Diana (whose personality could not have been expected to be fully formed by the time she became engaged, at the age of nineteen) can become girlish, even undignified. One royal insider has declared, "With Sarah she is all giggles and gossip. Diana is even starting to copy Sarah's way of digging men friends playfully in the ribs and rolling her eyes at them."

It seemed all to have got rather out of hand one summer at Ascot, the upper crust's favorite race meeting, when Diana and Sarah, done up to the nines, were spotted poking someone in the rear with an umbrella and giggling fiendishly. Major Ferguson set the record straight when he announced that "it so happened that the person they jabbed was a very great friend of theirs. He was just in front of them and a very natural reaction from them was to have a bit of fun. The press says you can't behave like that, which is ludicrous." Or is it?

The British monarchy today is still in a fragile position. Other European countries have decided down the centuries that their royal families are superfluous, exiling them or even (in more barbaric times) executing them. This is highly unlikely to happen to the current royal family, of course, but royal biographer Anthony Holden worries that the down-to-earth behavior of young royals means that people "are beginning to identify the monarchy with the gilded youth and the idle rich." In such an environment anarchy can flourish, if the public feel that the taxes creamed off their income (and then doled out in the form of Civil List payments to one of the richest families in the world) is being misspent on luxuries and high living. The British monarch not only rules the nation but is ultimately answerable to it. If the future king's wife behaves in a less than royal way, even to the extent of enjoying a little harmless horseplay, it reflects badly on the entire monarchy.

Lately, however, the evidence would seem to point to a distinct cooling in relations between the princesses' royal high-spiritednesses. Diana and Sarah aren't glimpsed together in public nearly so often, and for last year's skiing holiday each brought along her own pals for company; until then, they had seemed content with just each other (and their husbands). Again, Sarah is at liberty to mix with a much wider circle than is Diana. Along with old school chums like socialite Lulu Blacker (whom the Duchess chose to invite skiing), her friends include show-business personalities like Elton and Renata John and outrageous stand-up comedienne Pamela Stephenson, the driving force behind the Duchess's bachelorette party (when Diana, Sarah, and Stephenson donned uniforms and posed as policewomen). Ms. Stephenson, who lives with Scottish comedian Billy Connolly, famed for his blue jokes, is feared by talk-show hosts because of her penchant for attempting to take their pants off onscreen. The Duchess and Pamela share the same outrageous sense of humor. If the Princess of Wales chose such a friend, it would be frowned on and probably actively discouraged, by her husband, her mother-in-law, *and* the British press.

So Diana surrounds herself with the cozy clique of girls she knew before she was married, like her old roommates Anne Bolton and Carolyn Pride, who are all marrying suitably and having babies and whose reputations are as untarnished as her own. She could look enviously upon this freedom of her sister-in-law's to mix, unjudged and unimpeded, with whomsoever she pleases.

Even their weddings were different. Diana's was majestic and memorable, an undeniably magical day declared as a national holiday, but she exchanged vows in a cathedral full of strangers. Many of her friends and relatives were scratched from the list so the pews could be filled with foreign dignitaries, Commonwealth kings, and presidents' wives, like Nancy Reagan. Sarah's wedding was much more of a family occasion, in a smaller church, with pals lining the aisle, fewer overseas heads of state, and even old boyfriends to wink at, giving Sarah the satisfaction of knowing, as she glided by in the most stunning wedding dress anyone had ever seen (satin richly embroidered and sequined by Lindka Cierach), that at least one former love was probably wishing he'd snapped her up instead. Poignantly, there were no old boyfriends flanking the path as Diana, in a crushed ivory-silk dress by the Emanuels, made her way up the red-carpeted aisle. Even Diana and Charles's chaste Buckingham Palace balcony kiss was outdone by the lusty great smacker that Andrew and Sarah exchanged.

Everywhere you look, Sarah seems to be able to get away

with things Diana never can. Sarah (aware that her sister-in-law had already signed up the cream of British designers to dress her) was given permission to turn to the Parisian couturiers for her wardrobe—though her decision *not* to buy British has ruffled plenty of fashion business feathers in the United Kingdom. Diana must wave the British banner at all times. (When she switched her German-made car for a British model in the early days of her romance, it gave royal watchers a clue that Lady Diana was a serious contender in the marriage stakes.)

Diana and Sarah seem, at times, to be staging their own style wars. With Diana already the darling of the designers, loved for her fashion-model shape which shows their clothes off as perfectly as any catwalk model ever could, Sarah, rather than risk unflattering or unfavorable comparison, seems to have been driven to go elsewhere for her look. Even though her comely shape has earned her countless compliments, Fergie's curves have also resulted in criticism from fashion pundits. Sarah may already have cause to envy Diana's slenderness as she fights her own battle of the postbaby bulge. And although nobody can remember the last time a British royal shopped so extensively abroad—Paris, New York, Rome—it appears that this hasn't discouraged the daring Duchess.

Again, it is unthinkable that Diana should turn to a foreign interior decorator to furnish and design her homes, yet Sarah had the pick of the world's talent to choose from and initially settled upon Sister Parish, a chintz-crazed American.

So it looks to all intents and purposes as if there's more than a little royal rivalry afoot. Just as Sarah appears to be on the brink of stealing the show, Diana pulls another trick out of the bag. When the Duchess arrived at Ascot in summer 1987 in one of her winning numbers—a bright-yellow suit and cart-wheel straw hat—and had the photographers snapping away dementedly, Diana still made it a point to appear on the front page. Leaving the racetrack earlier than normal, she headed for the polo field to watch Charles play a chukka or two, hitched up her slim-line skirt and posed, on the hood of her husband's precious Aston Martin convertible, like a professional model in a pantyhose commercial. As Rat Pack member Arthur Edwards of the London *Sun* described it, "Then she flashed those gorgeous long legs and gave us what we call a real eyeful. Even the *Times* ran that picture next day on the front page." Fergie made it to the inside pages, but Diana had once again proved herself to be the unassailable star.

If Sarah has begun to revel in her celebrity status just as much as Diana, then Diana can still carry off the ultimate gesture of one-upmanship. When her husband is crowned king, Diana will be queen consort; she will wear the crown jewels and stand at his side during his coronation, knowing that she is not only married to a king but has given birth to one. One can only imagine the kick any woman would get from that. Sarah may at present cherish the freedom of her lesser role, but at times she may feel as green as Di's famous emeralds at Diana's privileged place in the history books. Every mother wants the best for her children, but Sarah's—so much further down the royal line—will forever be denied the ultimate prize: the throne. So near and yet so far. Diana and Sarah have literally injected new blood into the royal lineage. They have blown away cobwebs lurking in dusty palace corners and given the crown back its glitter. But they will have to beware that their spirit of competition—whether friendly or rooted in genuine, jealous rivalry—doesn't actually tarnish the royal image in the long run. And they must remember one crucial fact: that their celebrity status rests entirely on having made the ultimate match. Without royal husbands, they might never *once* have made the front pages, let alone monopolized them daily. But it would hardly be surprising if, occasionally, the pomp and circumstance didn't go to their tiaraed heads.

Diana has seen good times and bad during her eight years as a princess. Sarah is still learning the ropes and enjoying an extended honeymoon with the British media. Diana knows only too well that the glory days are short-lived. When any star shines too brightly, the British seem keen to shoot it down in flames. Diana saw that when the press tried to make a mountain out of a molehill of marital discord, implying that a short-lived hiccup (of the kind common to all but a handful of marriages) spelled doom and gloom for her match. Press speculation and pressure are said to have twice edged Diana to the brink of nervous breakdown.

Last year, Sarah too suffered her unfair share of criticism. She has had to learn the hard way that the simplest desire to please—her most basic characteristic, one demonstrated since childhood—can be wildly misinterpreted. In trying to appear natural (following her dad's advice), she was accused of being too downscale. Witty badinage exchanged with a Los Angeles audience when she was making a speech or off-the-cuff remarks about her husband have led to her being nicknamed the "Duchess of Yob" in the British press. All she did was talk about the royal toilets and, when asked if she had any pets, tell her interrogator that all she had was a Labrador named Tam, before pointing to her husband and adding: "apart from him." But Sarah and Diana have both had to learn the rough, tough lesson that a princess can't win. If she's too aloof, she's labeled haughty, unapproachable, and snobbish. Yet if she tries to act normally, she's unregal or undignified.

Despite the jewels, the clothes, and the luxury, Diana and Sarah have discovered already that the reality of being a princess is, in 1989, nothing like the fairy tale. There is immense pressure: to have a baby, to look wonderful, to act with dignity yet without airs and graces. They must contend with the fact that every gesture, every gown, every grin or grimace will be picked over by the press and public like hungry vultures. Love them or hate them, everyone is fascinated by the royals, and largely *because* of Diana and Sarah's appearance on the scene.

Diana is the only person who understands firsthand what Sarah's life is like, and vice versa. The ladies-in-waiting, the old friends, the celebrities, can only guess at what it feels like. It is something even their husbands can't really share; they can see what life is like for their wives inside that gilded cage, but Charles and Andrew, because they were born into royalty, cannot know what it *feels* like to have your life transformed forever. Sarah and Diana signed up. For good.

Being modern princesses is no picnic. In exchange for the love of their princes, they have traded their freedom. They are required to look good, do good, *be* good in public and in private twenty-four hours a day. There is little or no privacy from courtiers or reporters. It is like living in a beautifully decorated goldfish bowl.

If rivalry really develops between the pair, it will be tragic for both. Diamonds may be *thought* to be a girl's best friend. But Diana and Sarah know that when your jewel box is brimfull of them, all the diamonds in the world cannot offer comfort or share the jokes, the pressures, or the pleasure. Let's hope, for their sakes, that they learn to share the spotlight, not fight for it—and that the friendship forged between the Duchess and the Princess flourishes rather than fizzling out. Because without each other to lean on when the going gets tough, they may be condemned to the least enchanting ending of all—to live unhappily ever after.

Famous Lives

from St. Martin's Paperbacks

LIBERACE: THE TRUE STORY
Bob Thomas
———— 91352-4 $3.95 U.S. ———— 91354-0 $4.95 Can.

THE FITZGERALDS AND THE KENNEDYS
Doris Kearns Goodwin
———— 90933-0 $5.95 U.S. ———— 90934-9 $6.95 Can.

CAROLINE AND STEPHANIE
Susan Crimp and Patricia Burstein
———— 91116-5 $3.50 U.S. ———— 91117-3 $4.50 Can.

PATRICK SWAYZE
Mitchell Krugel
———— 91449-0 $3.50 U.S. ———— 91450-4 $4.50 Can.

YOUR CHEATIN' HEART:
A BIOGRAPHY OF HANK WILLIAMS
Chet Flippo
———— 91400-8 $3.95 U.S. ———— 91401-6 $4.95 Can.

WHO'S SORRY NOW?
Connie Francis
———— 90386-3 $3.95 U.S. ———— 90383-9 $4.95 Can.

Publishers Book and Audio Mailing Service
P.O. Box 120159, Staten Island, NY 10312-0004

Please send me the book(s) I have checked above. I am enclosing
$ —————— (please add $1.25 for the first book, and $.25 for each
additional book to cover postage and handling. Send check or
money order only—no CODs.)

Name _____

Address _____

City ———————————————— State/Zip ————————————————

Please allow six weeks for delivery. Prices subject to change
without notice.

FL 1/89